D1359431

Love or Loyalty

by
Joy Scott

For my thoughts are not your thoughts,
neither are your ways my ways.

For as the heavens are higher than the earth,
so are my ways higher than your ways,
and my thoughts than your thoughts.

For ye shall go out with joy, and be led forth with peace;
the mountains and the hills shall break forth before you into
singing,
and all the trees of the field shall clap their hands.

Isaiah 55, 8 – 13

"Love or Loyalty"

History books say the War Between the States ended in 1865. Even the computer machine, they tell me, says the same. But I know different. I was there, the day they fought the last battle of that Great War.

When was that? Since I didn't see daylight till the next century began. . .well you do the math, as they say today.

With people as old as me, knowing people who were alive then, well – it's not so very long ago, after all.

Truth be told – and I always tell the truth, you know – they got it wrong about the day the war started. No, I wasn't there for that first battle. But the ones who were told me all about it. Here's what they said. And this is their story. As they told it to me. So I'm telling it to you as it was in their time, how they talked, how they felt, and what they believed.

The Narrator

Table of Contents

Chapter 1
The Opening Salvo

The Great Conflict. It didn't start with guns and cannons and cavalry charges, like you might have read. You have to know about the first skirmish to understand what was to come. The Great Conflict of this story started one April day, in the Wilderness, before a Confederacy, before real bloodshed. That forest in Virginia so dense they say no white man has ever yet seen parts of it.

Only animals.

And Indians.

But those old legends didn't faze the Lewis boys that day. They roamed through that forest as if they owned it.

Lacking an enemy on that day – or so they thought – the boys wandered deep into the woods, playing their game of "Indian," enjoying a few carefree moments during the two elder boys' break from the University. For a few hours they could ignore the conflict that swirled around their familiar world.

Although still spring, the air was already hot and wet like one of those saunas people pay good money for nowadays. Yet to these proud Virginians, the weather – like everything about their beloved state – was as perfect as it could be.

Intent on their game, these cocky boys were blind to the danger that lurked a hundred strides behind them: an Indian on the warpath – dark hair in two long braids, war paint, tomahawk in hand, footsteps muffled on the soft forest floor.

Brave Wolf was that Indian's name. Stealing silently from tree to tree, Brave Wolf smiled grimly at the boys' foolishness. In a few moments, they would learn who the true masters of this land were. Eyes that had seen real bloodshed watched the boys with arrogance and not a trace of pity for what was about to be their fate. There was a score to settle, and Brave Wolf was the instrument of retribution.

"He must have come this way," claimed Jim, who as the oldest always thought he knew best.

"That's an old Indian trick. Break the branch and then go the other way," Zack disagreed, equally sure of himself.

"He knows the bog is down there. What do you think – he's holding his breath and hiding underwater?" argued Jim.

Brave Wolf, then uttering the bloodcurdling shriek of the savage Comanche, attacked. Before the boys could turn to face their assailant, Brave Wolf leaped astride Zack's back, one hand waving the tomahawk, the other covering the victim's eyes to maneuver Zack's head into scalping position.

Zack, however, wasn't making this easy, whirling in circles and struggling to get a grip on his invisible attacker. Luck favored him as he staggered into a tree, which whapped Brave Wolf a good one, strong enough to deposit the Indian into a bramble bush. Grabbing a fallen tree limb, Zack whirled to retaliate as Brave Wolf struggled to escape the clutches of the thorns.

"Zack, no," yelled Jim, grabbing Zack's arm just before Brave Wolf was about to be clubbed into unconsciousness. "Can't you see? It's Lenie."

Zack stared. The flailing savage was indeed his cousin Pauline – otherwise known as Lenie – glaring at him from underneath that war paint. Her wavy dark hair – so like Zack's own – was slicked down with water and some kind of grease, the origin of which Zack did not care to speculate. A praying mantis of a girl, her legs and arms seemed to stick out in all directions at once. Defiant blue-black eyes glared back into his own.

"You!" Zack sputtered. "What are you doing here? We told you the Wilderness is no place for a girl."

Lenie extricated herself from the bramble trap, ignoring the ripping sound that accompanied the loss of a good part of her skirt.

"Well, guess I showed you who the real scout in this family is!" she announced triumphantly.

At that auspicious moment, Alden Lewis, the third brother, broke through the underbrush into the clearing.

"I win! You didn't find me," he crowed, then stopped dead and stared at the spectacle of his eccentric girl cousin in savage garb. "What in tarnation?"

Ignoring Alden, Zack snapped back at Lenie, "You're no scout. You're just – just – unnatural, you are."

"Zack! She is our cousin," admonished Jim.

Indeed, as far as Zack was concerned, this was sadly true. Since her arrival from the wilds of Texas some months past, Lenie had proven herself to be as disruptive to the idyllic order of their Virginia home as a horned toad plopped in the middle of the Sunday dinner table.

"She's a wild – thing. No sense of her place and what's right and proper," fumed Zack, still feeling sorely the loss of his dignity.

"You just can't stand it that I know you're just playing! Pretending to be soldiers! Go ahead, Zack, show me what you know about real fighting!"

Her jaw thrust forward pugnaciously, she flung her challenge at Zack like a blow.

"Wouldn't I like to!" Zack muttered. "But you're a girl and Mother would – "

What Mother would do or think, no one ever knew. Brandishing the tomahawk, Lenie took off after Zack. He dodged, she attacked again, and he backed off. Jim, being the eldest and responsible for whatever damage to life and limb might result from this fracas, tried to separate them but then retreated to save his own hide – or scalp, as it were.

"You show her Zack!" yelled Alden, supremely confident in his brother's ability to subdue this upstart opponent.

Zack wasn't showing anything yet but some fancy footwork dodging Lenie's tomahawk.

"What's wrong, Zack? Go ahead! Pretend I'm one of those Yankees you hate so much," she taunted.

Zack grabbed a stick from the forest floor and deflected Lenie's tomahawk blows. As they parried, he backed up onto a log over the marshy bog. Lenie followed. As she lunged, he caught her skirts with his stick and pulled up. Off balance, Brave Wolf fell into the stagnant pond with a splat.

Jim, Zack and Alden leaned over the log expectantly, waiting for Lenie to surface. The pond was quiet. Too long quiet. Jim took Zack's stick and poked the algae-coated water.

"She could be trapped down there," Alden exclaimed, it must be confessed with more excitement than concern.

Belatedly realizing that Lenie was in real danger, Zack instantly jumped into the muddy water. Jim's cry of "Zack wait," faded as his impetuous brother sank into the murky swamp.

Underwater, the muck of the pond blinded Lenie's would-be-rescuer. He tried to swim, but in the thick mud he could barely move. His lungs burned with the strain of holding his breath. Finally, he bumped into the submerged tree limbs of the fallen log. Feeling his way, he encountered resistance – a gingham skirt, trapping Lenie underwater. Flailing arms blindly struck out at his head and torso. Despite this opposition, Zack managed to rip the treacherous fabric free. He tried to pull Lenie upward, but she struggled against him furiously. Mud filled his nose, his mouth. Lenie's escape efforts grew weaker. Was this death, Zack wondered, lucid despite his agony. Will I die because of a stupid game gone wrong?

Instead of his young life passing before his eyes, he saw the visions of what he had not yet done, the acts of heroism defending his beloved homestead, the valiant deeds that would earn his place in the family legends of famous ancestors. No, he thought, it's too soon . . . . .

Somehow the two combatants broke the surface, coughing and sputtering and wiping greenish sludge the color of a dragonfly's innards from their eyes as Jim and Alden pulled them to solid ground.

"If you two aren't the stupidest – Game's over!" fumed Jim. "You could have both drowned. Then how would I explain that?"

Their eyes two white circles in verdigris faces, Zack and Lenie could see each other now. Their gaze met as they realized their narrow escape. Still panting, Zack extended his hand to help Lenie up. Lenie studied his outstretched arm, then stared back into his eyes. Her dark brows met in a thunderous, mud-encrusted scowl.

"Brave Wolf never surrenders," she pronounced.

The Comanche cry once again resounded through the Wilderness as she grabbed her tomahawk and took off after Zack, bare brown legs – now almost entirely free of that skirt – flying. He fled for his life into the Wilderness.

At the edge of this primeval forest lay civilization. It was called "River's Rest." This small, ramshackle two-story frame house that looked for all the world like a stack of children's blocks, had been built by old Captain Lewis when King George III still claimed his allegiance. Now it was home for Lenie and her father.

To Lenie, these hundred-year-old wooden walls and the still, dense forest surrounding it represented the confinement that pressed in on her from everything Virginian – including the irksome sense of propriety that made everything she did so inappropriate and "unladylike."

On that afternoon, Lenie's father, Dr. John Lewis, focused intently on mixing medicines at the large desk from the rows of vials stored on its shelves. Over the mantle, his old sword with a heavy bronze handle hung in a place of honor.

Jeremiah, a muscular young man whose blue-black skin was to stay clear and ebony into his 90th year, like a cobalt shadow around his body, watched intently with his bare and swollen leg extended as if in offering to the god of medicine. Dr. Lewis completed the compounding process, applied the green concoction to Jeremiah's outstretched leg and bound it into place.

"It will hurt for a while, but in the morning, you'll be much better," promised Dr. Lewis. "Be sure to keep the poultice in place all night."

Jeremiah looked dubious.

"Are they any rattlesnake poison in this?" he asked timorously.

Dr. John frowned. "What? Was Lenie telling you that? No, Jeremiah, she was teasing you. There are herbs from her garden, though. Lenie knows as much about those kinds of medicines as I do."

Jeremiah looked unconvinced. "How come you don't put this on your leg?" he asked.

Dr. Lewis smiled, a bit wistfully I imagine. "I wish I could. My wound is too old. And it came from a cannonball, not a snakebite."

He never spoke about his wound, but as a man in the prime of life it must have been a trial to him to be so restricted.

Jeremiah gingerly rose to go. "Thank you, sir," he murmured, as though still not convinced of the efficacy of this treatment. John fondly patted him on the shoulder.

Thanks to his late wife, Dr. John was no believer in slavery. He was grateful that the Lewis family's patriarchal relationship with their slaves brooked no conflict with his – and their – belief in Christian charity and kindness. Indeed, their attitude towards the dozens of slaves who ran their huge estate combined the fondness for a beloved pet with the tolerance towards distant, impecunious relatives of an inferior social class. They took comfort in the knowledge that those who served them were fed, housed, and cared for when sick or old. That these people would have longings for freedom from their indentured status, even with its attendant economic uncertainties, never crossed their minds. Or consciences.

There's been plenty of great books written about the plight of these enslaved peoples as they found and fought their way to their God-given rights to freedom, here in the home of the free. You may know I've written one myself. But this story is not their story, I'll tell you right now. Just so you know what to expect.

So Jeremiah left, and we're back to the goings-on in the parlor. Dr. John rose with some difficulty. Once on his feet, he grasped his cane and hobbled to the sofa to join his brother, James.

James' wife, Sarah, and fourteen-year-old daughter, Nan, busied themselves arranging a large bouquet of flowers at the small dining table. Sarah, her carriage as erect as any soldier, gave no hint in her absorption of this household task that her keen mind held enough knowledge of Greek, Latin and literature to ready her somewhat unruly sons for university admission. Nan, softer in demeanor and appearance than her mother, bore the somewhat self-conscious look of the young girl poised to enter womanhood and all the responsibilities and uncertainties that this passage entailed. Together, they brought to mind the unlikely pairing of an elegant, watchful eagle with the sweet but undistinguished brown wren.

I knew that parlor well. The small fireplace, the rough-hewn mantle, and the letters that children painted around the walls and doorways, sayings and proverbs that they used to write on their slate tablets when they learned those revered three R's. I close my eyes, and it's all still there.

Sometimes when I think about that day, I can see them too, like one of those old-timey pictures when photographs were new and everybody looked like they had no teeth and had just eaten something sour, sitting primly on the straight Victorian chairs and horsehair sofa. A little moment of domestic peace and tranquility, before the great upheaval that was to come.

"What's the news, Brother?" asked John, sitting down heavily in the parlor chair.

News meant only one thing. What was Virginia going to do? Secede with the rest of the Southern states, or stay in the Union? The future and even the survival of the family hung in balance on that fateful question.

"The same. More talk of war," replied James. Abruptly he closed the newspaper, as if he didn't care to know more.

"Perhaps Lenie and I should have stayed in Texas. I picked a bad time to come home," John sighed pensively.

Sarah's reply was brisk. "Nonsense. There is no such thing as a bad time to come home. We are so happy to have family living again at River's Rest." Her tone left no doubt that she welcomed the return of the prodigal son and his offspring to their true homeland.

"Lenie's become like another sister for me, Uncle John," added Nan. She really meant it, even though with her demure manner and tidy clothes, Nan was as different from Lenie as a girl could be.

Despite their reassurances, Dr. John still worried. "I'm hoping that your ladylike ways, and some mothering from you, Sarah, might be a good influence. After Hannah – without Hannah, well, I thought about a convent school in New Orleans …"

Just at that moment, the door burst open and Zack raced in, breathless and covered in mud, trailing an aroma of swamp slime that quickly overpowered the scent of his mother's roses. He darted through the house and out the back door, calling contritely as he ran, "I told her not to go into the Wilderness, Mother. I truly did."

Before the startled family could respond, Lenie appeared in the doorway, wet, muddy, and mad. Paint dripped down her face and neck, staining what was left of her dress, remnants of which clung to her almost entirely bare legs. She spied the back door swinging shut, and with another war whoop took off in pursuit, leaving the family open-mouthed with shock.

"Maybe that convent school would have been a good idea," James observed drily.

How far had the Lewis family come since the modest home at River's Rest was built a hundred years before? A walk of less than a mile away from the Wilderness would have led you to velvet green lawns leading up to the porch of the Lewis family estate. Here was Virginia civilization at its finest. This was no antebellum, white-pillared, ostentatious mansion like the planters erected in the cottonocracy in the deep South. Yet, this home was the more impressive – precise Colonial angles, orderly windows and rooms quietly proclaimed "old money," if that term could be used in a country as young as America was in those days.

That particular afternoon, the family's slaves bustled about like a disturbed nest of ants, doing all the tasks that a big family and a large farm needed done to run.

Between the barn and the dense woods bloomed Sarah's carefully tended flower garden. Its blossoms adorned the table for every meal, and added color for every festivity. The garden was the unacknowledged heart of the household, its carefully tended plants with their delicate perfume symbolizing the essence of the family's ideals – beauty, truth, and loyalty – that permeated their lives like an ever-present scent of roses.

The huge lawn sloped gently down for an acre to the dirt road that connected the property with the rest of the civilized world, and ran along the edge of the thick woods that, by an unspoken agreement, was never violated with ax or plow.

Under the giant oak tree that spread its branches across the lawn, the littlest Lewis girls – Mildred, six, and Helen, four – hosted a tea party for their dolls. Their long dark hair hung in carefully woven braids, the handiwork of their devoted older sister. Juno, their nanny, enjoyed a rare moment of rest as she watched her young charges through sleepy, hooded eyes.

Mildred regally offered a teacup to Helen's doll. "One lump or two?" she inquired airily.

Nonplussed for a moment, Helen rose from her small chair, picked up her doll, and hit her more gracious sister with it, twice, over the head. Shocked, Mildred lost her balance and slid to the ground.

"No, you big baby, I meant sugar!" she shouted.

Helen's response to this insult would never be known because the tea party was at that moment interrupted by an unexpected guest – their big brother Zack, who paused in his flight to wipe mud and sweat from his face and catch his breath.

"Here Ackie, have some tea," ordered Helen.

Zack dutifully took the cup and sipped imaginary brew.

"What happened to you?" queried Mildred, one eyebrow raised in inquiry.

"A ferocious red Indian attacked me in the woods, but I escaped," Zack told them solemnly.

The girls looked at each other and then back at Zack.

"Are you and Lenie fighting again?" demanded Helen.

Peering around the tree, Zack spied Brave Wolf – er, Lenie – emerging from the woods that separated River's Rest from the larger plantation. Quickly setting down the cup, he was poised to take flight when a carriage drove around the bend in the road, its galloping horses kicking up clouds of dust in the dry lane. Helen jumped up.

"Look Ackie. That must be the Yankees Papa said were coming."

"I don't think so, Little Girl. Papa would never let a Yankee on our property," Zack replied, nevertheless studying the carriage suspiciously.

"Can't help it, Papa says. It's a wolf in a sheep's skin," intoned Mildred.

At that moment Lenie spied Zack on the lawn. With another whoop and threatening wave of the tomahawk, she darted across the road directly in front of the carriage. The driver tried in vain to stop the horses, but they were going too fast to do anything but neigh in protest as he jerked the reins. Just in time Lenie jumped aside, landing in the roadside ditch but safely out of danger.

The carriage finally stopped. As the driver struggled to calm the rearing horses, a man jumped from the carriage and ran toward Lenie with the speed of a wild bobcat, pulling her half-clad body from the ditch. Despite what appeared to be kicks and yelps of protest, he scooped her up into his arms and headed back for the carriage.

The little girls clutched each other in fear.

"Oh, no! The Yankee's got Lenie! Ackie you must save her!"

Their fear jolted Zack out of his shock and propelled him down the hill at a run. Regardless of his feelings for this renegade relative, she was family – and he would not hesitate to risk life and limb in her protection.

"Take your hands off her!" he yelled.

Hampered by the wet, muddy and slippery girl in his arms, the man struggled with the carriage door long enough for Zack to reach him. In a second Zack landed a solid punch on the stranger's jaw, knocking him flat. Lenie sprawled in the dirt road as well, but she was free. Zack braced himself for a counter-attack.

"Zack, no," screamed Lenie. Instead of being grateful for her rescue, she jumped Zack from the rear, pulling him off-balance. Completely surprised by her attack, Zack also collapsed on the road.

Now Jim and Alden emerged from the woods and stood staring at the scene in bewilderment.

"Help me! This Yankee was trying to kidnap Lenie!" yelled Zack, rolling in the dirt with his cousin.

That was all the feisty Lewis boys needed to know. Halfway back onto his feet, the kidnapper was knocked down again with both boys landing on his chest. The driver jumped down to help, but the flailing fists and feet convinced him not to interfere. The carriage door opened, and two other female captives peered out – young girls, their frightened faces framed with curls and bonnets. One sat frozen, immobilized with horror, but the second darted over to where Zack lay, struggling to free himself from Lenie's hold on his neck, and tried to pull them apart.

Helen and Mildred raced down the hill as fast as their chubby legs could carry them, followed by their frightened nanny, who added to the bedlam by shrieking unintelligible warnings of dire consequences.

"Shoot the Yankee, shoot the Yankee!" screamed Helen.

All the hubbub attracted the attention of the group at River's Rest. James was the first to arrive. Heeding Helen's advice, he drew a pistol. This story might have ended right there if he'd done what Zack thought his father was going to do. But instead of shooting the invading Yankee, James fired into the air. The struggling stopped immediately.

Dr. John hobbled into the now quiet group, and reached out his hand to the Yankee, helping him to his feet.

"Charles, I'm so sorry. What happened?"

Everyone talked at once until James raised the pistol again, an action which had the desired effect of stopping the arguments.

"There seems to have been a misunderstanding about my intentions toward Miss Pauline," said the man Dr. John called Charles. His cultivated, self-assured voice, with the trace of a broad Western accent, betrayed neither guilt for his intended crime nor acrimony for his treatment.

Lenie scrambled to her feet. "You idiot," she hissed to Zack. "This is our friend Mr. Delacourt, visiting from New York."

Zack recoiled in horror. "You're friends with a Yankee?"

This mysterious Mr. Delacourt dusted himself off. From the cut of his clothes and his bearing, he conveyed both aristocratic elegance and intelligence – even covered with dirt. Unlike the fashion of the day, he was clean-shaven, with dark hair and eyes and skin that while not quite olive, was several shades darker than the pale Celtic coloring which predominated in Virginia's ruling classes. Even in those old photos of him back then and later, he looks kind of wild-like. I'm sure that day was no exception.

To Zack, the interloper was a pirate – invading his family's kingdom with no respect for propriety or property. In short, a Yankee.

Bowing to Sarah and Nan, Monsieur Delacourt (as they called

him in New Orleans) smiled. His white teeth flashing in his tanned face did remind Helen of a picture she had seen of a wolf. She stared at this zoological wonder, fascinated. Then he spoke.

"Actually, I am a native of the South, same as you, but have been visiting in New York and other historic sites, introducing my nieces to the cultural attractions of that city."

The sardonic undertone of his comment acted like catnip to Zack's temper. But under his father's warning gaze, he remained silent.

"Allow me to introduce Miss Lucy and Miss Caroline." The two girls stepped forward. Now Zack saw the family resemblance in their brunette curls, brown eyes and fine-boned, slender build.

"It's so good to see you again, Lenie," said Lucy warmly, but refraining from embracing the exceedingly dirty Pauline. Zack recognized her as the girl who had tried to separate him from Lenie's neckhold.

"We've missed you so," added Caroline. "You are looking... well."

Another face appeared in the carriage window – skin the color of mocha, large dark eyes, and white even teeth. Charles acknowledged her presence.

"This is their governess, Miss Octavia."

Octavia nodded, confidently dignified despite her clearly inferior status.

James belatedly offered Charles his hand. "I apologize for the – attacks – of my sons."

"I understand. Nothing is as sacred as the honor of the Southern gentlemen and their duty to protect their property."

Again, the mocking undercurrent in his voice rankled Zack. Helen continued to study Charles as if he were an interesting specimen of insect.

"You do look like a wolf. But where is your sheep's skin?" she queried.

"Helen!" reproved Nan.

"That's all right, young lady," Charles addressed Helen as if she were an adult. "I'm afraid I left that outfit back in New York."

Over Helen's head, Charles caught Nan's eyes. Embarrassed at his attention, she dropped her gaze but could not quell the flush that crept up her cheeks.

"Well, please come inside. You and your nieces are very welcome to stay in our home," pronounced James, oblivious to the spark that flew between his beloved daughter, still a child in his mind, and this charming stranger.

"We're having a picnic supper later," added Nan, blushing as she felt Charles' eyes on her again.

"Lenie, we'll show you our new dresses from New York," offered Caroline. "Maybe you can wear one to the picnic."

Lenie's grimace told everyone just how much she looked forward to this prospect.

How I've often wished I'd been present for that first get-together of this odd and volatile meeting of minds. And ideologies. Could I, by quiet observation and intuition, have predicted the events that would change their fates in the years to come?

Probably not. Probably I would have been blind to the undercurrents of emotion and anger and attraction. Just the way they were.

Under Octavia's determined ministrations, Lenie emerged a few hours later from a hot bath with all traces of her swamp adventure scrubbed away. While Octavia took a comb to Lenie's tangled dark hair, Lucy and Caroline laid out their new frocks for Nan's admiration.

"See how the ruffle goes around the sleeve, like this? Isn't it cunning?" Caroline displayed the pale yellow gown by holding it up to Nan. Nan was impressed and a bit overwhelmed with such finery.

"It is lovely. Only, maybe too fancy for us here in the country."

"Who says you have to be old-fashioned if you don't live in the city?" protested Caroline.

"Ouch!" yelped Lenie. She grabbed the comb from Octavia. "I'll do it myself."

"As you wish, Miss Lenie. Will there be anything else?" inquired Octavia, her equanimity unruffled by this outburst.

"No, Octavia, you may go to our room if you like," Lucy

responded.

Octavia quietly withdrew, her dignity intact in the way only a person who's very sure of their position can be. Lenie watched her go. When Octavia was out of earshot, Lenie inquired, "I thought your uncle freed her."

"Oh, he did," replied Caroline, selecting a lovely violet dress and offering it to Lenie. "But she still serves us. Where else would she go?"

Lenie ignored the offer of the new frock. "She could have her own life."

"Don't be silly. Besides, she's like part of the family. Uncle Charles has always been very fond of her."

Both Nan and Lenie digested this remark in their own way but neither commented. Caroline picked up another dress, this one deep blue, and held it up to Lenie.

"This one matches your eyes. You should wear it for dinner today!"

Lenie made bug eyes by opening her orbs very wide. "You think so? You think because I live here now that I've turned into some simpering Southern belle?"

She pushed the dress away and stomped out of the room, slamming the door shut in a fit of adolescent pique that strikes girls sometimes for no discernible reason.

"I'm so sorry. She didn't mean to be rude, I'm sure," apologized Nan.

"It's all right. Sometimes it's hard for her," murmured Lucy, taking the dress and returning it to the bed. Neither looked at Nan nor explained this remark, and Nan was too well-bred to inquire further.

While the young ladies made their toilette, the wheels of the great plantation turned to create an afternoon's diversion for its owners. On the lawn, busy slaves laid out bowls of food on a makeshift picnic table. Others traipsed from the kitchen to the smokehouse to the garden and back in an endless dance, bringing culinary delights of Southern cooking to the outdoors. As the sun began its descent, the oppressive heat receded to a damp, blanketing

14

warmth.

Charles Delacourt lounged on the porch, observing the well-choreographed ballet. And he lounged well. Cleaned up, he was even more the picture of the gracious Southern gentleman.

As he contemplated the diorama before him, did he see the hand of divine order at work that the Lewis boys had been bred to believe in? Somehow I think not. Accepting authority was not bred into the Delacourt genes. No, they were a different species.

Charles' musings – whatever they were – were interrupted when Lenie stepped out of the big house, fidgeting uncomfortably in one of Nan's old dresses. At the sight of Charles, she stopped, for once at a loss for words. Charles gracefully straightened up and tipped his hat to her, a gesture that restored her powers of speech.

"Don't you go turning Virginian on me," harrumphed Lenie. "I've had about all the Southern gentlemen I can stand."

Her tone bespoke an old acquaintance. And indeed, Charles had held her as a baby and was one of the first people to look deep into those dark blue, penetrating eyes. His look now, which she could not see, was not the evaluation of a man for a young woman, but something else. Like searching for a piece of a puzzle.

She turned to look at him, and his expression changed in a twinkling. Now he grinned like a fellow conspirator. "Don't tell me you are yearning for our Texas wide open spaces in the midst of all this civilization?"

"Even a rattlesnake would be welcome at this point," groused Lenie. She plopped down on the step, legs straight out in front of her as Charles resumed leaning on the railing. Not looking at him, she picked at the hem of the hated dress.

"Oh, they mean well, I suppose. Just that they – all that's important to them is who you're related to. Then, it's how good are your horses. But most of all, it's that damn talk of war that gets my goat."

She stopped her litany of complaints as her cousin Nan approached the porch from the garden, carrying a basket of flowers. Charles turned and bowed to her, a courtesy that she seemed to appreciate, although her downcast eyes betrayed her lack of experience with this male attention.

"Your flowers are lovely, Miss Nan," he complimented her, with that grin that had set female hearts aflutter from the Gulf to the Eastern Seaboard.

Flustered with his attention and by being treated like a grown-up, Nan chattered to cover her nervousness.

"Mother's famous for her garden. The house always smells of flowers."

"You have a very beautiful home," he gestured to the big house, the lawn, but his gaze lingered on the slaves milling about the property. Nan, still bashful in his presence, didn't notice the focus of his attention. But Lenie did. She hoisted herself to her feet and stalked across the lawn, walking too far in front of Charles for him to take her arm. Instead, he turned his attention to Nan, who, somewhat hesitantly, linked her arm with his.

"Thank you," murmured Nan. "The little house at River's Rest is my favorite. Our great-grandfather built it. He fought with George Washington."

Lenie cast an "I told you so" glance toward Charles.

"Your family has quite a heritage," commented Charles, suppressing his grin.

"What about your family, Mr. Delacourt?" asked Nan.

Charles smiled as if at some private joke. "Oh – we were always moving, trying to stay one step ahead of – civilization." Long accustomed to hiding his past, he skirted any self-revelation with practiced ease.

Nan didn't know what to make of this remark, so she just kept talking. "Tomorrow, my brothers can show you some of our horses. They are quite remarkable, I'm told."

"Indeed, I would be delighted to see them." Lenie could barely keep from laughing out loud as she saw her prediction come true before they had even reached the picnic table, where the rest of the family awaited them.

Charles turned to Sarah. "Miss Sarah, I congratulate you on your skill in raising such beautiful Southern flowers."

Sarah nodded her head in acknowledgment while Nan smiled

her pleasure at the double meaning of his words.

From behind the house came whoops and yells as Zack, bearing Helen on his shoulders, and Jim, with Mildred on his, galloped around the corner. The little girls brandished sticks of wood as swords, while Alden served as their squire, riding his own imaginary horse as the posse charged around the table. Helen pointed her stick like a musket.

"Bang! Bang! I shot you and you're dead, Mr. Delacourt," she cried triumphantly. Charles clutched his chest and pretended to be wounded. Zack tumbled Helen on the ground; she ran up to Charles and stabbed him with her "sword."

"Take that, you no-good Yankee, and that!" she yelled.

"Helen! That's enough of this game," admonished Sarah, sternness covering her embarrassment.

"But Mama, it's not a game. It's war!" protested Helen.

"Hush, Helen. We must say the blessing," warned Sarah in quiet tones that brooked no argument.

Under the influence of her severe but loving presence, the family became quiet.

"Thank you, Lord, for this food, for our family, for our home, and for our good friends," said James. He hesitated a moment as if he wanted to add something else, but then closed the prayer with "Amen."

That formality over, the family dug into the food while several slaves stood at attention, ready to serve them the cornbread from Mr. Jefferson's own recipe, the prize smoked ham from the estate's plumpest pig, creamy succotash, peanut soup, and those maple pecan delicacies I've confessed to stealing from the cooling pan while Cook looked the other way. Two small boys waved gigantic fans – taller than they were – to discourage any flies from joining the feast. Trails of sweat poured down their dark, dusty faces.

"I understand you are studying at the University of Virginia?" Lucy inquired demurely of Zack.

Zack had the grace to swallow his mouthful of ham before replying. "Yes, Ma'am, I'm reading law. Jim here will take over the plantation, and I will have a profession."

"Our brother Will is at the University of Texas, studying the classics," offered Caroline.

"Well, Miss Lucy, we reckon the University of Virginia is the finest in the country, bar none." Zack glared at Charles as if daring him to disagree. "It being founded by Thomas Jefferson, and all."

Before Lucy could respond to this parochialism, Lenie chimed in, "Our schools in Texas are outstanding. More modern. That's where I'm going to medical school."

"Medical school? You can't be a nurse! You – have a family," protested Jim.

"I'm going to be a doctor," replied Lenie coolly.

This statement was so outrageous that her Virginia cousins could not even articulate a reply. James glanced at John, inviting a rebuke to the headstrong girl, but his younger brother merely shrugged haplessly.

"Mama!" Helen interjected persistently.

"Nan, why don't you explain the flowers you've chosen for the evening to our guests," suggested Sarah, ignoring her youngest child. Happy to bring the family together again, Nan obliged.

"Each flower has a meaning," she explained. "I chose lemon balm for the company of friends, pansies for good thoughts, and nasturtiums for patriotism."

"Wonderful choices," pronounced John.

Emboldened, Nan (who'd never before evinced an interest in anything anywhere even so far away as Richmond) ventured further into conversational waters and new geographies. "Tell us about your visit to New York, Mr. Delacourt. I've heard it's a fascinating city."

"It's a bunch of damn Yankees, Nan. Pardon my language," protested Zack.

"Oh, hush, Zack," interrupted Lenie. "I'm sure there are lots of people up North who don't have horns and a tail."

"I don't have anything against 'em, if they would just leave us alone," opined Jim.

"But they won't," retorted Zack. His outflung arm took in the house, River's Rest, and the cultivated fields. "They won't be happy till they ruin everything we've worked for. Our ancestors built this. It's about as perfect as a place can be. If we have to fight for our rights like the patriots did, we will."

Lenie eyed the silent black slaves.

"Do they think it's perfect, too?" she asked sarcastically. "Should they be fighting for their independence? Form the "'Army of the Emancipation?'"

"This way is the best thing for them," retorted Zack, getting heated again at this heresy expressed at his own family's dinner table.

"But Mr. Lincoln says he doesn't want a war," interjected Caroline. "We heard him say so. At the inauguration."

Too late, she realized her blunder as eight pairs of blue eyes gazed at her, wide with emotions ranging from mere shock to fury. That a guest in their home had actually attended the swearing in of the hated Yankee President was such an outrage that the normally outspoken boys were momentarily struck dumb.

The pause Caroline's faux pas engendered gave little Helen the opportunity she'd been waiting for.

"Mama, Mama, Mama, Mama, Mama," protested Helen.

"What is it, Helen?" asked Sarah.

"Ackie told me – he's going to be a soldier and shoot all the Yankees!" declared Helen proudly.

Again, unspoken surprise and dismay hung over the silent table. Jim and Zack exchanged discomfited glances.

"Zack and me, we talked with Captain Landis about joining his regiment," admitted Jim. "If – when – Virginia votes to secede."

"We can't stay at University when the War comes, Mother. We have to go. It's a matter of honor," argued Zack.

Sarah looked at James, who was silent. She dropped her eyes, accepting what she had known in her heart would come.

"Are you going to shoot Yankees, too, Mr. Delacourt?" asked Millie, as if she were inquiring whether he liked cornbread.

"I hope it won't come to that, Millie," Charles replied politely, his tone, for once, serious. "I would find it hard to take up arms against my own countrymen. On either side."

Zack's eyes narrowed with anger. He jumped to his feet.

"I knew it! You ARE a traitor! Anyone who takes their side is not welcome in this house!" he shouted.

He glared at Charles who, rather than being insulted, looked bemused. The girls, except for Lenie, stared down at their plates, properly horrified at this outburst of rudeness in a genteel Southern household.

James rose to his feet. He passed his judgment on the altercation by saying sternly, "Mr. Delacourt, I must apologize for the rudeness of my son. You are a welcome guest. Please forgive us."

"I understand. I was hotheaded too when I was a boy." Charles' condescending reply only infuriated Zack further.

"Mr. Delacourt fought with me, for our country, during the Mexican Wars. He saved my life," said John quietly. Zack, suddenly mortified, sat down abruptly, reining in with difficulty that quick temper I knew so well could flame in an instant.

Unnoticed by the participants in this contentious dinner conversation, Jeremiah had limped across the lawn as fast as his injured leg would allow. His blue-black skin shining with sweat, he stopped, panting, beside James, offering a beige sheet of paper for his perusal. Surprised, James accepted, but Jeremiah could not keep the news to himself.

"It's from Mr. Johnson, down at the telegraph office. That boy who deliver it – he say – he say – that Virginny done sus – sus – eeded. It join the Con fed see," he pronounced, stumbling over the unfamiliar words.

James looked at Sarah, willing her strength to accept the news that she dreaded, and others welcomed. For once oblivious to their mother's feelings, Jim, Zack and Alden erupted into triumphant cheers while Lenie eyed them with the revulsion of a Christian missionary observing demonic heathen rituals.

Sides had been chosen, battle lines drawn, in the first skirmish of the great conflict.

Chapter 2
Invasion

When the War Between the States first started, people thought it would be over in a season. Some folks even brought picnic lunches along to watch the first battles. I've seen those pictures. You probably have too. Those folks were sure wrong, weren't they?

For the new recruits – most of them still boys – sleeping in tents was a novelty that gave the entire affair the aura of a weekend outing. Jim and Zack Lewis were two of these boys. Virginia aristocrats for generations, these blue-eyed descendants of the Scottish Highlands saw the conflict as evil Northerners determined to destroy their way of life. They were true believers, all right.

As the days turned into weeks, they impatiently settled into a routine, always at the ready for the battle that would happen any day.

The summer sun was just fading away at the end of one long day as Jim sat diligently polishing the old family sword, a relic from before the first Revolution.

"Any more polishing and you'll wear the silver right off," warned Zack.

Neither looked up as a young man in civilian clothes ambled toward them. A serious-looking fellow with a wide, pale face and a forehead partially covered with a shock of chestnut brown hair, he paused for a moment before interrupting their conversation. Unfazed by their lack of welcome, he spoke in a soft, clear voice with the accents of the mountain folk.

"We're startin' our evening Bible reading soon. Would you like to join us?" he asked. Jim and Zack shook their heads "no." They were not here for religion.

Unfazed, the young man continued on through the camp, stopping to speak quietly to each group of soldiers.

"Lewis? You got a visitor from home," hollered one soldier. Sure enough, into the campsite galloped one of the Lewis family's fine thoroughbreds. And even better, astride that horse was a coltish figure with the grace of the experienced horseman they knew their younger brother to be.

"Alden! Do you have a package from Mother?" cried Zack. With Rebel whoops they fell upon Alden as he dismounted. His cap fell to the ground.

But this rider was not Alden. It was not their brother or father or uncle.

It was an abomination. It was a girl.

A girl they knew. Their embarrassing cousin, Pauline, recently returned "home" from Texas.

Lenie, as she was known, picked up her cap, replaced it on her newly shorn locks as Jim and Zack stared at her in horror and dismay.

"What are you doing here? What have you done with Alden?" demanded Jim.

"I used my excellent tracking skills to ambush him by Willow's Creek," boasted Lenie.

"You just turn around right now and get home. The army is no place for a girl," ordered Zack, glancing around in the hope that no one was watching this embarrassing scene.

"I'm here to help my father," announced Lenie. Her father and the boy's uncle, John Lewis, was indeed a surgeon assigned to their regiment. Zack suddenly remembered Lenie's stubborn silence as they rode away to war two months ago, leaving her behind, and her unspeakably inappropriate desire to become a physician herself.

This was bad. Very bad – for their reputation as well as for their errant cousin's safety.

Later that evening Zack and Jim expressed their displeasure by glowering at Lenie over their camp dinner. Samuel, the young man who organized the Bible readings, also observed her closely but with bemusement, not resentment. Dr. John Lewis, Lenie's father and the camp surgeon, presided over the meal as if he wasn't sure what would happen next.

"Uncle John, surely you can't let her stay," Zack burst out.

"Pauline, it's just too dangerous. This is no place for a young girl," began Dr. John.

"If I could help you at home, I can help you here!" retorted

Lenie, tossing her hair in defiance. Except she no longer had very much hair.

"Sir, we will need more help in the infirmary, once the fighting starts," suggested Samuel.

"Thank you, Dr. –?" queried Lenie.

Quick to correct her, and likewise to judge, Zack retorted, "He's no doctor! He's a hillbilly who hides back here 'cause he won't fight!" His words may have stung Samuel, but the boy made no reply, only looked down at his plate.

"Zack! Samuel is a Quaker. Please respect his beliefs just as he does yours."

At his uncle's rebuke, Zack subsided. Lenie looked at Samuel with new interest, noting his calm grey eyes and smooth brow, seemingly undisturbed by Zack's insult. Most of all, she noticed the kindness in his direct gaze.

"My mother was a Quaker," she offered.

But Samuel learned no more about Lenie's mother that night, because at that moment a very irate Alden burst into their circle, dirty, disheveled, and wearing only his long underwear.

"Where is she?" he demanded angrily. The others couldn't help laughing at his bizarre appearance, but Alden was more angry than embarrassed.

"Well, you didn't expect me to wear her dress, did you? She ambushed me!"

"I sure did!" exclaimed Lenie. "Tracked you all the way."

Alden ignored her boast and addressed his Uncle. "Uncle John, now that I'm here, I'm staying! I'm 13 and that's old enough to enlist."

"Well, I'm 15 and I'm staying!" retorted Lenie. Dr. John looked at Lenie's stubborn face and did not even try to argue. How could a father even consider allowing his young daughter to remain on a battlefield? Well, I guess you would have to know more about the history of Lenie Lewis' short life to understand. And you will.

"I guess the camp hospital is safe enough," he acknowledged. "If you think you can stand the sights you'll see."

Lenie smiled, triumphant, with a measured glare at Zack, to

underscore her victory.

John turned to Alden. "Son, your father needs you. You have a duty to help him take care of the farms and your family." Crestfallen, Alden knew his uncle was right.

"I have to go, and she stays? It's just not right," he grumbled, eying Jim and Zack resentfully. "This war will be over and I'll miss all the fun."

Zack put his arm around his younger brother and spoke prophetically. "Don't worry. I'll promise you we'll save some Yankees for you to shoot."

Chapter 3
Behind the Lines

Due to their knowledge of the local terrain, Jim and Zack became scouts, using their tracking skills to spy on the enemy on behalf of the revered General Jackson. Thrilled to be part of the entourage of this great icon and to earn their place in history, they wrote excited letters home of their exploits, taking care to leave out anything that might upset or worry their families, or dim their belief in the soon-to-be-won victory for independence.

With their fellow soldiers, they endured the hardships of war – all but one, for they had yet to fight in an actual battle. Lenie was the one who experienced firsthand the aftermath of the battles. While she reveled in the knowledge she acquired about the mysteries of medicine by serving at her father's side, her soul was roiled by the suffering of the men and her helplessness to alleviate it.

You may be wondering what people, men mostly, were thinking about this young girl in a soldier's camp. Well, in peacetime, the presence of a female in such an enclave – let alone a young female – would have precipitated its own rebellion within the genteel Southern society. But the men under her ministrations had no such concerns as they suffered and clung to life. Her father's protection and stature guarded her from any unwanted attention or lack of respect from the healthy enlisted men.

So she continued in her duties, snatching a moment of respite when she could, reading the few old books she had imported in her saddlebags that first night she appeared in camp, and roaming the nearby woods for the herbs that would help her patients.

And as cannons resounded in the distance and wagonloads of wounded soldiers arrived at the camp hospital, she was at her post, day and night.

The orderlies – Samuel and a patriotic old man from Fairfax County who'd been a postmaster in civilian life – made run after run from the frontline, bearing the wounded on their bloodied stretcher. Despite their haste, half the men were usually dead when they arrived. I say "men," but their faces were young – barely schoolboys. Realizing these patients were beyond help, Samuel and his helper unceremoniously threw the bodies to the side, beside a pile of amputated arms and legs and the voracious buzzing flies that hovered over this human refuse, to turn their attention to those they still might save.

Inside the tent, Lenie and Dr. John worked feverishly among the groaning, gasping and sometimes shrieking wounded. Plantation heirs, farmers, shopkeepers, schoolboys, rich or poor, all were reduced to the common denominator of wounds and pain.

Discovering that her basket was out of bandages, Lenie darted back to the supply cart, only to find it empty. Frustrated, she reached under her skirt, yanked off her petticoat, ripped it in half, and ran back to her father at the operating table. As she made her way through the cots, frantic hands grabbed at her ragged skirt.

"Water! Water! For the love of God," croaked a thirsty soldier. Samuel followed behind her, pushing a cup of water to the soldier's lips. The man released Lenie as he slurped greedily. Lenie and Samuel exchanged a look – very brief, but long enough for the tension in her face to relax. A bit.

So it was through experiences like these that Lenie and Samuel formed a bond that gave strength to them both. The fact that she was educated and privileged, and he was poor and uncultured, mattered not a whit to her. Something in Samuel's gentle yet firm commitment to his duties touched her wary heart. Whereas she was like a mercurial bubbling brook, making choppy waves as it bounced over rocks, trees and anything else in its path, he was like a placid and serene lake, under whose calm surface plants gently undulated on a broad sandy bottom.

She especially loved to sit quietly at night and listen to him read to the soldiers, watching his pale face, with its dusting of freckles, his thick brown hair flopping over his broad forehead, as he slowly, deliberately, formed each word.

"And I will dwell in the house of the Lord forever," concluded Samuel.

"Amen. Amen," murmured the soldiers as Samuel stood up to

leave, finally ready to retire. In the shadows of the tent, Lenie's eyes followed him.

"When you read to them, they seem to feel better. I'll remember that," she said softly.

Startled by her presence, and a little embarrassed, he responded shyly, "I'm glad they – you – find it – comforting."

"My father says you want to be a preacher," she queried, trying to engage him a little longer.

"Yes, if they will have me at the seminary," he shrugged. "I have a lot to learn."

"I could help you," offered Lenie, rushing her words. "My mother taught me – oh, you know, Latin and Greek and all those things."

Samuel nodded, hiding his happiness at her attention.

"I'll show you my books. Tomorrow," she promised.

I imagine that Dr. John was relieved rather than worried that this relationship took up Lenie's restless energy and soothed her volatile emotions. He probably quelled his fatherly concern by reminding himself that many girls Lenie's age were already married, and that this first interest in a young man on her part might be the first step toward a life path that was more in line with the expectations of a young woman from a good family in that Victorian era: respectable marriage and children.

Anyway, that's what I imagine.

Chapter 4
Christmas Dinner

That's how the Lewis boys find themselves in a real war with their unusual cousin on the front as well. Of the Delacourts they know nothing except that their former visitors had departed after Virginia's secession announcement for their homes in faraway Texas.

By their second winter, the War was no longer an outing to be over and done with after a few sedate skirmishes. As Christmas approached, Zack and Jim found themselves riding through the desolate landscape beside a frozen creek bank. The plumes and sashes of their uniforms dress were long gone; their garments now were shabby and frayed, their faces thin. The only sign of Christmas spirit was a light snow.

A lone rabbit hopped across their path. Zack grabbed his gun, but the rabbit disappeared before he could take aim.

"There goes our Christmas dinner!" muttered Zack, disgusted. Jim pulled hardtack from his saddlebag and gave a piece to Zack.

"This'll have to do."

Zack bit into the rock-hard lump, and heroically tried to chew it. Suddenly, he lifted his head, sniffing the air.

"What's that smell?" he asked. Jim also sniffed. The two looked at each other in disbelief.

"Roast goose!" gasped Zack. If Jefferson Davis himself had suddenly appeared before them, Zack could not have been more astonished.

Faster than that lucky hare, the two ragged boys were lying prone at the crest of a hill, looking out over a hollow where a white farmhouse nestled, smoke streaming from the chimney into the overcast sky. A dozen horses were tied in the yard. As they watched, more people arrived on horseback – several well-dressed women and two men in blue uniforms. The door opened, and sounds of Yuletide greetings wafted across the hollow along with the delicious aroma of roast meat. It was like a dream of past Christmases, back on their plantation, almost unbearable in its tantalizing sweetness.

Resolutely, Zack stood up and mounted his horse.

"It's time for my Christmas dinner," he announced firmly as he rode off toward the house. Jim, at first aghast at his brother's recklessness, recovered himself and quickly followed.

They dismounted in front of the farmhouse, tying their horses apart from the others. Zack marched arrogantly up to the door and knocked, as Jim followed more cautiously. The door opened – and there stood a Yankee soldier, his barrel chest straining against the buttons of the hated blue serge uniform, his eyes crinkling in a holiday grin.

"Merry Chris –" his greeting and his smile died as he gaped at the two Confederate soldiers – and their guns pointed at his portly chest.

As the other guests spotted the new arrivals, their cheerful conversation died in a shocked and fearful silence. A serving woman dropped a dish with a crash that echoed through the now quiet parlor. One soldier made a move toward the corner. Jim saw that this was where the soldiers' weapons were stored; he quickly moved in front of them to block the Yankee's way.

"No need to get up. We'll just have our dinner and be on our way," Zack informed the silent crowd. He took a seat close to the door, between the soldiers and their guns. Jim sat beside him.

The commanding officer locked eyes with Zack. He was a tall, slender man who cut a dashing figure in a blue serge uniform whose golden buttons and braids gleamed as if polished daily. Smiling, he showed pointed, white teeth in a lean, tanned, and watchful face. The hairs on the back of Zack's dirty neck bristled. He knew – and despised – this insolent, well-groomed man.

"Mr. Delacourt! You – you're –" Jim couldn't believe it. But Zack could. His suspicions had been right all along.

Zack glared his contempt at their former acquaintance. His finger twitched on the trigger of his rifle. But there were too many Yankees present for him to follow through on his urge to remove this traitorous – and useless – man from this earthly life.

Charles, seemingly oblivious to his danger, just grinned his feral smile and nodded in greeting as if Zack and Jim had stopped by for a holiday afternoon visit.

"These friends of yours, Captain Delacourt?" asked another soldier warily.

"Let's say I've enjoyed their family's hospitality in happier days. Go ahead, Sadie. Fix a plate for these two… guests," replied Charles.

The serving woman nervously selected two more plates, slopped food on them, and handed them to Zack and Jim, backing away quickly as if they were dangerous wild animals. The starving boys ate so fast they almost inhaled the food. No Virginia manners today – just ravenous appetites.

His mouth full, Zack encouraged the gaping onlookers. "It's really good. Go ahead, eat up."

Eying his gun, the other guests tentatively resumed their meal. In a few seconds, the boys' plates were clean, save for the biscuits. Scooping those tender, steaming morsels into their pockets, they backed toward the door.

"Much obliged for your hospitality," offered Jim, ever courteous.

Once outside, Zack slammed the door shut, blocking it with a piece of wood. The two raced to their horses and galloped off.

Soon as that door was closed, the Yankee soldiers leaped for their rifles. One aimed through the window at Zack and Jim. But Charles Delacourt stayed his hand.

"It's Christmas," he said, with that wolfish smile, watching the Lewis boys ride off into the woods. "Let them go."

Chapter 5
First Blood

Back at the Confederate camp, the closest the less fortunate soldiers got to a Christmas goose was hearing about Zack and Jim's heroic escapade and how they showed those arrogant Yankees what courage and bravery really looked like – Southern style.

"And there sat those Yankees, their mouths open like a row of dead fish. Jim and me, we just chewed as fast as we could," concluded Zack.

"Easter's comin'. Where you gonna go for dinner? Can I come, too?" asked a soldier. The others laughed raucously.

The laughter died away abruptly as their commander, Captain Landis, emerged from the shadows and stood expectantly at the edge of their group. Long respected as the local justice of the peace, he had won his men's allegiance with quiet competence and common sense. His very presence commanded their attention like the arrival of a preacher.

"Boys, you'd best get a good night's sleep. We're going into battle tomorrow morning," he announced solemnly.

Some greeted this news with silence, but Jim and Zack were jubilant. "It's about time," crowed Zack, smacking his brother heartily on the back.

Lenie and Samuel sauntered by, so deep in their private conversation they did not even notice the excitement among the men.

"Lenie! We're fighting tomorrow!" called Jim.

Lenie stopped, frowning. "Battle" meant something entirely different to her than to her naïve cousins.

"You be careful. Don't try to be heroes," she warned.

"Careful? Hah! There are no cowards in our family," claimed Zack, looking pointedly at Samuel. Samuel put his arm around Lenie, staying her retort – a move that irritated Zack even more.

"We're holding a prayer service in a few minutes. You are welcome to join us," offered Samuel.

Several soldiers rose and followed him. But Zack and Jim

stayed seated.

"Say some prayers for your friend Charles Delacourt. The Yankee. He'll be needing them tomorrow," Zack called after Lenie's retreating form.

Lenie turned back abruptly. "What?"

"It's true. We saw him. He's a turncoat to his own people," pronounced Jim.

"Maybe it's you who should watch out. He's one of the best shots in Texas," Lenie retorted.

Zack watched Lenie and Samuel disappear into the shadows, yet again puzzled and annoyed by his cousin's strange predilection for this awkward mountain boy.

"You don't suppose she's sweet on that hillbilly, do you?" asked Zack.

"Nah. There's no sweet in her," scoffed Jim. Zack stared after the couple, not so sure his suspicions might not be correct.

Before a battle, before the killing starts, they say it can be a pretty sight. The morning of the Lewis' boys first – and last – fight together, the infantry of both sides lined up in formation, making an undulating pattern of blue and gray across the huge field. Zack and Jim, on horseback with the cavalry, watched impatiently at the edge of the woods. Their fine Virginia horses pawed the pine cone-strewn ground nervously. Any fear Zack and Jim may have felt was transmuted by their excitement, and the belief in their own immortality that all young men have, even in the face of the gravest danger.

When he tired of straining to see the opposing army facing them across the field, Zack mentally took note of all the details around him – the quiet of the birds, the remnants of winter snow still clinging to the tree hollows, the cold bite of the air, the steam from his breath – to write to his family later about this historic and glorious event.

Finally the long-awaited bugle sounded. Hundreds of throats erupted in the Rebel yell. Swords drawn, the cavalry charged. The horses galloped fiercely over the dead winter grass, churning up a spray of dirt as they ran. For Zack, their sprint was suspended in time – like the moments between leaping out of the old tree by the river and landing in the cold water.

Suddenly, in fast motion, here was the enemy he had so long awaited. The cannons boomed, gunfire resounded. Zack did not even hear the sounds, so intent was he on striking his first blow for the beloved Cause.

The two armies collided in a frantic melee. Jim and Zack fought furiously. Zack was the first to draw blood as he struck down a young Northerner, whose cap fell off as he landed silently on the damp ground. Zack's triumphant expression dimmed as he saw the young face of the man he had killed, his lank blond hair spilling onto the brown grass.

Meanwhile, Jim succeeded in unhorsing a soldier with a swipe of his Uncle's lucky sword. He turned to Zack for recognition, but the "dead" soldier rose up, pulled a pistol from his belt and fired. Jim's horse reared wildly, and Jim disappeared into the smoke billowing across the battlefield. Zack tried to turn his horse to his brother's rescue, but his horse stumbled and fell, pinning him.

"Jim! Jim!" screamed Zack. There was no answer, only the explosions of firearms and the shrieks of the wounded, man and beast. A cannon ball exploded, exactly where Zack had last seen Jim. Zack freed himself from the fallen horse and staggered toward that spot, dragging his injured leg. He didn't see the approaching Yankee, the sword that struck his head, ending his desperate search for Jim and making him, too, one of the day's casualties.

By late afternoon, it was over. The meadow, now a field of blood-soaked mud, was quiet again. It was impossible to tell who had won by the state of that unlucky site, now littered with the dead and dying. Samuel and the old man trudged through the tragic debris, seeking the wounded, like stagehands clearing the set when the curtain has fallen on the play. As Samuel rolled over one more body, he recognized Zack. Samuel knelt beside him, and Zack's eyes fluttered open.

"Jim! Where's Jim?" Zack whispered groggily.

"If he's here, we'll find him," promised Samuel.

Samuel tried to lift Zack onto the stretcher, only to be pushed away with a sudden ferocious strength.

"Got to find Jim! Let me go!"

Perhaps secretly grateful for this opportunity to express his feelings without violating his beliefs, Samuel grabbed Zack by the shoulder, and slugged him, hard, on the jaw. At this "medicinal" blow, Zack collapsed, unconscious. Samuel and his helper hauled his inert body onto the stretcher.

So Zack found himself in the aftermath of his first battle, not recounting his courageous exploits as he had imagined, but enduring Lenie's ministrations in the field hospital amidst the smells of blood and worse, and the groans and screams of men with injuries much worse than his.

As the pain in his leg abated, the shame of being sidelined in his first battle increased, exacerbated by the impatience that is characteristic of boys of every era. The infirmary was a prison to him. Especially painful was listening to Samuel read the Bible to the other soldiers. He had no patience for words of peace, tolerance and forgiveness while his home and family were under attack by people he considered to be infidels, or worse.

Indeed, Samuel's quiet presence was a constant irritation. With his brethren fighting and dying on the field each day, Zack viewed Samuel's pacifism as a close cousin to downright betrayal of his Cause. Truth be told, he was most annoyed watching Lenie's dark head – her hair now long again and pulled back from her face by any strip of rag she could spare to use as a ribbon – bent close to Samuel's light brown one, in quiet conversation.

In his frustration, he was not above taking jibes at Samuel, almost hoping he would goad the other boy into an angry response. But Samuel exercised admirable restraint and irritated Zack mightily by consistently turning the other cheek. Except for one time.

On that day Samuel finished his reading to the other patients and moved to sit beside Zack's bed.

"Don't bother with me. I don't need any of that Bible stuff," warned Zack.

"But I found a passage just for you. Listen," responded Samuel, his calm eyes gleaming with an uncharacteristic mischief. He began to read from the worn Bible.

"I pursued my enemies and overtook them, and I did not turn back until they were consumed."

Samuel stopped and smiled, a little maliciously, if truth be told.

"If you hadn't stopped me, I would have found Jim," accused Zack.

"If Samuel hadn't brought you back, you would have died," snapped Lenie.

This incipient argument was interrupted when Captain Landis entered the cluttered ward, weaving between the wounded men. He carried a sword that he laid beside Zack. The metal no longer shown with the zeal of Jim's ministrations, but Zack knew that sword immediately.

"Did you find him?" asked Zack, almost fearful.

"No. But he could have been taken prisoner," responded Captain Landis.

"We... never... surrender," gasped the man lying next to Zack, a scruffy, stolid farmer from the backwoods of North Carolina who had somehow survived the night on the battlefield and the amputation of his left leg. With that effort, he fell back, unconscious. Zack picked up the sword reverently.

"Jim would never surrender," he murmured.

"Of course not! You'd all rather die for the glory of the cause!" retorted Lenie, the raw force of her emotions disguising what would have been a quiver in her voice.

"Pauline!" admonished Dr. John. She turned away so no one – and especially Zack – saw her face crumple in silent, angry sobs – not only for her missing cousin, but for the others who would not return home.

Chapter 6
First Loss

As Zack continued his recovery, he found distraction and purpose in helping the other men write letters home, imagining that somewhere, in some other hospital or even prison camp, someone would help his missing brother do the same. As for his feelings about Jim's future, or even his survival, I imagine Zack shut the door on those speculations as firmly as a clanging iron gate deep in the heart of a dungeon.

To his own family, his notes were always carefully worded to inspire and reassure those he loved so much. He treasured their missives deeply – especially those in Millie's and Helen's childish scrawls. I have been so fortunate as to see some of them myself – yellowed pages with spidery but vigorous letters forming words that speak through the years of the youthful hearts who created them.

Within a few weeks he was able to hobble from bed to bed, aided by a makeshift crutch. To Lenie's chagrin, and probably Samuel's, he was assigned to help in the hospital while he recovered.

This brings us to one fateful day in early summer, as Lenie enjoyed a rare quiet moment ripping cloth into bandages. Zack paced the tent, dispensing with his crutch for the first time, looking toward the front and waiting expectantly for the sounds of battle.

"I ought to be out there," muttered Zack.

"There will be action enough here for you later. Just wait," retorted Lenie. Her tone of superiority rankled Zack, but his planned reply was interrupted when Samuel ran into the tent, dodging the maze of cots as he made his way to Lenie's side. Breathless, he proudly reached into his pouch and showed her his prize: a cluster of green, prickly leaves.

"You got them!" crowed Lenie, taking his offering eagerly.

"Found them just in time," he gasped, out of breath from his mission yet enjoying the brief glow of happiness that lit up Lenie's face.

"I'll bet you high tailed it out of there when the shooting started," murmured Zack, just loud enough to be heard.

Lenie scowled at him, but Samuel focused her attention on a groaning soldier, grizzled and rangy, whose mountain stoicism broke down in the face of unremitting pain. Crushing the leaves in her hands, she pulled back his bandage and laid the crumpled herbs against his skin. Maybe it was her imagination, but it seemed to her that his moans grew softer.

"Do you mind how they talk about you?" Lenie asked Samuel, quietly.

"Well – yes. Sometimes," Samuel admitted. "But I just remember about turning the other cheek."

"How's the battle going?" grunted the injured soldier through clenched teeth.

"Too soon to tell. Would you like me to read to you?" asked Samuel. The man nodded, his face pale with effort as he struggled not to moan.

"Can't you help him?" Zack burst out in frustration.

"There's no more morphine. Our ships can't get through the blockade," snapped Lenie crossly, as if to an irritating and slow-witted child.

"Damn Ape Lincoln," Zack swore fervently.

Samuel opened his worn Bible and began to read, offering the only relief available.

"*I have set the Lord always before:*
Because he is at my right hand, I shall not be moved.
Therefore my heart is glad and my glory rejoiceth,
My flesh also shall rest in hope.
For thou will not leave my soul in hell,
Neither wilt thou suffer thine Holy One to see corruption.
Thou wilt shew me the path of life.
In thy presence is fullness of joy
At thy right hand there are pleasures for evermore." (Psalm 16: 8 – 11)

I imagine these words that people today read so seldom, acted like a balm to the soul back then. Especially since that was about all they had to soothe their fears.

Just as Lenie had predicted, within a few hours the field hospital was a madhouse. Samuel and his elderly helper staggered in with another stretcher, depositing one more casualty on the ground, as Lenie barked orders to Zack.

"Faster! Tie it tight!" she snapped. Zack's clumsy hands were all twisted in the frayed bandages. Only his concern for his injured comrades kept him from throwing the ragged cloth on the floor in disgust. The old man wiped his sweating face with his sleeve, breathing hard.

"Here, Grandpa, take my place. I'll spell you for a while," Zack eagerly hobbled over and picked up the stretcher.

"Zack!" called Lenie. Zack turned to her, impatiently. She spoke softly so Samuel couldn't hear.

"Take care! For both of you." Her words were both an order and a plea.

Zack nodded quickly, not really listening in his eagerness to be off to the battlefield. Samuel and Lenie exchanged a quick, poignant smile as he and Zack set off. As she did each day, Lenie impressed the memory of this smile onto her malleable heart.

Zack's second battle was as filled with smoke and noise as his first – with one big difference. He wasn't fighting this time. Emerging from the woods, he beheld another scene of bedlam – another pristine field transformed to a site dedicated to the organized extermination of human beings. The two boys made their way through the chaos, booming cannons, and screaming men and horses to a fallen soldier, limbs spread out at odd angles and mouth agape. Quickly they loaded him on to the stretcher and headed back to the hospital.

Behind a hastily dug earthen barricade, Zack's comrades in arms crouched, firing their rifles into the smoky melee. Samuel ducked low as he ran, while Zack craned his head to see over the little mound to where the conflict continued.

"Samuel! Stop!" he yelled, barely audible above the battle's din. Galloping toward them was a magnificent chestnut stallion, its rider expertly, invisibly guiding the horse through the noise and chaos. The men recognized his stone-faced handsome visage, the long flowing beard. They turned from their murderous work and waved. Some cheered, and a few whistled and tossed their worn hats into the air.

"Holding this ditch like a Stone Wall. That's right, General," hollered one rambunctious boy in faded butternut. The General solemnly nodded in approval, heedless of the danger and the target he made to the enemy.

"Hold the line, boys. Hold the line," he called in his authoritative, deep voice as he galloped on. Zack stared transfixed after his hero, remembering the days when he was an important part of the General's scouting team. Belatedly he thought to wave, but General Jackson was already out of sight – a memory to be carried for a lifetime.

Meanwhile Samuel's attention was focused on the man in the stretcher, whose sightless stare announced that he was beyond the help of any field hospital.

"Zack! We'll leave him here and go back," he ordered.

They deposited the body under a tree. Samuel took a moment to close the dead soldier's eyes and murmur a quiet prayer. The man's rifle fell to the ground. Without thinking, Zack picked it up, then found himself expertly removing the ammunition from the soldier's belt.

"What are you doing?" shouted Samuel over the deafening noise.

"You believe what you believe, and I believe what I believe," Zack retorted. He hobbled off toward the earthen barricade, crouched, and took aim at the enemy. Samuel watched him in frustration, then threw down the useless stretcher and climbed over the barricade.

"All right then, you cover me," Samuel hollered to Zack.

"Go back! Get someone to help you!" Zack waved him back but Samuel ignored him, heading out into no man's land.

Shrugging off Samuel's instruction, Zack reloaded his rifle. He had only gotten off a few more shots when Samuel reappeared through the smoke, dragging a wounded soldier by the feet. Zack fired again, another Yankee down. Samuel continued on. He was

30 feet from the line when abruptly he froze. Slowly he fell to his knees as if beholding a vision, then crumpled face forward into the dirt.

Zack's heart beat once, really hard, as he realized Samuel had been hit. Too late, he remembered his promise to Lenie. Quickly, he leaped over the barricade and raced to the fallen orderly. Samuel's eyes were open, but unfocused. Hooking his arms under Samuel's, he managed to drag the wounded boy back to the line. Other soldiers dropped their rifles long enough to help him lift Samuel over and behind it. One obligingly helped Zack drag Samuel to the stretcher. Unlike Zack, he was probably grateful for a break in the fighting. Together the two headed back with their wounded charge toward the hospital.

It seemed an eternity, but it was only a few minutes before Zack limped inside the hospital and lay Samuel's bloodied body on the ground, by the spot where Lenie was working over a young blacksmith, now a loader of cannons, whose face and hands bore the red burn marks of an exploded charge.

"Oh, Lordy!" gasped the old man in dismay at the site of Zack's charge.

"No!" whispered Lenie, as she fell to her knees beside the wounded boy. The spreading stain on Samuel's chest told her his wound was serious. As her hands worked dexterously to pull the wet cloth from his body and replace it with a thick bandage to stanch the scarlet flow, she looked fiercely into his glazed eyes.

"Don't you even think about dying on me. You're going to be all right," she commanded. Samuel looked for her face, but could not focus.

"It's all right. Lenie – say our prayer with me," he whispered.

She held his hand tightly, desperately, while her other hand covered his heart, in a vain attempt to stem the spreading tide of red liquid. They began to pray.

*"I shall not want. He maketh me lie down in green pastures.
He restoreth my soul.
Yea, though I walk in the shadow of the valley of death
I shall fear no evil."*

Samuel's voice fell to an inaudible whisper. Lenie continued on, louder and stronger as if her voice could give him life.

"For thou art at my side, thy rod and thy staff shall comfort me. Thou preparest a table before me in the presence of mine enemies. Thou —"

She peered into Samuel's eyes, willing them to see her. He whispered, very low.

"Lenie – remember – remember –" Samuel's voice faded. His eyes stared fixedly, no longer at this world but into the next.

Lenie's own heart stopped with his. Imagining her agony, her bravery, my own heart breaks for her across the years.

But not so her cousin. Watching, Zack's heart irrationally made a little leap at the knowledge that Samuel was removed from Lenie's life. He told himself quickly it was because he didn't think Samuel was a good influence on his volatile cousin. Then, his own guilt flooded his heart. This was a man, a good man, regardless of his own judgments about Samuel's beliefs. And his cousin had cared for him. Tentatively, he reached out and touched her shoulder in probably the first tender gesture he'd ever made across the gulf of judgment that separated them.

Lenie responded to the unfamiliar touch, looking up through eyes desperately bright with tears. Instead of his contrite expression, however, she only saw the rifle slung over Zack's shoulder.

"You left him, didn't you?" she affirmed rather than asked. Her grief changed to rage as she threw herself at Zack, beating his chest with her bloodied fists until Dr. John grabbed her arms, pulling her back and confining her in his strong embrace. Then she collapsed, weeping violently on her father's chest.

Dr. John glared accusingly at Zack, as if his nephew were the source of his daughter's bitter grief. The words "I'm sorry" formed in Zack's mind, but he could not make them pass his lips.

"Pauline! You must be strong!" ordered John. But Lenie could no longer hold back her desolation at losing this most personal and heartbreaking battle against death. For the second time in her young life, the only person who could calm her heart was lost to her.

Chapter 7
Bitter Good-byes

If Zack felt guilt over Samuel's death, it didn't stop him from sleeping soundly that night. Perhaps he comforted himself with the old platitude, "She's young. She'll get over it."

Only the whinnying of frightened horses finally woke him, proving that a Virginian is more attuned to the moods of his horses than to his womenfolk. In a second he was alert. Grabbing his sword, he limped off to investigate. In the darkness, he could discern a figure untying one of the precious beasts.

"Halt! I've got you trapped!" he waved the sword threateningly.

"Don't try to stop me! I'll shoot you! I swear I will!" cried a shrill, high voice in the darkness.

Lenie stepped forward from the blackness, leading one of the regiment's priceless horses, the flaring nostrils in its chestnut-colored face reflecting her agitation. After all, it wasn't every day that an Army horse was led out for a nocturnal ride by a crazy Texas girl. And one who was wearing only a nightgown and a pair of boots. And carried a gun.

The female in question pointed her pistol at Zack.

"I'm leaving. Getting away from this hell. Don't try to stop me," she announced.

"That's a capital idea. But can't you wait until morning?" inquired Zack, countering her hysteria with logic. "Go back to bed. You'll feel better in the morning. I always do."

His advice was not well received. Lenie's face closed as she turned to mount the skittish animal. Zack rushed over, grabbing her legs to stop her. She fought him, swinging the pistol. He dodged. The gun fired, shattering the night quiet.

At the explosion, the somnolent camp sprang to life. Soldiers came running, aiming their rifles at Lenie, now half hanging off the horse, as it shied and whinnied in fear. Despite the encumbrance of his cane, Dr. John pushed Zack away and pulled Lenie to the ground.

"She's acting crazy, Uncle John," explained Zack. "She wants to run away –"

"He killed Samuel! He wants to kill everybody!" Lenie wailed, her rigid self-control broken at last. Dr. John enfolded her in his arms, shushing her.

"No, Daughter, it was God's will," he murmured. "The Lord giveth and He taketh away."

"They're out there, in the dark, waiting for us," Lenie cried, dread and terror in her voice. "I can see their eyes."

Zack peered around suspiciously, but saw no one lurking in the shadows.

"No, no. There's nothing there. I'm here now," murmured Dr. John, stroking her wildly waving hair. Lenie's sobs subsided; she looked up into her father's eyes, pleading.

"Mama's dead. I couldn't save her. I couldn't – save him either." Lenie swallowed but could not continue. His arm firmly around her thin shoulders, her father began to lead her back to her tent.

Respectfully, even gently, the men stepped aside to make way for this brave girl whose crusty manner belied her generous heart.

At the edge of the silent crowd, she turned back and glared at Zack, very calm now, her blue eyes blazing like the point of a sword.

"It was your fault. You and your stupid War. I'll never forgive you for what you did to Samuel. Never."

Whether she had any idea at that moment, her words cut a rift that would last a lifetime. Zack almost winced but was too stubborn to react to the verbal blow. He just stared wordlessly at her retreating, white figure as her father led her away.

Then, he suddenly remembered his own culpability for her pain. "I'm sorry," he muttered, forcing the words from his tired mind into speech. But it was too late...

Dr. John's concern for his daughter overrode his physician's commitment to helping the wounded soldiers. Perhaps he remembered his old friend Charles' advice to head west, toward the frontier, and away from the dangerous Virginia battlefields. Perhaps he was just driven to escape with his precious daughter. Whatever his reasons, within a few days father and daughter had packed and

43

left the battlefields of Northern Virginia for their distant, adopted home in Texas.

Although he professed great relief that his young cousin was bound for safety and presumably, a life more fitting for her age and sex, Zack sometimes found that he missed their constant arguments. Now he realized how the presence of his cousin and his uncle had been a tenuous connection with his home and family. With them gone, and Jim still missing, he was truly alone. Nevertheless, he carried on with his duty as he saw it, the lone representative of his family on the battlefront, fighting for the Cause they all loved.

Chapter 8
Re-connection

Now it was that Zack's career as a soldier began in earnest. The battles raged all around the towns and farms Zack had known as a boy, taking one village, losing it again in a few weeks, each acre a bitter, blood-soaked fight.

The old family sword proved lucky for him, as he grimly defended his homeland on courthouse steps, across fields, on rough bridges and in country lanes. Secretly, he harbored the wish that he might find that turncoat Charles Delacourt at the opposite end of his sword in one of these encounters, but that hope had yet to materialize.

While we have today so many things to capture and distract our thoughts – more and more of them involving that infernal computer machine – people in those days had only themselves, and their own thoughts. Once when Zack was entertaining me with his war stories, we'd just been to see one of the first of those old-timey (so considered nowadays) moving pictures. Images rapidly flickering by, like thumbing the pages of a book. That was how he said the pictures in his head flew by when he fought to keep away the reality that surrounded him.

Before each encounter, Zack played his own mental movie. In his mind's eye he saw again the tranquil fields, heard the lazy hum of bees in his mother's flower garden, and smelled the blossoms that spoke the language of their hearts and souls.

At night in camp, while others tossed on the hard ground or cried out from tormented dreams, Zack summoned more serene scenes to strengthen his spirit: the rustle of his mother's purple taffeta skirt, the cool slate tablets in the nursery as she taught him his lessons, and the hardness of the saddle as his father balanced his small body on his favorite horse, Ezekiel, while he toured his farms and spoke with the overseers.

Sometimes the plot of this movie strayed to more sentimental scenes: stringing popcorn for the Christmas tree, holding Helen's chubby hand as she took her first steps, and presenting his parents with the crudely carved wooden dog he had once made for their holiday present. When a rush of emotion threatened to bring a tear of loneliness to his tired eyes, he resolutely turned his imagination to the most powerful images of all: the vision of his sisters, married and happy and with families of their own, safe and secure at the old homestead.

What would my movie have been? Could I have persisted, day after day, hour after hour, in this dance with death? Well, I'll be honest with you. No, I could not. No commitment to glory or home could have kept me there. Maybe I should be downright ashamed, but I promised to tell the truth.

In "real" life, Zack dutifully continued to write brief, comforting letters to his parents and family, never mentioning his hardships and always optimistic about his faith in an ultimate victory. Whatever their private doubts, they were confident in the belief that Jim had only been captured and would someday soon be able to smuggle a letter to them proclaiming his survival. The letters Zack received from home echoed the hope that victory was inevitable, and any deprivations were minor compared to that ultimate goal.

Occasionally, his thoughts turned farther South, to the frontier of Texas, as he imagined his wayward cousin returning to her former life and – what? There his imaginings stopped, for there were no details shared about their Texas relatives in his letters from home, after the news that they had arrived at their destination and set up house at their old home in Galveston.

While Lenie and her father may have been safely away from the front, that was not the case for Zack's Virginia family. They lived in constant suspense of warfare erupting in their neighborhood as the two armies chased themselves back and forth between their respective capitals. Several times, the elegant mansion saw use as a field hospital for the wounded from nearby battlefields. Once, an errant cannonball landed so close to the barn that some valuable livestock, including two prized horses, were killed. This news the family did not share with Zack. As for the animals, it did not matter, for those that were not donated to the Rebel army were soon confiscated by marauding Northern troops.

46

So it was that two more years of bitter fighting found Zack even shabbier and more exhausted, but undaunted in his resolve or commitment to his Cause. The inexperienced boy soldier was replaced by a hardened, tough veteran. Due to his scouting skills, Zack became a valued advisor to his commanding officers for his knowledge of the countryside and his ability to track the movements of troops between battles.

On a sultry summer evening, when Captain Landis summoned him to personally brief the men on the terrain for the next day's battle, Zack went dutifully, not expecting the following day's events to be any different than a dozen other skirmishes.

"They call this place the Wilderness. Trees so thick you can't see the sun," Zack explained to his silent, bone-weary comrades.

"Any spark from a gun will set off a fire. Orders are to keep fighting and leave the wounded to fend for themselves," said Captain Landis. "Could be a trap. Could be a Yankee callin' for help."

The Captain paused. "We may not be able to get to you before the flames. Best to keep one shot in reserve. For yourself."

As the horror of this advice sank in, the men sat motionless, with not even the sound of an indrawn breath to disturb the silence. This time, there was no Samuel to offer them spiritual solace before the next day's ordeal. They were left with only their own thoughts and imaginings of what the following morning would bring.

Could you have gone into battle the next day, knowing the probability of suffering the most painful death that fate can deal a man? Those ragged, hungry, passionate scarecrows did.

At their posts in the dark, pre-dawn hours, the Army of Northern Virginia found that the foliage was indeed so thick that only a few muted rays of sunshine penetrated the umbrella of interlocked branches. With his comrades, Zack crept slowly through the dense underbrush as guns and cannons sounded in the distance.

Dislodged from its hiding place within the layers of dried leaves, a hard object rolled toward the supine soldiers. It came to rest precariously in a small hollow, illuminated by one pale ray of sun: a skull, grinning hideously in the washed out light. Was it an Indian brave, first denizen of the vast forest? A casualty of the Colonial war for freedom? A friend or foe from last year's battle?

No one ever knew. Suddenly, a cannonball burst through the trees, landing with a thud and then, a second later, an explosion. Bodies and tree branches flew through the air. As the sparks landed in the dry brush, small, wispy fires broke out.

Keeping low to the ground, the crouched soldiers tried to beat out the flames, but there were too many. They could only continue to advance, their escape route now cut off as the flames spread beside and behind them. The sounds of gunfire intensified. Another cannonball exploded, then another. More fires began. Now the shots were punctuated with men screaming. Soldiers fought on, grimly, as the tormented shrieks resounded on all sides.

"Where are those damn orderlies?" shouted Zack. He coughed, wiping his streaming eyes. His face was as black as one of his family's darkies. The smoke, the darkness, the mute trees, the inhuman howling – it was all like that hell they described in the Bible.

"Help me! Help me! For the love of God, help me!" cried desperate voices in the shadows, behind the undulating flames.

Zack could stand it no longer.

"I'm going in there. Cover me," he ordered the comrade next to him.

"You'll just get trapped yourself! We've got our orders!" argued the soldier. His white, frightened eyes gleamed in the darkness like a terrified forest animal. Zack ignored his warnings, vaulting over a fallen log and disappearing into the strange twilight.

Immediately he was lost, unable to see his comrades or distinguish the enemy. The shrieks of wounded soldiers came from every direction. The smell of something sweet and repulsive filled his nostrils, lending urgency to his search.

Keeping low to the ground, he crawled in the direction of where he'd heard a cry for help. Unexpectedly, he came to a clearing where, through the grey smoke, he thought he saw a figure moving toward him. The cry came again.

"Help me! Help me!"

It was indeed a fellow soldier, pulling himself along the ground with his one good arm, the other hanging limply beside him, and his useless legs dragging in the dead leaves that covered the ground and served as kindling for the ravenous fire. He was just ahead of the flames, his terrified young face lighting up with hope as he thought he saw his rescuer through the hazy air.

But at that moment, the wind shifted, and the flames leaped with malevolent glee across the clearing. Suddenly, the wounded soldier was on fire, lighting up the clearing like a ghastly human torch. His mouth formed an "O" of agony but no sound could be heard among the madly crackling inferno. As the flames raced toward him, Zack felt the heat of a huge bellows sear his face. He had no choice but to run for his life.

With Satanic malevolence, the flames raced after him. Unconsciously, Zack's knowledge of the woods took him through it as swiftly as any Indian brave. Until abruptly he stumbled, as the ground gave way beneath him and he fell headfirst into a boggy pond.

As Zack sank into its murky depths, its cool waters soothed his seared skin with instant relief. Only problem was, he couldn't breathe. The thought flashed through his head: better to die by drowning or by burning? The answer was easy.

Holding his breath until his lungs seared with pain, he swam with all his might toward the center of the pond, knowing by instinct where it was. Finally, self-preservation forced him to the surface. Gasping in the hot air, unable to see, he was relieved that no flames singed his muddy face. Wiping his eyes, he surveyed his surroundings. All around the green-slick pond, fires raged, stopping when they reached his watery bivouac. If he could just stay afloat until the fires passed him, he would be saved.

That night, a full moon eerily gleamed above the smoke and the horror of the day's events, belatedly providing more light than the shriveled sun had all that day.

On the bank of the river, a deer was startled by the sight of a pair of alien white eyes in the blackness. Their owner crept cautiously to the water's edge. His face blackened with soot and dirt, his clothes

49

covered with mud, Zack knelt down on all fours and drank greedily from the water, like an animal. Once sated, he rinsed his face in the cool stream.

Behind him, the dying fires glowed eerily and the sounds of battle receded. His mission of mercy had failed. He had not saved a single one of his suffering comrades. In a rare moment of piety, he silently said a prayer for their souls, especially the boy whose face he would never forget and whose name he would never know. Of the outcome of the battle, he knew nothing.

Looking up with a face now smudged grey instead of ebony, he recognized his surroundings. Like a childhood dream, the memory began to come back to him. But this was not a dream.

He staggered a few paces along the bank, around a curve in the river, and there it was. River's Rest. Now deserted, with boards across the narrow windows, still it drew him to it with an irresistible force. Home.

Chapter 9
A Tragic Reunion

Little Helen was the first to awaken that morning. Slipping out of bed, she crept to the window where she liked to watch the sun come up, and say her prayers for the safety of her beloved brothers. But this morning was different. Her eyes wide with horror, she let loose with a high, childish shriek, and flew from the room as her sister Millie woke with a start.

Dispensing with the propriety of knocking, Helen burst into her parents' room and catapulted like a polecat onto the bed.

"What in tarnation – HELEN!" admonished James.

"Papa, get your gun! There's a Yankee on the front lawn!" she yelped frantically.

James leaped up, grabbing the rifle that rested on the chair by the bed.

In a moment the entire family, clad in their nightclothes, was downstairs peering through the curtains onto the wide lawn, the terrified house slaves clustered behind them. Alden took the rifle from his father and measured the intruder in its sights.

What were they looking at? A sleeping soldier lay in a crumpled heap on the green grass, not so carefully trimmed since the War had tapped their resources for other purposes. The soft waving fronds had no doubt beckoned as a comfortable bed.

The family dog warily approached the trespasser. Nan stayed Alden's eager trigger finger.

"Don't shoot! You might hit Rex!" she warned.

Teeth bared, Rex stalked the unconscious figure. Getting closer, he sniffed. Then, he began to lick the soldier's dirty face.

"Rex! You traitor! You're supposed to bite him," accused Mildred. But Helen had recognized that soldier.

"Ackie! It's Ackie!" she cried joyfully. She darted outside, the rest of the family close behind.

From very far away, in some realm where there was no war and no more death, Zack's soul stirred at the familiar sounds of childish voices mixed with softer adult tones. With great effort, he opened his eyes. There, surrounding him, was his family. Truly, he was in Paradise.

That day's luncheon was a Thanksgiving of the heart in the Lewis household. James led grace with a special fervor, touched with the tinge of sadness that always permeated the family now, since the loss of their eldest son.

"For your bounty, and for the safety of our loved ones, we are truly thankful, Lord."

"Praise God," responded Sarah, her quiet voice unexpectedly husky with emotion. "Nan, would you explain the flowers today?"

"Lily of the Valley, for the return of happiness. Sorrell, for the affection of parents, and woodbine, for brotherly love," proclaimed Nan. "Everything we are celebrating today."

Zack inhaled the scent of the blossoms, another sensory anchor in this world that he had so long dreamt of and was now, once again, real. Feisty Helen, sitting at his elbow, flanked by her constant companion Millie. His parents, with lines of worry he had not remembered creasing their beloved faces. Nan, smiling so radiantly she gave off as much light as a sunbeam. And Alden, growing like a colt and boasting a new authority as his father's right hand. It was real, and yet it was like a dream.

Juno poured a steaming mixture into Zack's bowl. He sniffed it suspiciously.

"Yankees stole all our livestock," explained Helen.

"Looks delicious to me," replied Zack. He took a sip, and was seized with the desire to drink the entire bowl in one famished gulp. But his first mouthful was interrupted when Jeremiah dashed into the room.

"They's Yankees in the yard!" he cried, his eyes wide with the horror of this vision.

"That was this morning!" declared Millie authoritatively. Juno, peering through the drapes, backed away from the window as if she had just beheld a three-headed demon. The serving bowl of precious soup slipped from her hands, spilling on the now worn rug.

"They's a whole army out there! With guns," she wailed. Alden darted to the parlor window to see for himself.

"She's right. Zack, you've got to hide."

"Stay quiet, everyone," warned James as Zack raced upstairs. Nan whispered to her little sisters. "Don't say anything about Zack. Not a word." They nodded in solemn understanding.

In the dusty attic, Zack looked frantically for hiding places and opened the door to an old wardrobe. A frightened mouse scurried across his ragged boots, its frantic feet scrambling so hard to escape he could feel its claws through the worn leather. Military discipline asserted itself and he made no sound of surprise – or disgust.

Downstairs, James strolled out with feigned nonchalance to meet the small enemy squadron, while the family watched warily from the porch.

"Good day, Mr. Lewis," said the leader. James gazed up into the man's face. It was Charles Delacourt. His skin was still tanned and his teeth still flashed white in the sunlight, albeit his figure was more slender, even gaunt, than before the War. However, their former guest had not lost his gallant manners.

"I am sorry my return visit to your home is under these circumstances."

Although he knew from Zack and Jim's letters that Charles had sided with their foes, it was still a shock to see his former guest in the navy blue uniform of their enemy. But James recovered quickly, and nodded slightly to acknowledge the greeting. Behind him, the family glared balefully at the invaders.

"He IS a damn Yankee!" hissed Alden.

"Shh," warned Sarah.

Charles shifted slightly in his saddle, as if beneath his suave manner, some uneasiness about his relationship with his former hosts ruffled his equanimity.

"We're looking for Rebel soldiers. You wouldn't happen to have any here, would you?" he asked. James hesitated only a second.

"Rebel soldiers? No, no rebels."

Mildred's eyes grew as large as the buttons that served as eyes for her dolls, in shock at this paternal falsehood. But she made no sound. Not so her more boisterous sister.

53

"Go 'way! We don't want no damn Yankees round here!" shouted Helen.

"Helen! We do not use such language! Apologize to the captain at once!" admonished Sarah.

Embarrassed, Helen hid her face in Nan's skirts.

"Apologize? Mother, they're on our land, stealing our property!" protested Alden.

"That's enough!" ordered James. He turned his attention back to Charles. "Once again, it seems I am apologizing for the rudeness of my children."

"Damn Rebels! No matter how bad we beat 'em, they're still polite," murmured a Sergeant, his broad jaw jutting outward in disapprobation. Four years in the field and away from the streets of New York City had done nothing to nurture a fondness for these strange people and their two-edged gentility.

Ignoring him, Charles ordered, "Take the family to the barn while we search the house."

Several soldiers dismounted and led the family toward the barn as the rest of the troop entered the house. The terrified house slaves followed their masters into a new type of captivity.

"Papa told a lie!" whispered Mildred, incredulous.

"No, he didn't," Alden whispered back fiercely. "Zack's no rebel. He's a patriot."

Inside, soldiers searched the well-appointed rooms, mightily impressed by the luxurious furnishings and pocketing small items as they went from room to room. Several of the invaders inspected the pot on the fireplace, still bubbling with its varmint stew, and quickly helped themselves. One soldier spied Zack's sword in the corner. He picked it up, studying its fine workmanship.

In the attic, two soldiers conducted their search by overturning the discarded furniture and running their swords through the dusty cushions. One approached the old wardrobe and tried the handle. It was locked. He shook it. Still the door remained stubbornly closed to him. His companion pulled out his revolver and prepared to shoot the annoying lock open, but his partner stayed his hand.

"Save your shot," he instructed. Instead, he took his bayonet and stabbed at the thin wood. It broke easily; he jabbed it repeatedly. Then he peered inside.

"See anything?" asked his companion.

"Nah. Nothing worth taking either," replied the soldier, withdrawing his head from the ragged frame. Disappointed at the lack of plunder, they made their way back downstairs.

Meanwhile, in the front yard, the Sergeant reported to Captain Delacourt.

"Didn't find anyone, sir. Should we try to smoke 'em out?"

"No. Finish the search. We'll check the woods," responded Charles. He seemed reluctant to enter the home that had once offered him hospitality.

"But our orders –" protested the Sergeant.

"There's nothing here," Charles cut him off. He turned his horse and headed toward the woods he remembered lay between the big house and River's Rest, taking a few men with him to assist in the search.

Ostensibly obedient, the sergeant re-entered the house. From the parlor window he watched Charles ride away. Then, ignoring his orders, he took a brand from the fireplace and, grinning malevolently, held it to the fine fabric of the draperies, until the flames caught.

Up in the attic, thousands of dust specks filled the air as the afternoon sunlight bathed the devastation the marauders left behind. In the silence, Zack cautiously emerged from UNDER the ransacked wardrobe. He crept to the window and peered outside. Several enemy soldiers still loitered in the yard, watching the house with interest. Then he smelled it. Smoke. Visions of the horror in the forest, only days before, filled his mind.

He darted to the door and flung it open. Flames and smoke already greedily climbed the stairs, blocking his escape. He ran back to the window, eying a branch of the large oak by the house.

In a moment, dried leaves from the oak tree drifted down onto the head and shoulders of a Yankee soldier standing below it. He peered up into the thick foliage as he brushed off the leaves, then back to the burning mansion. The other Yankees didn't notice. They were too enthralled in watching the progress of the flames consume this once beautiful edifice to the Southern culture.

Confident that their mission was accomplished, the troops rode off. One soldier detoured by the barn to remove the barricade to the wooden door, releasing the family from their captivity.

Blinking in the sunshine, their eyes quickly adjusted to the light only to take in the horrible sight of the flames leaping high above their beloved homestead.

Helen was the first to remember his missing brother. "Ackie! Ackie!" she cried. As heedless of danger as her brothers, she ran up the steps and into the burning manse.

"Helen! Helen! Come back!" screamed Sarah. James and Alden raced after Helen as the women watched, horrified.

Belatedly, Zack dropped to the ground from the bushy oak tree, where he had been hiding all along.

"Zack! Helen ran in to get you!" cried Nan.

Instantly, Zack darted inside the burning house as Sarah hugged her other terrified daughters fiercely, as if afraid that she might lose them, too. Never in all the years her boys were in danger, had her heart constricted in this horrible pain.

After a few endless moments, James and Alden emerged, coughing, soot-covered – and empty-handed.

Behind them, timbers fell into what was once their parlor, burying the site of so many happy family gatherings. Nan braced herself to uphold her mother, while Sarah tightened her grip on both daughters, her fingers like iron claws binding their flesh.

Wiping their streaming eyes and coughing up soot and ash, Alden and James studied the family tableau and with horror, realized that Zack and Helen were still missing

Then, at last, Zack appeared in the doorway, holding Helen in his arms. Behind him, with a boom like a distant cannon, the roof caved in, sending a billowing cloud of soot and ash into the air like one final shot from the enemy army.

Laying Helen gently on the ground, as if putting her down for her nap, Zack wiped soot from her grimy face and looked desperately for signs of life. Shaking her firmly, he called her name.

But Helen's spirited little voice, finally, was still. Sarah stared at James, horror and grief in her face, looking for reassurance where there was none. Zack cradled the tiny body.

"Come back, little girl, come back," he urged. "Remember your promise." Maybe Helen did remember that far-off morning and their childhood pledge. She opened her eyes and stared deeply at Zack's face, her gaze radiating love and wisdom as slowly the life in them died.

The crackling of the flames and spitting embers was the only sound in God's world at the moment Helen's soul left us. Even the birds were quiet.

For Zack, time stopped. For something happened as Helen's spirit rose from her body. It moved up and straight through Zack. He felt her go as if a miraculous, sacred perfume wafting through his very being. Stunned by this supernatural feeling, and the events of this horrible day, he could not think. Only feel. For a few moments.

The family slowly looked into each other's eyes, unable to believe this great tragedy had happened right here, before the sacred homestead that was always their sanctuary.

Then behind them, horses' hooves thudded dully on the hard earth as a small contingent of the enemy troops rounded the curve around the old barn and stopped in front of the stunned family. Still enthralled by this – his first otherworldly experience – Zack did not even look up.

With horror and fury, Charles surveyed the still smoldering ruins of the Lewis family mansion.

"Why did you do this? I gave you orders –" Charles angrily barked at the sergeant.

"Uh… must have been an accident," muttered the sergeant guiltily.

Realizing that there was no way he could undo the loss of this once beautiful home, Charles turned his attention to the family. In the face of his underling's perfidy, no apologies seemed relevant. Instead he held out Zack's sword to James.

"One of my men – ah – accidentally picked this up. I believe it belongs to you."

James did not move, his shocked and disbelieving eyes staring dully at Charles as if he were speaking in a strange, foreign tongue. Finally, Charles noticed Zack holding Helen.

"Told you we could smoke 'em out!" crowed the sergeant, vindicated by the discovery of their Rebel quarry. Dismounting, several soldiers moved towards Zack. Seeing the small, still body in his arms, her long hair trailing almost into the dust, the Yankees realized that something was wrong, very wrong. They stopped.

The approach of the enemy finally broke the spell of Zack's communion with the essence of his baby sister. Helen's eyes were truly lifeless now. Her spirt had flown.

Charles and Zack locked eyes at the same moment, and recognized each other. Zack's stunned expression changed to one of pure hatred.

It was Nan who broke the stalemate.

"Give her to me, Zack. I'll take care of her," she promised softly. Zack slowly handed little Helen to Nan, who accepted the burden gently.

Charles dismounted and approached Nan. Disbelieving, he gazed from the living sister to the face of the lost one. For once, he could not speak. After all, he was not heartless. No doubt he remembered Helen's lively presence from his visit in another life. Perhaps he recalled his young nieces, when they were chubby children whose unconscious innocence tugged at the heart.

But only Nan saw his grief and horror, the shock that rendered him oblivious to the danger to his own life.

As two soldiers started to bind Zack's hands behind his back, an almost superhuman strength took possession of their would-be prisoner. Fueled by rage and grief, he broke free, grabbed the ancient sword, and lunged for Charles.   The sword swept the air with such force and wind that Charles blinked, but his normally quick reflexes did not have time to react and defend himself.

More quick-witted than their captain, the other Yankees quickly overpowered the renegade Rebel; one clubbed him with a rifle, and

Zack fell to his knees. More soldiers restrained Alden, who tried to go to Zack's assistance.

Now helpless, Zack glared at his nemesis with such hatred that Charles stepped back. Zack's gaze only broke as the soldiers tied his hands behind his back and lifted him onto a horse.

Through the blood running down his face, he watched his family silhouetted against the smoldering house, his final view of his old home and the keeper of his heart. Immobilized by her own grief, Nan still held the limp body of little Helen in her arms. The family gathered around her in a silent tableau of despair. The touch of spirit – Helen's last gift – was forgotten, as an imagined event that had no reality. His helplessness in the face of their tragedy was like a brand searing his heart.

Chapter 10
The Lost Shall Be Found

How this loving family coped with the loss of this bright, innocent spirit, I cannot imagine. No one really spoke of it to me. I imagine that the Lewis family mourned their loss quietly, with the dignity and faith that was their heritage. The loss was deep – of Helen, of their home, of their way of life. The women, in the way I have observed in this so-called weaker sex, probably kept their hearts alive and filled with the love they had lost in honor of the child who had left the earthly life. They know – love never dies.

Nowadays, they have a name for this condition – when a body has seen just too much horror and loss to withstand it any more. They treat people who come back from war for it. But then, it was just about enduring, with an iron discipline to continue each day and to live by the code in which they believed.

The night of the fire, the family moved into the small house at River's Rest. Mildred clutched a ragged, soot-stained doll – the only remnant of the old life.

Without the money to buy seed and lacking the other resources to effectively farm their lands, Alden was able to convince his parents to let him enlist. There were no plumes or fancy dress uniforms for him, and no effusive good-byes with expectations of a quick and glorious victory. Dressed in a plain homemade uniform, Alden stepped down from the porch at River's Rest to set off for the front and his long-awaited chance at glory, past the flowerbeds of untended sticks and thorns that had once been his mother's pride, as the family silently witnessed his departure.

Zack's journey to prison camp was, for him, a blur of endless horseback rides, throbbing headaches, and nights where he lay unconscious, rather than sleeping, on the rock-hard ground. Dazed from his wound, the sharp memory of Helen's death pierced his soul in those moments when he surfaced to consciousness. The image of her lifeless little form, her poignant, loving last look, was always accompanied by the face of the man he hated above all others, the one who had robbed his family of their home and happiness – Charles Delacourt.

Maybe you read about those prisons. Long before countries got together and agreed on how to treat their captives, they were more like a place to be slowly starved to death than a settlement for captives to be held until release. But Zack knew nothing of this.

By the time he reached the prison, his head wound was still serious enough for him to be assigned to the infirmary, where a merciful sleep obliterated his memories.

On his second day, a miracle occurred.

Zack slowly emerged from his deep slumber to see a pair of dirty male hands trying to feed him a brown liquid that passed for soup.

"Come on, Soldier, you got to eat," said an authoritative voice, firm in the know-it-all patronage born in an eldest son. Zack grimaced in pain, but opened his eyes wider. Gradually he focused on the man sitting at his bedside, squinting in disbelief into blue-black eyes like his own.

"Jim? Am I in heaven?" croaked Zack.

"Heaven? More like the other place," replied a wan soldier, supine on the next ragged cot. The others snorted in derision. Zack tried to focus on the man feeding him.

"Jim! It is you!"

"You know who I am?" asked the young man, incredulous, pushing his hair back from his forehead in a gesture of bewilderment.

"Course I do! You're my brother," exclaimed Zack. Despite the return of his stabbing headache, Zack weakly smacked Jim's shoulder in what he meant as a gesture of masculine affection. Jim – for it was indeed Zack's long lost brother – still looked puzzled at this effusive affection as the precious soup slopped on the ragged bedclothes.

I couldn't say that this miraculous reunion lifted Zack's spirits, but it gave him purpose – the sense of duty that propelled him through the most serious obstacles of his young existence. No longer able to fight, and robbed of the chance to help his family, he made Jim his new Cause – to bring back the lost memories and regain the brother he had feared gone forever.

Compared to life on the battlefront, prison routine was stiflingly boring – the same privations but without the intermittent excitement of battles and the gratification that their simplest chores were contributing to the ultimate victory in which they all believed. Despite the poor food, unsanitary conditions, and invading hordes of insects, Zack's natural vitality asserted itself and he quickly recovered.

So as the days shortened and the temperatures dropped, Zack worked diligently all that winter to bring Jim's memories back. At least it helped keep their minds off the freezing temperatures that turned their breath to frost even with the sun high in the grey heavens.

Outside the prison, a light snow fell, even though by the calendar it was supposed to be spring. On the window ledges, an entire community of wooden figures and buildings was displayed, the product of many hours of tedious work. The other soldiers whittled as much to keep their freezing fingers active and a little bit warmer as they did to pass the time , while Zack tried to help Jim remember their past by re-creating scenes with the carved buildings.

"Remember, the big house – our house – was on the river where we used to swim. All the land you could see belonged to us. On Sundays, we'd have smoked ham – I loved that smell!" Zack almost smiled at the memory.

"I only remember – sometimes – the smell of flowers." Jim frowned with the effort of chasing the wisps of remembrance, running his hand through his shaggy hair, this time in frustration.

"Mother's garden. You've got to remember, Jim. This is why we're in this War," encouraged Zack.

Zack's lesson was interrupted by the entry of two Yankee guards belligerently sauntering into the room, inspecting the prisoners who in turn glared at them with quiet resentment. Zack hated these men – not only were they Yankees, but they looked and acted like feral jackals, routinely stealing the few gifts the prisoners received from home, helping themselves to the supplies that were meant to keep the scrawny inmates healthy enough to survive.

An uneasy man in a minister's collar followed them, his jiggling double chin and portly figure attesting that he suffered no privations due to the War.

"Who's on top now, Johnny Reb? You boys listen good to the preacher man here," advised one of the guards. The prisoners stared sullenly at the minister.

"Bein' locked up here and all, I thought you could use some spiritual comfort." The minister nervously opened his Bible, and began to read. Some prisoners sat up to hear more.

"I will love thee, O Lord, my strength.
The Lord is my rock and my fortress, and my deliverer,
My God, my strength, in whom I will trust,
My buckler, and the horn of my salvation and my high tower.
I will call upon the lord, who is worthy to be praised..." (Psalm 18)

"Why are you preaching to us? Go tell Ape Lincoln to be charitable," Zack called out defiantly. "Let the ships through the blockade with medicine for our wounded."

Behind the minister's back, another prisoner imitated the Union President, hopping and scratching like an ape. His fellow captives laughed and hooted. The minister, mystified by their behavior, shook his finger in admonishment.

"There's no need for blasphemy. Oh!" he cried as the "ape" reached out and pinched his ample rump. "God damn –" The words escaped his lips as he jumped and whirled on the attacker. The prisoners roared.

"You don't need to worry about us, Reverend. We pray every day. Don't we, boys?" hollered Zack.

"We do?" asked Jim. This was news to him.

"Hell, yes. Every day we send this prayer to God. 'Damn the Yankees'," retorted Zack.

"That's right! Damn the Yankees!" cried the prisoners. They took up the chant, growing louder and more threatening with each repetition.

The frightened minister pounded on the door to be rescued from these infidels. As the doors opened, he gratefully escaped to tell his tale of the godless Southern riffraff who rejected the word of the Lord and taunted His representative on earth.

The guards re-entered, perhaps puzzled by the minister's strange retreat but nevertheless grinning with pleasure at the happy news they bore.

"You lazy boys going to get some exercise," one leered. "Work detail. Come on, get up."

They roughly poked and prodded the prisoners toward the door. Jim started to obey, but Zack stopped him.

"Wait, you can't go. You're not well yet," he argued. He faced the guard. "He's too sick. Supposed to rest. Doctor's orders."

Zack's ruse worked. Thank goodness, 'cause it's unlikely as a sunflower in winter that poor Jim could have withstood the coming ordeal. The guard reluctantly nodded, then roughly pushed Zack out the door of the communal cell.

Outside in the cold air, the prisoners shivered in their ragged clothing, the snow clinging to their hair and eyelashes. The guards herded them forward into open wagons, where they huddled together for warmth. With their captive cargo, the wagons rolled out the prison gates, accompanied by enough armed riders to preclude thoughts of escape.

Indeed, uneasy sleep was the only respite for the prisoners on that long ride. Through the night they bounced along the rutted roads, darkness hiding the sights that might tell them their location. No one suspected their destination would be in the heart of the hated enemy territory. That was until, as dawn was breaking, they could see the outlines of the pristine white dome, and then the huge White House that housed the leader of their enemy. The irony of being in the Yankee capital, named for his ancestor's old friend and patriot, was not lost on Zack. But the worst insult was yet to come.

Right in front of these hated landmarks, the wagons stopped. The guards prodded the exhausted prisoners out into the muddy street.

"You all gonna make the city purty for President Lincoln's ee-nog-er-a-shun," announced one.

The prisoners sat motionless, stupefied at this appalling news.

Their forced labors would actually help honor their despised enemy.

Ever resourceful, Zack's mind flew to thoughts of escape, bearing back to his brethren valuable news of the enemy stronghold. However, these fantasies dimmed as more Yankee soldiers arrived to triple their guard detail.

Under their captors' watchful eyes, the prisoners had no choice but to comply with their work orders. The gaunt laborers toiled through the days preparing the roads to bear the wheels and weight of all the visiting carriages expected to roll down the streets on inauguration day. They sawed and hammered, building the stands for the spectators. Zack worked as slowly and sloppily as he could. I can only imagine the mental torture he must have endured to have to force his traitorous body to labor for his hated enemy. At least, he comforted himself, Jim's fragile mind and body were spared these privations as well as the stinging disgrace.

Constantly watchful for the opportunity to sabotage the proceedings, Zack's plot was frustrated by the vigilance of the guards. Each night the prisoners were herded back into their wagons, unable even to stretch out their cramped legs, their skin chafed by the meal sacks that were their only covering – donated (or confiscated) from local merchants, motivated not by charity but by the need to keep the captives from freezing so they could continue working.

So Inauguration Day dawned, both cloudy and windy – typical of the capricious month of March. To their chagrin and humiliation, the prisoners found themselves standing at attention, like trophies of war, in full view of the gaily decorated stands housing the warmly dressed spectators, who waved miniature American flags and chattered expectantly.

About to come face to face with his great enemy, Zack had one wish.

"If there is a God, He should give me a pistol," he whispered to the man on his left. "I could end this thing right here and now."

One of the guards poked him, hard, with his rifle to silence him.

And then, there he was. The Devil himself. Tall, gaunt and as ugly as his reputation claimed, Lincoln stepped up to the dais, followed by a round, petite woman so short she seemed only as tall as her gigantic husband's waist.

Zack's hatred burned so strongly that a buzzing started in his head. Or maybe he was just so hungry and tired he was about to faint. The figures on the temporary stage swam in his vision and their words ran together in a slow hum. He steeled himself against the humiliation of collapsing by a sheer effort of will.

By the time his mind cleared, Lincoln stood alone on the podium, tiny spectacles on his huge nose, reading from a simple piece of paper.

"With malice toward none; with charity for all; with firmness in the right, as God gives us to see the right," he intoned in a surprisingly high voice for someone so tall.

His words of tolerance burned into Zack's brain, but not his heart. Silently his mouth formed the words, "Damn the Yankees. Damn you, damn you, damn you."

Perhaps his raging desire for revenge connected with the same fire alight in another heart. But suddenly Zack's attention was caught by a handsome young man, standing a little away from the crowd of respectful spectators. His eyes, too, smoldered with an emotion that was not fondness for the great President. But what captured Zack's eye and made his heart leap was the pistol that the young man quietly, slowly raised and pointed at the tall figure on the dais.

As he watched that elegant finger curl around the trigger, Zack could not breathe in anticipation of vengeance, at long last. But instead of the expected explosion, there was nothing. The gunman aimed again. Silence. Slowly the failed assassin lowered the gun, stuffed it into his coat, and stepped out of the crowd to be lost from view. Zack exhaled, his disappointment palpable.

So it was not yet Lincoln's day to meet his Maker.

After the ceremonies and the balls and the festivities were over, the prisoners had one more day to clean the city again and restore it to its grim wartime efficiency before returning to their prison fortress.

Upon their arrival, Zack rushed to the barracks, eager to tell Jim of his adventure, his sighting of the despised enemy leader and Lincoln's narrow escape. He found his brother seated on his rickety cot, a piece of paper in his hand.

"Jim, we've got to get out of here," Zack announced. "They made us – I saw him myself – if I had had a gun –" his thoughts came too fast to be coherent. Jim did not respond, only stared at the paper with a dazed expression. Fear stabbed Zack's heart.

"What is it? A letter from Mother?" he asked.

"No," Jim looked up from the document in disbelief. "I've been paroled."

Zack whooped with excitement.

"But that's good news. You can go back to the front!"

"But I don't want to go. I just don't want to kill anybody, anymore," said Jim, as if amazed at his own feelings.

"Of course you do. It's your head. You're just not yourself yet." Zack had an inspiration. "You know, I could go in your place. How would they know?"

Jim nodded slowly. Sure enough, their trick worked a second time. The Yankees didn't know or care which Lewis was which.

Although it's just about unbelievable to me, Zack's resolve and hatred of those damned Yankees had not abated one whit in the last four years. Eschewing a visit home, Zack's goal was to get back to help his fellow soldiers as quickly as possible, land a decisive blow against the enemy that had so humiliated him with forced slave labor, and atone for the idleness and wasted time of prison camp.

Chapter 11
The Cause Undone

So Zack found himself back at the front, but with a different army than the one he had left.

These Confederate troops, ragged and hungry, moved like zombies. The fervent drilling and the discipline of regimental camp life was just a faint memory to these exhausted, idle soldiers, who seemed too tired and weak to even endure a march to the latrines.

Zack walked among them, searching this ragamuffin army with growing unease. Where was their heart? Their spirit? Their will?

Then, in a small group of reclining men he spotted a grimy, lanky boy who staggered to his feet, staring in disbelief at the new arrival. Then, with a rebel yell, the dirty soldier threw his arms around Zack.

"Zack! I knew those Yankees couldn't keep you locked up. How's Jim?" asked Alden.

Zack recovered his balance. His "little" brother was now as tall as he was.

"He'll be fine once we get him back. How can I get my hands on a rifle? And some ammunition?" asked Zack, always one to have his priorities straight.

Overhearing his questions, the other gaunt and filthy men chortled grimly.

"You and the entire Confederate army," guffawed one ragged, skeletal figure whose head reminded Zack of the skull he'd seen in that cursed day in the Wilderness. Another waved a stick with his scarecrow-thin arm.

"Here's my rifle, right here."

"While you're at the supply station, get me some new shoes," demanded another, wriggling his bare toes. The soldiers chuckled, sarcastically, as the two brothers sat down on the bare ground.

"What's the matter with them?" asked Zack in a low voice.

"We don't have any supplies. Or ammunition. Right now. But I do have this," Alden produced the regimental flag and spread it out proudly. Zack examined the shredded cloth, so torn with bullets it was a large checkered rag. He scanned the bedraggled soldiers and Alden's bare feet.

"Do you think General Lee will retreat until he can get some more supplies?" asked Zack.

"Supplies from where? But he'll never retreat. We'll keep fighting with our bare hands if needs be," boasted Alden.

And then, a noise like a low growl seemed to start at one end of the ragtag camp and rolled down the line toward them. An old man on a very thin horse rode up, tears sliding down the crevices of his wrinkled face.

"It's over, boys," croaked the horseman, his voice cracking with grief and his eyes bearing the piteous, lost look of the severely wounded. "General Lee has surrendered."

The men staggered to their feet. Some began to cry. Zack and Alden looked at each other, incredulous.

"It can't be true," said Alden, his mind unable to take in this devastating news.

"It's true. It's true. It's all over," wailed the horseman, tears rolling down his stubble-covered cheeks. Alden set his young face so that he would not cry. Zack merely stared straight ahead. I reckon there were just no tears in him.

All the swords he had escaped in battle suddenly re-united to pierce his heart at once. The world turned over, like a pancake. Zack fought the nausea with the same iron-strong determination that had driven him these last four years. He willed his heart to close and his feelings to subside.

"No. It will never be over," he vowed with fierce finality.

Chapter 12
Homecoming

After all these brave souls had been through, it was a deadening and heartbreaking denouement to be faced with the long walk home. Their grand plans of four years ago sat like dust in their mouths. Zack and Alden, the folded regiment flag hanging over his shoulder, found themselves part of a long procession of wounded and disheartened men.

As they trudged south along a dry, dusty road sprinkled with prickly weeds and foot deep potholes, a loaded wagon approached, pulled by four black men. There was something familiar about that overcrowded wagon and those men.

"Isn't that Jeremiah?" croaked Alden, his voice raspy with dust and thirst.

"I think it is! Ho!" Zack called out.

The wagon was stacked high with household goods, tools and baggage that threatened to topple over with each rut in the road. Beside and around it trudged three generations of Jeremiah's family, laden with more baggage and sundry children too small to walk.

"Mr. Zack, Alden!" Jeremiah seemed genuinely relieved to see them.

"Where you going, Jeremiah? Is everything all right at home?" asked Zack fearfully.

"Well as it could be, Mr. Zack."

Alden incredulously examined the goods in the wagon.

"Where'd you get all this?"

"Mr. Lewis, he gave it to us. 'Cuz the Yankees took all the land," explained Jeremiah defensively, as if fearful of the loss of these precious possessions.

Zack's temper blazed up, re-igniting from somewhere within his frozen soul, his latent fighting spirit. "What! They can't do that!"

Jeremiah answered, avoiding his eyes with perhaps shame, perhaps compassion. "Bank says it can. 'Cuz the Confederate money ain't worth nothin' no more."

Alden rested his head on the wagon in despair.

"It's true, Zack. Father mortgaged all the farms at the beginning of the war. Everyone did."

Zack's anger died as quickly as it came. Of course. Another defeat. Was there to be no justice in the world?

"So we have nothing to go back to," he murmured dully.

"Yo family, they still got the little place. It belong to your uncle," offered Juno, by way of consolation. If either boy had looked closely, they would have seen the expression of guarded sympathy in her large dark eyes. "They be needing you."

"So Jeremiah, you're leaving us?" accused Alden.

"We goin' north. No work for us here," Jeremiah responded, still not meeting Alden's eyes, a lifetime of deference at war with his newfound independence.

"What will you do there? You think Ape Lincoln is going to give you a job? Make you white?" asked Zack spitefully. Now Jeremiah met Zack's eyes.

"No Suh. But he make us free."

Zack had no answer to Jeremiah's proud declaration. Memories of the Greek tragedies their mother had taught them, floated incongruously to his mind. The gods had surely turned their capricious backs upon the South. But his mouth set in a bitter line at what he viewed as yet another betrayal to his family.

The Lewis boys' journey was shorter than most of the other soldiers, since their family had lived so close to the front. While exhaustion dogged every step, worry at what they might find drove them on – and the heartfelt desire of every lost creature to reach its home.

A few days after the encounter with Jeremiah, they arrived at their destination: the burned skeleton of their former home. The once carefully manicured lawn was now awash with weeds, as the verdant Virginia forest rushed to take back its own. Zack refused even to look at the ruin of the old homesite, keeping his eyes doggedly fixed ahead.

Stepping out of the woods at the edge of Sarah's flower garden, now overgrown with waist-high weed invaders, they spied their future: River's Rest, seemingly just as they left it, tranquil and untouched. Alden sniffed the air, at first puzzled, then thrilled.

"Mother's roses!"

There was a new clearing amidst the flowering bushes. A small cross marked Helen's grave. On this morning, as luck would have it, Nan knelt beside it, gently arranging freshly cut roses over the little mound. At the sound of Alden's voice she turned abruptly, startled at the sight of two grimy veterans.

In a moment she recognized them and – despite their filthy condition – flung herself into their arms. Zack's eyes stung with bitter tears. His arm around Nan told him she had lost the soft plumpness of her youth, another reminder of the theft of their hopes and dreams. She should be married now, thought Zack dully, knowing the prospects for his sisters having the life they had accepted as their birthright, were dim indeed.

But there was no room in Nan's heart for anything but joy this day. As if they were children again, she grasped her brothers' hands and pulled them in a run toward River's Rest, calling as she ran,

"Mother, Father – they're home!"

James, Sarah, and Mildred emerged from the little house. To Zack, his parents suddenly looked old – still ramrod straight in their posture, but their spirit was changed, diminished by their losses. Little Mildred – now the "baby" of the family – had grown tall, with a new maturity about her that belied her years. Painfully absent was the presence of little Helen, her lively antics and irrepressible, feisty spirit. Zack only had a moment to make these observations before the family was reunited in hugs and tears, and he allowed himself to feel a tiny bit of the joy of their bittersweet reunion.

Chapter 13
A New Offensive for the Cause

With Jim's return a few weeks later from prison camp, the last missing son was home. While Jim's memory of their old life was still misty, he heroically pretended to remember more than he did, hoping that in time, his recall would return. Perhaps it was a blessing that he could not compare the existence of the gentleman farmer to which he had been bred with their present grim reality.

No one spoke of their defeat and its terrible price, although each individual had it constantly on their minds. James and Sarah stoically reminded themselves and their brood each day of what they still had – each other. Accustomed to living in hope during the War years, and to the circumscribed routine at the small house at River's Rest, their daughters followed suit. Their faith in a better life after death, and in the virtue of righteous living no matter the circumstances, sustained them.

But the boys felt differently. Freed from the stress of the battlefield and the constant threat of legitimate murder or dismemberment, they found this new life – a very different one than they had ever expected – to be a most unwelcome reality. There was to be no reward for their bravery, nor for the sacrifices of thousands of their comrades. They had risked everything to protect their birthright – and lost it all. As menfolk do, they put great store in their pride. Once lords of this land, now they were serfs. The bitterness stung worse than the fattest, maddest hornet.

Even the news of Lincoln's assassination – as that debonair actor had better luck with his pistol at Ford's theater than he had the day Zack spied him at the inauguration – was of little comfort. While Zack may have viewed this event as an indication that justice did sometimes triumph, it mattered for nothing in their new world. And indeed, unbeknownst to them at the time, their future was to be the bleaker once the President and his openness to reconciliation was replaced by others seeking revenge and profits from the defeated Southerners.

Even without this foreknowledge, Zack felt deeply that God had betrayed them. Still never doubting the rightness of their Cause, the cruelty of the outcome poisoned his heart. He could not accept, as his parents did, that His will be done. I think his hubris was still that he could change that Will.

And did little Helen's spirit speak to him, now that he was back in the old home and the lands where she had played all her short life? Did the merging of their spirits in her last moment, sweeten his memories? No, he was deaf with bitterness to those ethereal feelings.

Nowadays we have a name for this kind of malady. Sometimes people go crazy and start shooting things up. Back then, it was just life. You had your rules, your code to live by, and it didn't much matter how you felt about it. So they followed the precepts of good behavior they'd been taught, but their souls were dead inside.

However, the need to feed and protect their family quickly drew the returning soldiers into their new way of life. With no slaves, all work had to be done by the family members. There were no more picnics by the river bank. Instead, they gathered daily to till the meager fields remaining to them.

Oblivious to the signs of nature's spring rebirth, Zack awkwardly planted seeds in the moist earth while Mildred instructed him.

"Make them further apart. Like this." She demonstrated. I reckon Zack felt doubly insulted – being instructed by a girl child, and doing the work of a slave. Instead of complying with Mildred's instructions, he straightened up and walked over to his mother as she carefully placed the seeds into a neighboring row of ploughed earth. Her bonnet shaded her face, but still the sun beat down through the thin material of her worn dress.

At Zack's approach she straightened up to face him. Zack took her hands in his. The calluses on those once pristine hands wounded him like a blow.

"Mother, go sit in the shade. You shouldn't be out here, doing this," he ordered tersely.

"It's all right, Son. You know I've always loved gardening." She smiled reassuringly.

"This isn't gardening. It's work for a field hand," responded Alden, disdain dripping from his words.

"At least we have River's Rest. Our neighbors have nothing," James reminded his resentful sons calmly, but firmly.

"We have nothing, Father. Damn the Yankees. They set out to ruin us, and they did," pronounced Zack, as he stalked away in disgust, too embittered to even tolerate the presence of his beloved family.

No one knows where Zack went that day. My guess is he wandered deep into those dark woods, following the long-cold trail of Brave Wolf and his boyish dreams. Wherever he went, something spoke to him and he came to a decision that would change his family's history for generations.

Zack did not return until the family had gathered that evening, eating their Spartan meal. He stood in the doorway, as if by joining them, he would again admit defeat. His face was calm, but his eyes bespoke a stubborn determination.

"Father, Mother, I've decided I'm going to Texas. They're still fighting down there."

James and Sarah exchanged worried glances. "Son, it's only a matter of time before all the Confederate troops surrender. Please –" James began.

"Then I'll go to Mexico! I'll enlist in the French Navy! I can't – I won't – live under the damned Yankee flag!"

The family silent in the face of his outburst, he continued, more calmly.

"I'll send you my pay. It'll help you more than having me here as a hired hand. Without some money, you'll all starve."

His parents did not even try to argue that the dying Confederacy had no money to pay anybody. Zack's mind was made up.

That night, Sarah lay abed silently staring into the darkness above her. She had miraculously gotten all her sons home, alive and whole, and here was one taking off to risk life and limb for a lost Cause. But knowing her, I believe she was more worried about Zack's soul, mourning the idealistic boy who had become a man obsessed with revenge.

James, eyes closed, reached over and took her hand.

"Zack's life has been in God's hands these last four years, and it will continue to be, wherever he goes," he murmured wearily.

"I know, I know," she sighed. "But it's his heart that worries me. I wish I could help him feel – not defeat, but acceptance. And then forgiveness."

"You could wish that for the entire Confederacy. Without much success," responded James dryly. Untwining her hand with his, Sarah slipped out of bed, gathered her wrap around her, and made her way down the dark hallway by feeling the wall in search of her wounded son. For four years, her constant prayer was to release her boys into the safety of the Almighty's arms. But tonight, her faith failed her.

And God was silent to her beseeching soul that night. Reaching her sons' room, she peered inside. Zack's bed was empty.

While his worried mother searched for him in a vain quest to heal his wounded heart, Zack was already outside in the overgrown garden, standing before Helen's grave. Having made his decision, he decided to leave at once, skipping yet another painful leave-taking from his family. He wore his ragged soldier's uniform with his belongings in a pack on his back. But the family's priceless sword did not hang by his side. He had decided that it was of more value left here, for his family's defense.

A crackling sound from the darkness startled him from his reverie. He whirled around, immediately on guard.

"Hell's bells. You scared me. You're lucky I don't have a gun," he snapped to the slender figure now illuminated by the moonlight. It was Alden.

"I'm coming with you," announced Alden, stubbornly.

"You can't come," Zack retorted dismissively. "Who will help Father? Jim can't do it alone."

"Well, all right then," Alden admitted. "Only one of us can go. Let's flip for it."

"With what? Have you got any money?" asked Zack sarcastically. For answer, Alden ripped a button from his soldier's coat, showed Zack both sides.

76

"Heads, tails. Call it."

"Heads." Alden flipped the button, turned it up to see in the moonlight. His face fell. Zack clapped him on the shoulder in farewell.

"It's meant to be, Brother. Besides, I've got shoes and you don't," he noted.

As if still reluctant to leave, he gazed around at the tree branches soaring over their heads. "Remember when we played Indian in these woods? I still say I was the best scout."

"You would. Actually, I always thought that was Jim," replied Alden, disagreeing as usual.

"Remember that day Lenie followed us and then chased me all over the plantation? She was a hellion." Zack mused, betraying a thought I suspect was on his mind much more than anyone imagined.

"Well, you can find out when you get to Texas." Alden retorted, still stung to be left behind.

"Umhh." Actually, Zack had already thought of this. Indeed the image of his feisty cousin, her thin form drenched and muddy from her fall in the swamp, had only been temporarily buried during the war years.

Both young men started at another noise in the underbrush. Another figure stepped into the clearing. This time, the intruder was female.

"You, too? Why don't we just have the entire family out here for tea?" suggested Zack, his sarcasm covering the sudden lump in his throat.

"I brought you something." Nan offered Zack a misshapen hunk of metal. "I think it's a doorknob. I found it after the fire."

"Thank you, Nan. I will treasure it always," said Zack, dubiously fingering her gift before dropping it into his pack. Nan plucked a flower blooming under the moonlight and tenderly tucked it into Zack's jacket, blinking rapidly.

"We just got you back! Now we're losing you again. Please don't forget us." She was trying hard not to cry, but not quite succeeding.

"Never," Zack responded fervently, his voice husky with emotion. His fingers stroked the petals of the rose in his buttonhole, as if memorizing their velvety softness. With one more fierce hug for Nan, and a brusque nod to Alden, he disappeared into the darkness. Alone, and called to duty as he saw it.

Chapter 14
Going South

Texas was a long way from Virginia. It still is. But Zack had plenty of company for his journey. The Army of the Confederacy was on the march, going home.

In later years, he never spoke much about this heartbreaking trek. At least until I came along, a willing audience for an old man's memories. That's proof that he never forgets the sights he saw on that long walk to Texas as one of the parade of emaciated veterans, many of them wounded. Some died on the trail and never saw their homes again. Maybe they were the lucky ones, spared the reality of ruined farms, burned homes, deserted slave quarters, and the very real threat of starvation for the families they had loved and fought for.

The unremitting suffering of his countrymen and the betrayal of what he believed in hardened Zack's resolve to fight the Yankees to his dying breath. His hatred drove him to put one foot in front of the other, mile after exhausting mile.

Sometimes, he hitched rides in rickety wagons, or on the backs of long-suffering horses or – once – a skeletal mule whose owner proudly claimed was just "too ornery to die."

Trekking through the mountains, he spent a night at a remote, ramshackle cabin, inhabited by a Confederate widow and her two small daughters. Unbeknownst to Zack, her forbearers had also fled the hills of Scotland two hundred years before to escape to freedom across the water. Only when the gaunt, quiet woman pulled out their family's last cherished possession – an old fiddle – and wistfully played the Celtic songs from their shared homeland did he awaken to their kinship.

He never knew that a few miles away, around the bend and by the creek, lay another rundown mountain home, where a sad-faced, quiet family mourned their son Samuel, who would never realize his dream of becoming a preacher man.

As Zack descended into the red-earthed fields and low hills of the Deep South, the heat returned, along with the plague of insects that thrived in the damp, moist climate. After hearing of his quest to find and join the remaining Army of the South, one family lent him a canoe so that he could travel by water down a nearby river. Gliding through the silent country, watching the dragonflies flit along the calm surface of the greenish brown water, Zack imagined himself one of the early settlers of this place – exploring the virgin land, before the War had ruined it all.

His plan was twofold: to find his relatives in Texas and enlist in the Texas army. His goal was Galveston, a town on the edge of the state that, unlike Virginia, was rumored to be relatively untouched by the devastation of the War.

Whatever thoughts Zack had about seeing his unruly cousin again, he quickly suppressed – relegating her to a corner of his mind that dealt with minor annoyances like stinging insects, a sweltering sun, and irritating relatives. He willed his thoughts towards memories of his true home and family and his vow to the Cause.

As Zack approached his destination, the warm heavy air of the South slowly lightened, becoming drier and easier to breathe. The hazy light of the sun sharpened, brightening to a penetrating ray that bored through his thin clothes and stung his eyes. Zack welcomed this new kind of heat, imagining that it burned away the humiliation of defeat and signaled a new offensive for the indefatigable South.

Then one blindingly sunny day, a new smell assailed his nose. Hard as it is to believe for those of us who grew up with this tangy scent, in the eventful two decades of his life Zack had never seen the sea. Somehow the salty air invigorated him, signaling that not only new experiences but also good fortune lay before him. Maybe he thought back to the school room, translating Julius Caesar under his mother's stern eye, and imagined himself to be crossing his own Rubicon. For indeed, that was what he did.

For me, making that crossing to the mainland was as natural as a carriage ride. But for someone who had never crossed a body of water with waves, tides, and hurricanes, it must have been a daunting prospect.

Arriving at the edge of the bay that separated Galveston from the mainland, he faced another unanticipated obstacle: how exactly was he going to cross the grayish-green waters with waves like tufts of grass? He had no money for the ferry, and no prospects of acquiring any. Even he was not daring enough to imagine that he could swim across – the playful romping in the rivers at home hardly qualified him for that adventure.

So he sat, disheartened, at the wharf as the ferryman waited for paying fare. It was not long in coming as two businessmen arrived, valises in hand, vests bedecked with gold watches on shiny chains. Zack watched them dully, mightily impressed – and a bit suspicious – at their obvious prosperity. Sort of like those scoundrels in Mr. Twain's book, you know, "The King and the Duke."

Whatever they really were – carpetbaggers or just successful profiteers – they saw only a dirty, disheveled tramp. Until one of them looked more closely and recognized his tattered rags as the remnants of a Confederate uniform.

He paused, taking Zack's measure.

"Going home, Son?" he queried.

Zack wanted to explain his quest, but exhaustion was stronger than the power of speech required to tell his story one more time. He merely nodded.

"Come on, then." The gentleman gestured with his bewhiskered head, topped with its shiny black hat, toward the ferry.

So Zack, swallowing his immediate reaction to pridefully reject any offer of charity, shuffled toward the boat and mumbled his thanks.

Although the sea looked calm, the ride was unexpectedly rough – at least to Zack. Noticing the greenish tinge in his face, his benefactor advised him to keep his eyes on the horizon as the skyline of Galveston grew closer. This did indeed help, along with several swigs from the water bottle the strangers offered.

As the ferry dipped and rocked across the bay, he shared with them his immediate goal to find his uncle. Fortunately, they both were of his acquaintance, and upon landing at the busy harbor, directed him toward Dr. John's medical office.

Debarking at the busy wharf into a bustling Victorian metropolis, Zack was startled and heartened to see evidence that this was a real and thriving city. Except for all the people dressed in black, he could almost imagine that the War had not happened. Horses and carriages filled the streets. There wasn't a burned house in sight. The citizens looked reasonably well-fed, unlike the starving wraiths Zack had encountered in his march through the South. Houses curiously built on stilts with small children playing in the shade of the raised foundations gave way to solid brick mansions on broad boulevards.

Galveston in those days – indeed, in any day – never had the glamour or decadence of its big sister city, New Orleans. Yet it has always had its own personality, you'd say today. Unconsciously, Zack was invigorated by its energy, its civic pride, its own brand of Southern charm blended with the optimism of the Wild West.

The townspeople, startled by his ragged appearance, gave him a wide berth which he, in his excitement, did not even notice. Those who recognized his rags as the remnants of a butternut-colored uniform tipped their hats in recognition of his military service. He didn't notice that either.

Like a horse approaching its stall at the end of a long ride, Zack's mind was only on his destination. Thinking of his uncle and cousin, Zack experienced more relief than he expected, assuming them safe and unchanged in their old home.

By the time he spotted the white frame house with the sign in the window reading, "John Lewis, Physician," his heart was thumping with an agitation that could not be explained solely by the length of his journey. Palms sweaty, he approached the door, but was really and truly frightened by his own reflection in the glass window – a wild man, bushy beard sticking out in all directions, so covered with dirt that when he moved, a fine cloud of dust rose from his clothes. Appalled, he retreated to the street and leaned over the horses' watering trough, splashing his face and head in a vain attempt to improve his appearance. It didn't help. Oh well. Drying his hands on his dusty trousers, he squared his shoulders and entered the office.

Inside, the small parlor was crowded with patients awaiting attention and fidgeting on half a dozen straight-backed chairs. This modest structure was one of those that served its owners with two functions – an office in the daytime, a parlor at night with sleeping quarters above stairs.

Zack queried an old man with watery eyes and sun blotched leathery skin studded with white whiskers.

"Where's the doctor?"

"Back there," the man pointed with his scrawny neck and stubbly chin, "Be out soon."

Zack's eyes returned to the door as it opened and a strikingly pretty young woman peered into the room. Who was she – a nurse? A patient?

Then, with a shock, he realized that this attractive female was his wild cousin Lenie. She had grown up, in every way.

The bones of her face and slender body formed a series of perfect angles. Her startling blue eyes were sharp and penetrating, made lovelier by long dark lashes and ivory skin. Dark hair fell in lustrous waves around that classic face, some strands carelessly pinned back, as if she had not time for the niceties of personal care. But her manner was perfunctory, unconscious and uncaring for her physical appearance that literally took Zack's breath away. The memories of his hellcat cousin vanished in the face of this vision.

As for Lenie – well, she had no such epiphany. She took in his ragged uniform, his grimy bewhiskered face, his bewildered expression, with no trace of recognition.

"What is it, Soldier?" she asked curtly. As Zack stared openmouthed, Lenie stepped closer, peering at him.

"Is it a war wound? Can't you speak?" She leaned over to look him in the eye. Blue eyes as dark as her own stared back at her. Now, long-dormant memories leaped into her awareness.

"Zack! Father, it's Zack!" she cried. About to throw her arms around him, she reconsidered.

Still too stunned to speak, Zack spied his uncle in the doorway, limping forward with a hearty welcoming embrace despite his nephew's filthy condition.

Suddenly remembering Zack's past betrayals, Lenie's memory flew back to the scene she strove to forget: the dark, stifling army tent, Samuel's bleeding body on the cot, their last prayer – and the cause of her loss. Her exuberance disappeared as fast as it had come. A guarded expression replaced her momentary happiness as she stepped back and watched her father welcome Zack. Overwhelmed to have finally reached his destination, Zack did not notice the emotional wall his cousin threw down between them.

Chapter 15
The Battle Resumes

And what of Lenie, these past four years? Yes, she grew up. That happens. How did that broken child who fled the battlefields of Virginia recover the strength that now radiated from her as a young woman?

The answer was... complicated. Her despair and grief over the loss of Samuel pierced her soul with such violence that her poor father feared for her life. And her sanity. Sometimes, as he well knew, when too much grief comes too quickly, even the strong can break and shatter.

Then one day, riding in their carriage and staring out with dull, hopeless eyes, something caught her attention. As homes with black wreathes adorning the windows passed her view, and somber pedestrians filed by listlessly on the wooden sidewalks, she spied a young woman. A girl not much older than she was herself, wearing widow's black. A small boy held her hand, following dutifully at her side. His eyes mimicked his mother's lost and wounded expression. And in the young woman's other arm was a well-wrapped bundle that could only be another child, a baby.

Lenie instantly recognized her own grief in this broken-hearted young wife. And felt shame. Shame at her own self-indulgence, and inspiration at this young woman's quiet courage, putting one step in front of the other despite her own devastation, for her children.

Samuel's face flashed before her. And this time, instead of heartsick grief, she remembered – strength. The shared purpose that inspired them both. And the answer to her despair presented itself to her. Carry on his purpose, so that it – and their bond – would live beyond both their earthly lives.

It didn't happen all at once, but day by day, Lenie taught herself the discipline of channeling her grief into action – turning inward pain into outward acts of service. She announced that she would be assisting her father in his practice, overcoming his desire to protect her with that willful insistence that he never could withstand. And whenever the sadness threatened to overtake her, she learned to envision her heart – and all that it had once contained – being locked securely in the little jewelry box where she kept her mother's wedding ring, the sole legacy of her beloved parent.

So Lenie started a new life, with a renewed commitment to conquer the sufferings of others, and in so doing, to – well, not heal herself, but to bury her own frailties in the strength of her resolve. Thus, her heart slowly tightened and hardened within her, conferring a perfunctory, curt and distant manner that served her admirably as a shield against the entanglement of pesky emotions.

And so it was this reserved, emotionally controlled young woman who replaced the impulsive, outspoken girl who had so irritated Zack in their youth.

Lenie was not only her father's trusted medical assistant, but she was also the efficient manager of their small household. It was in that capacity that she saw to it that Zack's first experience in the Lewis home was a shave and a hot bath in the tin tub wheeled out into the kitchen for such occasions.

While Zack luxuriated in the warm water, the door opened unexpectedly. Startled, Zack submerged himself into the bathtub as Lenie marched over to the pile of filthy rags that was once his uniform and gingerly picked them up.

What are you doing?" he gasped.

"I'm going to burn these before they start a plague," retorted Lenie.

"That's my uniform! Come back!" He started to rise, remembered he was naked, but it was too late. Off balance, he tipped the tub over and landed on the floor in a pool of suds, helpless as an upended swamp turtle. Lenie escaped out the door, laughing at his come-uppance.

After a night in a featherbed that to Zack was as decadent as the court at Versailles, he appeared at breakfast the next morning, wearing civilian clothes and a scowl to show his displeasure. Only his shoes – tied together with string given him by a grieving mother somewhere in a Louisiana bayou – remained of his traveling clothes. Seeing his cousin's cool blue eyes assessing his appearance, he flushed, remembering the scene in the bath.

86

"My old clothes fit you well," commented Dr. John. Zack threw Lenie a dirty look as he sat down. Then, hunger conquered table manners as he dug into the first real meal he could remember having in – well, maybe since that Yankee Christmas dinner so many years ago.

Lenie and John watched him but made no comment on his voraciousness.

"You know, I can help you get a job here," offered his uncle. "There's going to be lots of opportunity for an enterprising young man now that the War is –"

Zack swallowed, interrupting him before he could finish. "Thank you, Uncle John. But I'm here to enlist in the Texas army and keep on fighting."

Dr. John and Lenie exchanged glances.

"You're too late. The troops surrendered," Lenie informed him brusquely. Zack paused in mid-chew, stunned. Lenie shoved the newspaper toward him, pointing to the headlines to confirm her words.

"Guess you'll have to find a career that doesn't involve killing people for your honor," said Lenie with mock concern. Her sarcasm went unnoticed as Zack swallowed again, more slowly, taking in this horrible news. Lenie expertly sliced a pat of butter and spread it on her bread.

"You might consider surgery as a career, Zack. The knife slides through flesh just like butter. But you probably already know that." She stood up, letting her macabre taunt hang in the air like a wound, and then left the room.

John studied Zack's devastated face, noting his crushing disappointment.

"I'm sorry, Son. Very sorry,"

Zack blinked rapidly, pretending to study the newspaper, and feeling the familiar despair clutching at his soul, the specter he fought every day. Then, other headlines gave him new hope.

"I'll go to Mexico then. Says the French and the Mexicans are going to declare war on America. I'll fight the damn Yankees for them," he declared defiantly.

Realizing the futility of argument, Uncle John tried another approach. "Well, at least let me buy you a pair of shoes before you go. It's a long walk to Mexico," he offered.

And what of Zack's feelings, to be back in the bosom of family that was well-fed, contented, almost a flashback (yes, I know about those) to a normal life? Well, it must have been mighty strange, I imagine. After battling to preserve this way of life for four years, he couldn't wait to escape it again and return to the fray. But I reckon he was just too scarred up inside to even feel the peace of a home. Not yet. His strong will just continued to obsess about getting back to the front – any kind of front – where he could carry on that sacred struggle.

Due to his uncle's generosity, later that afternoon Zack found himself walking gingerly along the boulevards of Galveston, his feet adjusting to the unfamiliar feel of real shoes. Dr. John hobbled beside him, gesturing to the bustling street activity with his cane.

"You know, with the blockade gone, this city's port will be booming. You could get a job, even send some money home," he noted with studied casualness.

"I made a vow, Uncle John. I'll die before I'll live on Yankee soil," Zack responded, his face set with his typical stubbornness.

"I see. Well, technically, Galveston is an island. So it's not really part of the United States," argued Dr. John.

A distant thudding turned quickly into a staccato thunder of horses' hooves as a troop of Yankee soldiers galloped by. The civilian horses neighed in fear while pedestrians scattered to avoid being trampled. The blue uniformed men rode on, unconcerned. Zack instinctively ducked in a doorway of a store, reaching for his non-existent gun. Dr. John stayed his arm.

"We're at peace now, Zack," he warned, glancing about to be sure no one had seen Zack's reaction.

"Hah! The Army of the Occupation don't think so," retorted the storekeeper as the soldiers disappeared down the road.

"The what?" asked Zack. The storekeeper spat on the ground to show his contempt, nodding to the hotel next door where more Yankee soldiers lounged on the veranda.

"They're movin' in to take over this town. And the South," said the storekeeper.

I reckon the sight of all those bluecoats was mighty unsettling to poor Zack. One more piercing of his already lacerated soul.

Dr. John probably sensed that too, as he took Zack's arm, leading him on as the seated soldiers watched them suspiciously.

He quickly changed the subject. "You know, Lenie is determined to go to medical school. She goes out at all hours tending sick people, even the Negroes. Many of them have no jobs and no homes."

He was trying to distract his nephew with a new line of conversation, yet his concern for his feisty daughter was surely genuine.

"Thanks to the damn Yankees. And their Emancipation," growled Zack, glaring back at the reclining bluecoats.

"If you stayed here, you could help me look after her," suggested Dr. John.

"I don't think she wants any looking after," declared Zack, but his irrational heart gave a tiny leap at this prospect.

The two men turned up a residential street to see the troop of blue-coated Yankees halted before a large home with narrow white pillars bordering its wide veranda, green shutters around its windows, and iron grillwork that reminded Zack of pictures he'd seen of New Orleans. A husky sergeant stood on the front porch, arguing with a young woman whose passion for this discussion was evident in her sharp, staccato gestures. Behind the gesticulating officer, a platoon of his men stood at attention, their rifles at the ready. Neighbors gathered in the yard and on the sidewalk, murmuring angrily. The threat of violence hung in the air.

"Is that Lenie?" asked Zack, squinting into the blazing sun.

Of course.

It was indeed Lenie on the porch, giving up her debate with the stubborn sergeant and now pounding on the door. Two young women peered from an upstairs window while their servants watched nervously from behind the drapes.

"Lucy! Caroline! Open up or they'll break down the door.

Please!" shouted Lenie.

Following Lenie's gaze upward, Zack realized that he knew these two young ladies – his cousin's friends and visitors to his home, on the eve of the War. Even from a distance he could tell – or maybe sense – how the years had changed them from the demure young girls on the cusp of womanhood who had flirted with him in happier times.

"Never! We'll burn this place before we let Yankees live in it!" shouted Lucy with the passionate defiance that immediately roused Zack's chivalrous instincts. Leaving his uncle stranded on the sidewalk, he raced down the block (despite the discomfort of those new shoes) and bounded up the steps and onto the porch.

"Leave these women alone and go back where you belong!" he ordered the surprised officer, as the men bristled at his intrusion.

"Couldn't be soon enough for me," sneered the sergeant, his arrogant tone made all the more insufferable by his Yankee twang. "But orders are to take this house for the Army of the Occupation. Along with any other property we want from these rebels."

Zack fought back the urge to strike him then and there.

"You can't do that! It's illegal," he argued, falling back instinctively on his limited law studies.

"No it ain't. This city's under martial law and what's legal is what the army says is legal." The sergeant's jaw jutted outward in righteousness, making a tempting target for Zack's fist. However, he managed to control this impulse and turned to his skill in debate.

"Look, I studied law at the University of Virginia…"

"You be studying in jail, Johnny Reb, if you don't shut up," warned the Sergeant, pulling himself up to his full height to make his point.

He gestured to his men, who pointed their rifles at the house. Lenie threw up her hands in frustration, glaring at Zack as if this were all his fault.

But the heavy front door suddenly opened, revealing Lucy. Her eyes looked frightened, but her hands were steady as she raised a rifle from the folds of her skirts and pointed it at the soldiers.

"You'll have to kill us to get this house." Her voice dripped with genteel rage. Proving that even Northerners had a sense of chivalry, the soldiers hesitated. Zack stepped forward.

"Please, Lucy, give me that gun," he asked softly. Lucy stared deeply into his clear blue eyes. The romantic young woman from before the War recognized the idealistic soldier who had caught her fancy at a riverside picnic. His commanding presence communicated to her that everything would be all right.

"I'll protect you," he spoke softly so that only she could hear. Her fingers released their grip on the gun and allowed Zack to grasp it. Instantly he whirled on the invaders, pushed Lucy and Caroline behind him back into the house. The soldiers aimed their guns at him. But Zack's rifle pointed directly at the Sergeant.

"I suggest you call off your dogs, Sergeant. It's a stalemate," ordered Zack, his tone dripping Southern disdain for how easily he had tricked his adversary.

The watching neighbors gasped and began a hasty retreat to avoid the impending bloodshed.

"Zack, for God's sake —" called out Dr. John, who had come forward as fast as his disabled leg would allow.

"He's not right in the head. Don't hurt him," Lenie announced with medical authority. "I'm his doctor."

At this bizarre pronouncement, the men looked from her to her armed cousin and back to her, not sure which was more dangerous – his gun or this crazy woman under the delusion that she was a physician.

Behind them in the street, a gleaming chestnut horse trotted swiftly toward the house. With the agility of the experienced horseman, its rider leaped off before his mount had stopped. In a few quick strides he reached the porch. The retreating crowd parted to let him pass, their contempt palpable on sullen faces.

It was that former Yankee captain, Charles Delacourt. Still lean and feral, looking as debonair as a riverboat gambler (which some said he had been), he mounted the steps two at a time and paused, taking in the scene – his beleaguered nieces, Lenie's belligerent and exasperated stance, the red-faced Yankee and the trigger-happy troops. And this rough-looking man-boy with the fierce gaze and the lethal rifle.

"Captain Delacourt, talk some sense into this boy," begged the Sergeant.

Zack and Charles locked eyes. Zack recognized the man who, in his mind, had murdered his little sister. The man who had destroyed his family's home was now standing before him, unarmed and delivered up to justice. This time, Zack was not afraid of retribution. The worst had already happened. The deliverance of his enemy to his hands must be God's will and His long-awaited justice.

All this crossed his mind in a second. Without hesitation, he turned the rifle on Charles, cocked it, and pulled the trigger. The shot resounded through the quiet street.

Yet somehow his adversary still faced him, unhurt. Then he realized that Lenie had knocked the rifle askew and sent its shot into the air, over Charles' head.

Seemingly oblivious to his latest brush with death, Charles leaped forward, grabbing the rifle from Zack's hands. The Yankee soldiers quickly pinned Zack by the arms. The Sergeant relaxed.

"Thank you, Captain," he twanged fervently.

"It's Mr. Delacourt now," responded Charles coolly. Lucy and Caroline ran to him like ducklings seeking the shelter of their mother's wing.

"Uncle Charles, they want our house!" cried Lucy.

"Said we could live in the stables!" added Caroline.

"All Rebel houses are subject to confiscation for Army barracks," explained the Sergeant defensively.

"Take my house, then," offered Charles, a protective arm firmly around each of his nieces.

The Sergeant shook his head. "You ain't no rebel, Captain. Orders are orders. Take the house, and take Johnny Reb to the jail."

And so once again, Yankee soldiers marched Zack away into captivity.

Chapter 16
A New World

Within a day of arriving in Galveston, Zack's gallantry – some would say impulsiveness – had landed him in another jail cell where he now sat alone, brooding. His grand mission had come to nothing. So far. He had to get out of this cell and to Mexico. With nowhere to go, his newly shod feet tapped impatiently on the floor while he pondered his plight.

An elderly guard shuffled up to the cell and peered in as if to make sure Zack was still there. Zack ignored him. Then, wheezing and snorting like a dying horse, the old man took out his huge key ring and unlocked the door, stepping aside to allow two young women to enter, their frocks rustling like mice across the rough floor. Surprised, Zack rose politely.

"Mr. Lewis, I wanted to thank you for your help," announced Lucy, her eyes demurely downcast, only her firm grip on her parasol revealing her emotions. Several inches shorter than her companion, Lenie, her petite frame made her seem even smaller. Yet she held herself with a quiet dignity that both impressed and calmed those in her presence. Tactfully, she made no mention of Zack's attempt on her uncle's life.

"I'm afraid I didn't help you much. What happened with your house?" asked Zack.

"The Yankees moved in. Caroline and I are going to live with Uncle Charles," Lucy informed him, watching his reaction from under dark lashes.

"Your uncle, the Yankee?" asked Zack bitterly. Now Lucy looked Zack squarely in the eye, but her voice remained soft.

"I know people hate him for that. But he has always been kind to us."

Watching this exchange, Lenie interrupted before Zack could reply. "Lucy and Caroline lost their brother William in the War, Zack. That's why they lost their home."

Lucy dropped her eyes. "At Shiloh. With so many others."

Zack bowed his head briefly in deference to her loss. "Then

you'll understand why I have to get out of here. I'm going to Mexico to fight the Yankees there."

"Hmmph. That war's off, too. They reached a truce," Lenie announced triumphantly, watching Zack's face fall as he took in this devastating news. Lucy sensed his pain and impulsively touched his arm.

"But you could stay here, Mr. Lewis. Finish your law studies. We will all need your help. Our Cause is not dead, especially now that we are a conquered people."

Lucy's heartfelt plea touched Zack, despite this new grief. For the first time, it seemed, he really looked at her. Thankfully, he saw no resemblance to her hated uncle in her face. In fact, her calm brown eyes and sweet smile reminded him a little of his beloved sister, Nan.

The aged guard shuffled up to the cell, rattling his keys. Once again, he unlocked the cell door and this time, held it ajar.

"Come on, Johnny Reb. You're free," he wheezed.

"What? Why?" asked Zack incredulously.

"I know you'd rather be a martyr to the Cause, Zack, but I explained to them that you were hit in the head during the War and can't be responsible for your actions," explained Lenie quickly. Zack glared at her, but he followed the women out of the cell nonetheless.

"You got some rich friends in high places," muttered the surly guard as Zack passed him.

Lucy turned to Zack, honesty compelling her confession. "I spoke with Uncle Charles, and of course he was glad to do what he could to get you released. After what you did for us."

Zack stopped dead. "I don't need his help," he said coldly.

Lenie took a firm hold of Zack's arm, pulling him out of the cell. "Hell's bells, you are so stubborn. Come on. You're no use to anyone in jail."

Chapter 17
A New Life

Dr. John was right about Galveston. With the War over and the blockades lifted, the city's port was busier than it had ever been. Ships from Europe crowded the harbor to load huge bales of cotton – Dixie's gold – while blue-coated soldiers on horseback and on foot arrogantly supervised the process. The island city's renaissance would see it grow to become Texas's largest city, renowned for its commerce, its gentility, and its beautiful homes.

But that was many years in an unimagined future.

Zack never spoke again of his dreams to try to rescue the failed dreams of the South. From outward appearances he was "getting on with his life," as we say of those who have suffered a great loss and still manage to stumble through the chores of daily life.

Zack found work quickly in the cotton warehouses, counting the thousands of bales piled high to the ceilings. So, without ever acknowledging the defeat of his beloved Confederacy, Zack carried on in this new locale, sending most of his earnings back to his family in Virginia. His contributions to their welfare were sorely needed. Jim's memories of their childhood had not returned, and he resigned himself to creating new ones as a subsistence laborer, not the gentrified plantation owner everyone had assumed he would be. Going back to the University was out of the question with the decline of the family's fortunes. With the help of Alden and his longsuffering father, he dedicated himself to the demands necessitated by their fallen fortunes.

To Zack's relief, his mother and sisters gave up their roles as field hands and established a school, putting their intelligence and learning to the economic betterment of the family, and the enlightenment of a younger generation. Their impoverished neighbors often paid in eggs, vegetables, and even firewood, but all contributions were gratefully accepted.

River's Rest was soon a busy hub of learning, with both day-students and boarders who slept in beds in the old attic. Their lively antics added a laughter and lightheartedness to what might otherwise have been a somber residence. Zack, never a witness to the joy that brightened his family's lives even in their reduced straits, completely missed the reality that his beloved homestead was once again a place of happiness. He only remembered their losses.

Instead, he zealously resumed his law studies in the evenings, determined to find a way to better their economic lot. That is, when he wasn't busy with his second job, keeping his promise to his uncle to look after his willful cousin on her trips to tend to the sick.

After her initial impulsive welcome to Zack, Lenie quickly erected the prickly barriers that existed between them before her departure back to Texas. While she would never refuse hospitality to a family member, her belief that Zack had caused Samuel's death was an ever-present barrier between them. As acrimony crept back into their relationship, Zack's initial infatuation was supplanted by the habitual annoyance at her obstinacy and un-ladylike ways. Yet a trace of those softer feelings remained, fascinating him in quiet moments like the sinuous, dangerous dancing of a cobra.

Yes, I can imagine those feelings, even if the cause is foreign to me. The delight and the agony of our wayward hearts – the inspiration of song, of art, of the most moving and inspiring great books. Yes, I know it.

But Zack, as you probably know by now, did not think in these terms. He was just unsettled and could not understand why. If he had had the power to peer into her mysterious mind, he would have seen a determination to reach her mission – becoming a physician, despite the handicap of her sex – that rivaled the depth of his zeal for his own Cause.

Her fierce determination sometimes conveyed a hardness, even callousness, as she marched inexorably toward her self-made destiny. Only the plight of her patients pierced her emotional armor, and she never forgot the power of the comfort that Samuel gave to the wounded soldiers in the hospital tents and open air wards of the battlefield, with his counsel, his Bible readings, and his calm presence.

Normally, I reckon, a woman of her eccentric inclinations would have been ostracized by the good Victorian citizens of Galveston – or any other city in America. But respect for her war service, admiration for her devoted father, and distant memories of her mother's kindness, stilled tongues that may have otherwise gossiped her into social exile.

At the end of one long day on the wharf, as the orange-rimmed sun lingered above the water's edge, Zack wearily unlatched the gate to the modest Lewis home. His dark hair, plastered to his head with sweat, bespoke another grueling day spent in the sweltering cotton warehouses. The quiet house assured him that all the patients had left for the day. As he turned to close the gate, Lenie emerged from the front door, carrying a small black bag.

"You're going out? Now?" he asked, incredulous.

"Yes, now. Mrs. Gruber's having her baby. You don't have to come." Lenie marched rapidly around Zack and out the gate. With an exhausted sigh, Zack turned and followed her.

"I promised your father I'd look after you. Slow down!" he called.

"She should be having this baby in a hospital. I told her she shouldn't be having it at all," fumed Lenie, grousing to herself more than speaking to Zack.

"You shouldn't be gallivanting around the streets at night. It's not seemly. Why don't you just behave like other girls? They're getting married..." Zack stopped in mid-sentence, unwilling for some reason to put these ideas into Lenie's head.

"I'm not like other girls. And there's no one alive I would even think of marrying," Lenie snapped at him. Too late, Zack remembered Samuel, and was quiet.

Despite Lenie's rapid pace, it was dark before they arrived at their destination in a disreputable part of town no decent woman should set foot in – if you asked Zack. Lenie, of course, had no interest in his opinion.

Inside a shabby rooming house, all was bedlam with six unruly children leaping on the threadbare furniture and running amuck – a domestic chaos Zack had never seen in his strict and ordered upbringing. The oldest girl, looking to be about 12, admitted Lenie and Zack. Ignoring the children, Lenie headed straight for the bedroom, the source of distressed moans.

"Charlotte, boil some clean sheets," ordered Lenie.

"We don't have any clean sheets," responded Charlotte, looking confused.

"Then boil some rags. And come in and help me. Zack, you take care of the children. Play war or something," she ordered.

Lenie disappeared into the bedroom as Zack haplessly surveyed the disheveled, scowling children. One pugnacious little boy glared at him with particular ferocity.

"Are you a Yankee?" ventured the tyke, venom dripping from his shrill tones as he said the hated word.

"Hell – uh, no. I'm a Confederate soldier," replied Zack defensively.

"They took our house. Cause we couldn't pay our taxes. Damn Yankees," said the child fiercely. Zack nodded in sympathy.

"Well, just what would you like to do to those Yankees?" he asked.

The boy raised his eyebrows and grinned in anticipation of his revenge. He let out a Rebel yell that drowned out the sounds of his mother's moans. The other children immediately took up the cry, and Zack joined in, his spirits restored as the old adrenaline coursed through his veins.

The sun was just beginning its morning ascent as Zack slept fitfully in a sagging chair, his arms around the youngest child. The other children, toy weapons in hand, sprawled about the room in various postures of sleep. Something – maybe the unaccustomed silence – woke Zack. He gently untangled the boy's arms from his and placed the tot back into the chair; then quietly crossed the room and peered into the tiny bedroom.

Lenie sat beside a drowsy Mrs. Gruber, whose prematurely lined face had finally relaxed as she held a small – but quiet – bundle in her arms. Lenie opened her Bible and placed her hand on the exhausted woman's forearm. The new mother's eyes – dull but spellbound – watched, breathing in an invisible strength, as Lenie read in a soft but clear voice.

"Behold, my servant, whom I uphold.
My chosen one in whom my soul delights.
I have put my spirit upon him;
He will bring forth justice to the nations."

The harshness had drained from her face; there was a power in her voice that awed even Zack. Moved despite himself, he watched silently from the doorway, remembering the many nights in the camp hospital when words of faith were the only medicine to offer the suffering soldiers. He had always scorned these efforts, believing only in the power of the sword. Now he was touched by a different kind of force.

In his mind, maybe for the first time, he glimpsed his cousin not as an adversary, but as a fellow warrior, fighting her own battles. A feeling of kinship – not blood relationship, but a sympathetic spirit – took root in his heart. Maybe there was something more than shared family ties linking them together, after all.

Sometimes Lenie's nursing visits took place during the day, when Zack was at work. Occasionally, others accompanied her. Of these visits, he fortunately knew nothing. For this knowledge would have greatly disturbed his peace of mind, and perhaps, have occasioned an episode of violence.

On one such day, the Delacourt carriage – all shiny leather and black wood, with a spirited team of horses whose coats gleamed as if they, too, had been polished –pulled up in front of Dr. John's house. Charles leaped out and walked to the door with his graceful yet stalking stride, and an adventurer's suppressed excitement for the next conquest. He reached it just as it opened and Lenie, carrying her ubiquitous black bag, emerged.

"Good afternoon, Miss Pauline. Might you be at home?" asked Charles, formally but rakishly tipping his hat, as if subtly mocking the formal Victorian manners that governed every aspect of their lives, and which he knew Lenie despised.

"Course I'm at home," Lenie replied brusquely. "But I'm leaving. Father's out too."

"I see. Perhaps I can offer you a ride to your destination?" he offered, flashing his sardonic grin that still thrilled loyal

99

Confederate ladies of Galveston, despite their condemnation of his traitorous allegiance during the War.

But Pauline Lewis may have been the only female in Galveston who was immune to his charms. "I'll walk, thank you. It's not far."

Charles followed her, undeterred. "Mind if I walk with you, then?"

"I'm going to see a sick woman. May not be where you want to go." replied Lenie, continuing on without waiting. Charles quickly caught up and fell in step with her. Despite Lenie's rapid, purposeful pace, Charles appeared to be merely sauntering.

"I think anywhere you go would be very interesting. You're famous, you know, as the young lady who wants to go to medical school."

"Notorious, you mean. Well, I don't care as long as the old men let me in," she declared, the young person's disdain of the establishment dripping from her tones.

As they marched down the street, the omnipresent Yankee soldiers nodded in acknowledgment to Charles. Several old-time residents also passed them, their disapproval almost tangible. Charles nodded in recognition; they reluctantly returned his greeting.

Lenie observed all this in silence. Then her curiosity burst forth as she asked bluntly, "Why did you come back here, after the War? You could have stayed away, and you wouldn't have to face them every day."

Charles paused only a moment before responding lightly, "It's my home. And they're still my neighbors."

"You turned against them. Why?" asked Lenie bluntly, voicing the question no one had dared ask before. Charles was about to make a flip response, but stopped, held by Lenie's direct gaze.

Before them, a family of newly freed blacks drove by in a wagon. Some were very dark, some light. Judging from their shabby clothes, freedom had not improved their lot. Breaking his gaze with Lenie, Charles watched them, studying their dusky skins and the range of hues their complexions represented.

"Every year in New Orleans there used to be a ball. Young

women of color, all shades, were sold to white men who wanted to buy them. Can you imagine living that life?" he asked, his eyes still following the wagon wobbling down the dusty street.

Lenie watched them too. And she thought – really thought – about what such a life would be like. How confining, how degrading to an independent spirit like herself.

"No," admitted Lenie, "I can't."

"The Confederates were fighting for survival. But the North was fighting for freedom. So I guess – like your young cousin – I'm an idealist at heart." This admission seemed to be wrung from him against his will.

Lenie studied his angular face, for once unmasked of its veneer of charm. Satisfied with his sincerity, she murmured, "I always thought it was wrong. For one man to own another. That's what Mother said."

"Yes, I remember," Charles replied with quiet understanding. Now he caught her gaze, in a moment of insight that, despite their long acquaintance, could not be put into words. Yet.

The moment passed. As if shaking off her own memories, Lenie resolutely resumed her walk. Charles knew he had impressed her, yet he felt strangely embarrassed by it. Shedding his momentary vulnerability, his normal aplomb re-asserted itself in his jaunty stride and tone.

"You're very much like your mother, you know. A woman of convictions. I pointed that out to the committee when we reviewed your application. For medical school."

"What?" asked Lenie, stopping dead in her tracks.

"I am one of the trustees at the university. Still – despite my perfidy during the War," Charles reminded her. Lenie's heart lurched within her, but outwardly she gave no sign of joy at what she realized was Charles' declaration of support. Then another thought struck her.

"Don't do this because you feel sorry for me."

Charles seemed to understand what she was trying to tell him without her speaking the words. He bowed, holding his hat over his heart.

101

"I assure you, my support comes from my desire to have another fine doctor in our town."

Looking into his dark eyes, Lenie was satisfied with the frankness she read there and his declaration. She resumed her walk to cover her elation.

"Well, if you can get them to let me into medical school, maybe you could convince them to build a new hospital."

Behind her, Charles grinned, shaking his head at her audacity. He needed no convincing that her efforts in every realm would be successful.

Despite Charles' assurances, Lenie was nervous, snappish, and borderline sickly waiting to hear about her acceptance to medical school. Although her knowledge of anatomy told her this was impossible, she honestly felt that her heart had risen up into her throat as she accepted a letter from the postman with the university's insignia stamped upon it.

With cold, awkward fingers she pried it open and peeked at its contents. Her pale face broke into a triumphant smile and then a rebel yell of exuberance. She threw her arms around her father so enthusiastically that she threatened to knock both of them to the floor. Dr. John clung to her for balance, enormously relieved that this long-cherished, but unusual, dream of his eccentric daughter would be realized.

That night in her room, Lenie – unable to wait for classes to start – opened her brand new medical books for her first evening of study. I guess she was realizing that her life was finally changing forever. Like when there is electricity in the air, before a big storm. She bent the binding slowly, reverently, savoring the moment, inhaling the slightly spicy smell of the leather cover. Her dream was coming true, opening a new life before her. From that moment on, the scent of a new book would serve her as a reminder of the excitement of discovering the unknown.

Inside Zack's room, he too was studying – reading his worn secondhand law books. They held no tart scent of fresh leather, only the musty smell of ancient tomes long stored and then re-sold in a secondhand shop. Where Lenie was inspired by her victory over the prejudices of her time, Zack was motivated only by his sense of duty to his family. His own dreams of justice had vanished in the smoke of his old homestead.

The melted doorknob from his old home sat on his desk, a constant reminder of that loss.

That night, he fingered it absentmindedly, his mind uneasy and unable to concentrate. Without even realizing what he was doing, he opened his door and looked at the light peeking out from under Lenie's closed door.

At that moment, Dr. John's cane tapped on the wooden floor as he emerged from his room and caught sight of Zack before his nephew could duck back out of sight. Startled and embarrassed, Zack stepped out into the hallway as if he had been on his way downstairs all along.

"Uncle John, I think it's better if I get a place of my own," he blurted out. "I don't want to crowd you and Lenie."

John sensed his agitation but misread his concern.

"Nonsense! Why spend money on rent that you could send to your family?"

Zack had no answer for this logic. John put his arm over Zack's shoulder.

"Besides, you're the only one I trust to look after my willful daughter. She's not the tomboy you knew in Virginia."

"Yes. She is – different," agreed Zack fervently.

"Come have a drink with me. Let's celebrate your future." Zack followed John down the stairs, with a confused backward glance at the closed room and its mysterious and vexing occupant.

Chapter 18
Epidemic

Others were less than enthusiastic about Lenie's admittance into the medical school, viewing it as an insult to the established order that was already weakened by the sad outcome of the War. Very well, she was about as welcome as an elephant at a debutante's ball. But she did not care.

Whatever overt hostility her presence inspired, Lenie was oblivious to it. Until one day...

It happened in the old hospital ward, as an officious professor led a group of medical students, Lenie among them, to the bedside of a groaning patient. With distaste, Lenie observed the outdated fixtures, crowded wards, slovenly nurses, and dirty floors.

One particularly beefy nurse deliberately tossed a pail of dirty water into the path of the gawking students, forcing them to jump to avoid its stream. In an outraged whisper, Lenie scolded her.

"That water is full of germs! There are sick people here. You should..."

Looking down her nose disdainfully as if Lenie were a peculiarly offensive insect, the nurse insolently interrupted.

"Doctors here don't believe in germs, Miss." She nodded to the retreating backs of the other students. "You'll be missing your class."

Lenie gave up the argument – at least for now – and hurried after her group, no doubt vowing to herself, "It will be different when I'm in charge."

"Diagnosis, please? High fever, delirium, swollen glands –" snapped the Professor. Lenie stared in horror at the yellowish-faced, panting sick man on the cot before them, and raised her hand.

"I've seen this before."

The professor threw her a scornful look and turned toward the male students for an answer. No one responded. He sighed in frustration.

"A local fever. Not serious with proper care," pronounced the Professor authoritatively.

"You're wrong," protested Lenie. "My mother died of this. It's yellow fever."

"Nonsense, young lady. You will remember your place and speak when spoken to. Yellow fever is much more serious. Toward the end stages the patient emits black vomit..." droned the Professor.

The patient suddenly jerked half-upright, spewing viscous black liquid on the horrified professor. The medical students stared in shock – then one turned and ran from the room in terror. One by one the others broke rank and followed, leaving only Lenie and the speechless professor, as the exhausted patient collapsed back onto his cot.

Within weeks, the deadly yellow fever epidemic was rampant throughout the city. The activities of commerce and daily living ground to a halt. Almost every house had a yellow rag tied to the porch railing. The streets were deserted except for the workers wearing kerchiefs over their mouths and noses, loading sheet-covered bodies into wagons. One of those sheets fell away to reveal the body of the arrogant professor, jaw agape and eyes wide and staring as if amazed at his own demise.

Inside the overcrowded hospital, once again Lenie and Dr. John worked side by side in their battle against death. At least this time they battled a sickness, whose origin was as yet unknown, and not wounds inflicted by other human beings upon their fellow man. Some brave members of the community assisted them, Lenie's dear friend Lucy among them.

"Lenie – come quick!" Lenie followed Lucy to a bed where her cousin Zack lay groaning, staring fearfully at an invisible scene.

"Helen! Helen! Don't go in there!" he cried. Repressing her own fear for her cousin and her horror at the memory she knew he was reliving, Lenie felt his forehead, pushing him back on to the bed.

"What is it?" asked Lucy fearfully.

"Delirium. He's still living the War," replied Lenie, not completely aware of how true her statement was.

"Is he – will he –" asked Lucy, tremulous with anxiety.

"I don't know. He's very ill." Lenie's voice was dispassionate, even as she fought an unexpected emotion rising in her throat.

Lucy sat down heavily, exhausted, but never taking her eyes off Zack.

"You remember. We all had it. It was so – horrible…"

Lenie kept her eyes fixed on her patient. "I remember. But now you can't get it again. Neither can I."

"Thank goodness. They need you to take care of them," Lucy spoke fervently, her tone expressing her gratitude as she took a cool rag and gently wiped Zack's stubbled face.

"And you. Thank you – for your help," said Lenie, turning toward her friend. She rested her hand briefly on Lucy's shoulder. Lucy clasped it, still eying Zack's pale, sweaty face with trepidation.

Both women looked up in surprise as Charles made his way towards them through the crowded cots, ignoring the groans of the suffering and the malodorous smells. He was followed by a teenage boy, a mulatto, with chiseled cheekbones and skin the color of light chocolate. The boy held his head high despite the stares from even the sickest patients, telling him wordlessly that he did not belong here.

Lucy regarded the boy and Charles with surprise and even dismay. Charles, less sure of himself than usual, looked unusually brittle from some tightly held emotion, his face marked with new lines of – grief? Worry? Lenie could not tell.

"Miss Lenie, Lucy. I brought Phillip to help you. He's a good nurse," he explained quietly.

Suddenly embarrassed, Lucy quickly returned her attention to the patients. Lenie looked Phillip up and down, back at Charles, then at Phillip again, noting the angles of his face and his intelligent dark eyes. So like Octavia, Lucy and Charlotte's old nurse. Having seen much more of the world than her sheltered counterparts, understanding of what this meant dawned on her.

"Phillip – Delacourt, is it?" asked Lenie. Phillip met her eyes, unblinking. Lenie extended her hand to him. He hesitated only a moment before taking it.

Charles seemed to relax a little as he perceived her matter-of-fact acceptance.

"How do you know about medicine?" Lenie asked the still silent youth.

The boy answered readily, in accents that bespoke an education considerably above his station in life.

"I took care of my family. But they all died." Trained by a life in the shadows to hide his feelings, his voice held no trace of the grief he must be feeling inside. "I'm going to be a doctor." He stared back at Lenie, proudly, daring her to react.

"Oh? Then we have something in common. Neither of us knows our place."

At that, Phillip smiled. White teeth flashed in a grin reminiscent of a wild canine.

In admiration and relief at Lenie's acceptance, Charles nodded his gratitude.

"Thank you," he said quietly, with no trace of his trademark irony. His hand rested on Phillip's shoulder briefly before he turned to go. Watching his stiff figure make its way among the crowded cots, Lenie saw that his step lacked its usual insouciance – instead it was almost sedate, labored. Suddenly she realized that this man, her friend from childhood, was indeed as old as her own father.

Shaking off her concern for Charles' health, she returned her attention to Zack's bedside, as Phillip stood a step behind her, watching with an analytical and observant stare. Zack opened his eyes.

"Who's that?" asked Zack groggily.

"His name is Phillip. He's helping me," said Lenie, feeling Zack's forehead.

"I don't want you going out at night without a chaperone. It's not decent," murmured Zack. Despite his intent to lecture his cousin, his eyes drooped closed.

"Still telling me what to do. That's a good sign. I think Zack's going to be all right." Lenie's gruff words hid her own sense of relief that Zack was out of danger.

Lucy's anxiety melted with a sigh of thankfulness as she smiled her gratitude.

107

Past midnight, Phillip still stood at Lenie's elbow, exhaustion plain in his face and stance. He struggled to keep his own eyes open as Lenie closed the lids of a tired patient. Then she surprised him by taking out her worn Bible. Settling in a rickety chair, she began to read.

"The spirit of the Lord God is upon me;
because the Lord hath anointed me to preach good tidings unto the meek;
He hath sent me to bind up the brokenhearted, to proclaim liberty to the captives, and the opening of the prison to them that are bound."

Phillip was not her only audience. Finally conscious, but still very weak, his head feeling heavy as a cannonball, Zack watched his unwomanly, constantly surprising cousin through hooded lids, listening to the proclamation of her mission with a strange, soft look on his face that she never saw.

Chapter 19
An Uneasy Truce

Once Zack passed the crisis, his recovery was rapid. A grudging respect for Lenie's dedication as a healer and a growing awareness of her as a woman was the legacy of his illness. Unable to articulate his feelings, let alone act on them, Zack continued in the pattern of their established relationship: muted irritation coupled with sporadic arguments over their differing views on life, work, and the appropriate behavior of women. I guess he was afraid to change, or just plain didn't know how.

Of this inner conflict, Zack communicated nary a word to his family back in Virginia. Nor did he ever acknowledge the loss of the War or its aftermath. His letters were determinedly cheerful and optimistic, sharing progress with his studies, carefully neutral observations of the activities of his uncle and cousin, and queries and comments on the lives of the loved ones back home.

When not studying, working or writing home, he continued to sacrifice precious time that should have been devoted to studying to accompany Lenie on her evening calls. More often than Zack realized, Phillip took that responsibility during the day, becoming a stalwart assistant to Lenie.

So the years of their studies passed, and the approach of their mutual graduations brought the unspoken understanding that life was about to change once again. How it would be re-arranged, no one could possibly have guessed.

This momentous turn of fate began late one afternoon as Dr. John entered the little white frame house, suppressed excitement in his face.

"Lenie! Zack!" he called. Lenie slipped in from the kitchen, Zack from the upstairs landing.

"I have a surprise for you. A present for your graduations."

He opened the front door with a flourish. There stood a young woman, smiling with quiet radiance and excitement, and a young man, tall as Zack, but thinner and more muscular from daily labors on the farm.

It took Zack a minute to recognize his siblings from Virginia –
Nan and Alden. Their clothes were older but respectable – no longer
the rags left after four years of war. Their faces had lost the
gauntness of semi-starvation and returned to the healthy proportions
of their more prosperous youth. Alden had outgrown the coltishness
of his boyhood and into his height as a man. The responsibilities of
running a farm and leading his family had given him a new gravity.
Nan seemed more placid and content, with the fear of losing her
brothers and the daily fight for survival now behind her.

To Zack, they were a vision of the home and the old life he
revered. After a moment of shocked silence, the young people ran
together in welcoming hugs.

As the excitement abated a bit and the visitors and guests seated
themselves in the small parlor, Dr. John poured glasses of his
favorite port for Alden and Zack. Alden saluted Zack and Lenie.

"Here's to the new doctor and the lawyer in the family," he
toasted.

"It's us who are proud of you. Working the farm, running a
school with your mother," countered Lenie.

"We couldn't have survived without Zack's help. Thank you for
bringing us here," said Nan, smiling her gratitude at her older
brother.

"But I didn't –" responded Zack. Dr. John looked uncomfortable.
The cook appeared in the doorway.

"All the guests here for dinner?" she asked. The doorbell rang.

"That must be the rest of them now," said Dr. John, with relief
and a little trepidation. He opened the door and welcomed the new
arrivals: First Lucy and Caroline, expectant, slightly nervous smiles
on their faces, which were framed with large bonnets matching their
frocks. New dresses from Paris, different styles but similar colors to
the ones they had proudly showed Lenie and Nan in Virginia, many
years ago.

If Nan contrasted these beautiful gowns with her own brown
dress, now faded and "turned," the practice of wearing the dress
inside out when it was too faded and worn, she betrayed no sign of
it. Her habitual calm expression only altered when she recognized

the tall figure following them. It was Charles Delacourt. Zack's expression, I've been told, was almost comical – like he'd bitten into a luscious apple and saw in the remaining fruit, the remnants of a worm.

Lenie jumped up to greet her friends as Alden recognized his family's nemesis. His initial shock gave way to anger.

"You!" he sputtered. Lenie quickly interrupted, stepping between the two young women to include them in the gathering.

"You remember my friends, Lucy and Caroline. And their uncle, Mr. Delacourt. Whom you also know."

There was a pregnant pause as Alden, incapable of forming human speech, simply glared at Charles. Zack shot visual daggers at this insufferable villain for spoiling their family's sacred reunion. Then Nan stepped forward, offering Charles her small hand.

"I'm glad to see you again. Under pleasanter circumstances," she said, sincerely. The blushing young girl had given way to a poised young lady. Charles kissed her hand, gallantly acknowledging her acceptance of his presence.

"I have to confess. This was all Charles' idea. He paid for your train tickets," said Dr. John with false heartiness in his voice.

"I hoped that our families could resume the friendly relationships we had before the War," explained Charles, doing his best to look guileless.

"Well then, thank you, Mr. Delacourt, for your kindness. It has been so long since we were all together," responded Nan, only realizing the double meaning of her words after they had escaped her mouth.

"I'm sure we all feel the same," said Lenie, glaring at Alden and Zack. The two young men were silent. Neither offered their hands to Charles, but neither did they leave the room nor attempt to act on the anger showing in their tightly held expressions. Zack quelled his violent impulses with difficulty, his desire for revenge tempered with gratitude for the generosity of his uncle these last several years. How, he must have wondered, could he maintain civility – even dine with – the one man in the world he longed to murder? No doubt Alden's thoughts ran along the same vein. An uneasy silence reigned.

"Please, come in for dinner," pleaded Dr. John. "Cook has prepared a special feast."

"Yes, Dr. Lewis. It smells delicious," declared Lucy. She offered her arm to Zack. Woodenly he took it, accompanying her to the dining room. Alden took his cue from Zack and extended the same courtesy to Caroline.

Chapter 20
True Confessions

After an awkward dinner and evening of conversation that alternated between politely formal and quietly hostile, the Delacourts finally left. Truth be told, Nan was pleased that the olive branch had been offered and accepted, if only between some members of the family. The four young ladies had happily resumed the acquaintance begun in the old Virginia mansion, as if they had never been parted, and the tragic events and deprivations of the last decade had not occurred. Ever the peacemakers, they all – except Lenie – made an effort to include the men in the conversation, trying to spin a web of renewed friendship between the stubborn warriors. Too polite to openly reject the efforts of their womenfolk, the men gruffly complied with their overtures. Lenie, sitting next to Charles, made a point of devoting her entire attention to him all evening, a spectacle that almost drove Zack to apoplexy, if not violence.

Emotionally exhausted by the stressful evening, Zack chased sleep for several hours but could not catch it. Instead, he found himself sitting alone in the empty parlor, staring into the dying fireplace, trying to make sense of the emotional maelstrom within his soul.

As if sensing his distress, Nan stole silently down the dark staircase, her small feet making nary a sound as she entered the parlor and seated herself on the sofa, pulling her robes around her and waiting for her brother to speak to her. In her comforting, quiet presence Zack realized he finally had someone to whom he could reveal his heart.

"Nothing is the way it should be anymore, little sister," he sighed.

"I know. But Uncle John and Lenie want to be friends with the Delacourts. So we must accept it. Besides, Charles seems to be quite taken with Lenie," she observed, as if hoping Zack would deny it. Zack jumped up.

"Over my dead body! He's not fit to – to – touch her shoe.

113

Besides, Nan – he killed our baby sister!"

"That wasn't his fault, Zack. It was the War. Anyway, it seems that Lenie will do what she wants to do." Nan still watched her brother carefully, waiting for his opinion. Zack's rage burst forth.

"I won't allow it! He can't marry her. It would betray everything our family fought for!"

Nan looked suddenly guilty. "But the War is over. Surely, we can forgive and for –"

"Never! Besides, he can't marry her because – because – I love her!" Zack blurted out. Shocked speechless at his own revelation after years of silence, Zack stopped. Nan's eyes widened in surprise. She, no more than Zack, had expected this.

"Until I die, I'll never understand how this happened. It's like my heart has a mind of its own," confessed Zack.

"Our hearts know what we need, Zack. It must be right," responded Nan, as if trying to convince herself.

"Nan, I don't know what to do. Everything used to be so clear. Now, it's upside down."

Nan thought quickly, evaluating the practical matter at hand, oblivious to Zack's philosophical distress. "Well, if you do nothing, I think Charles will. So you must woo her. I'll help you."

Zack looked up at her, almost pathetically grateful. A female ally in this battle for Lenie's affections – he had not expected this boon. Fortunately for his peace of mind, he remained quite oblivious to Nan's self-interest in the matter.

Chapter 21
Brave Wolf Returns

As the days lengthened and the temperatures rose, Lenie grew more snappish than usual. Nan noticed her moodiness but had no idea of the cause. She did not know that an anniversary was approaching, that for both her uncle and her cousin drew them back to the saddest events of their lives.

Dr. John seemed especially tolerant of his daughter's mood. That is, until she announced her intention to visit her family's old homestead and the herb garden that she believed still possessed some of the plants that she required for her medicine bag. Surprisingly, her father's reaction to her plans was, for once, to interject himself between his daughter and her objective, with a firm refusal to let her go. The place was abandoned, he argued. Nothing would be left there. Outlaws and renegade Indians still roamed those areas. It was far too dangerous.

Charles, seeing an opportunity and desiring to keep the peace between his old friend and his headstrong daughter, offered a compromise. He would organize an outing for everyone. The group could travel together and camp on his property that adjoined the Lewis' old farm.

Under Charles' assurances, Dr. John's resistance gradually wore down until he, still somewhat reluctant, gave his permission.

And so, early one morning, the party found themselves traversing the wild, scrubby Texas countryside, the women riding in wagons and the men on horseback.

In contrast to the verdant, lush Virginia woods, the dry Texas hills boasted only short, gnarly oaks separated by scraggly-branched bushes, as much brown as green. A veritable desert, thought Zack, thoroughly unimpressed by the aesthetics of the landscape and its potential for producing anything useful to human beings. I see the same landscape, and it is beautiful to me.

Then, coming over a hill, the women gasped collectively at a springtime vision – acres of violet-blue flowers known as bluebonnets. Alden surveyed the open, spacious countryside with wonder.

"Is all this yours?" he asked, incredulous.

"Yes," responded Charles. "Someday, I had in mind starting a ranch. Breeding longhorn. But I never got around to it. Yet."

"When I think of how hard we work to raise a few crops – with cattle, you just let them graze." Alden contemplated this new idea. To Zack's chagrin, he could see that his brother's resentment of Charles was weakening.

Charles halted their trek beside a creek under a grove of majestic cedar trees.

"This is my favorite spot on the property."

"It's beautiful!" exclaimed Nan. Perhaps in her imagination, she saw a rustic ranch house there in the future, with dogs and children playing in the yard.

"Hmph. I hope no Indians feel the same way," groused Zack, surveying the horizon.

"There haven't been Indians around here in years," snapped Lenie. "So sorry to disappoint you. I know how you relish a good fight."

Despite every effort of his will, Zack felt himself flush bright red under Lenie's rebuke. Lucy quickly intervened.

"Let's see what our cook packed for lunch. I'm so ravenous – I could eat a bear!"

Caroline stared at her genteel sister, shocked at this unladylike comment. Nevertheless, it served its purpose of defusing the tension.

The gentlemen quickly unloaded the wagon and the ladies spread out the carefully packed dishes. In no time the group was enjoying a delightful picnic luncheon. Conversation drifted back to another picnic, in Virginia, a lifetime ago. Only Charles noticed how quiet Lenie had become.

"I remember how you and your mother knew a meaning for each flower! It's like a language," mused Lucy.

"What about our bluebonnets?" asked Caroline.

"I think they mean... new friends," surmised Nan.

"I remember how Lenie was hell-bent on showing us she really

116

was the best scout in the family," declared Alden. "You remember, Zack? I thought she was going to scalp you for sure."

For the second time that day Zack felt himself flushing in embarrassment. But Lenie was in no mood to gloat. She rose swiftly.

"While you all are resting, I'm going to the garden," she announced, avoiding eye contact.

"What garden? I haven't seen anything growing here that isn't either prickly or poisonous," questioned Zack.

Charles studied Lenie's back as she stalked to her horse. "Dr. John's spread is next to mine. Lenie's mother had quite an herb garden."

Lenie didn't answer. As she mounted one of the horses, Zack sprang up.

"Well, you can't go out there alone," he said although this was clearly what Lenie intended to do. She was already riding off as Zack hastily mounted another horse and galloped after her.

As they rode through gnarled trees and low hills, Zack nervously watched in all directions, further irritating Lenie.

"Hell's bells, you act like some Yankee sniper is going to pop out from behind a tree," she snapped.

"You heard your father – there could still be Indians in these parts. Shooting would be merciful compared to what they might do," Zack retorted. And indeed, even as a latecomer to Galveston he had heard the stories of the savage Comanches and how they cruelly tortured the settlers they captured only a generation ago.

Lenie did not answer, but threw Zack a look of such scornful contempt that his other warnings died on his lips.

At the crest of a hill, Lenie reined in her horse. Below them was a beautiful panorama of the Texas hill country, green hills, low trees with twisted branches, with a stream running through it. A small house, an afterthought to God's beauty, sat by the stream.

"This is it? Where are the slave quarters?" asked Zack, incredulous.

"My mother didn't believe in slavery," Lenie explained, her voice very quiet.

117

"No wonder this farm failed," muttered Zack. Lenie spurred her horse onward, ready to face whatever ghosts lurked here in the light of day.

The small herb garden beside the house indeed still flourished, in the shade of the east wall. Inside the little house, some simple furnishings still remained, covered with dust and cobwebs. Lenie, ignoring the dirt and the bizarre and perhaps poisonous creatures who might be inhabiting the house's hidden places, went directly to the corner where rested some ancient gardening implements. She quickly set Zack to work harvesting plants as the afternoon sun blazed down on them and cicadas hummed ceaselessly.

"Cut them close to the root, but not too close. Then they'll grow back," instructed Lenie.

Zack's hoe hit the ground with a dull thump that was definitely not soil. He chopped away to more metallic clangs. "There's something here," he called to Lenie.

Puzzled, she knelt beside him, pulling at the overgrown plants and brushing black dirt aside. Her efforts revealed a square stone, engraved with simple letters.

Lenie's fingers caressed the stone, tracing the lettering as if it were that language invented for the blind. "He did this," she whispered in quiet amazement.

Zack read slowly, "Remember. Hannah Lewis, 1859."

Suddenly aware of what these words meant, he leaped up and jumped away from the site.

"This is your mother's grave? I'm sorry – I didn't know."

Lenie remained kneeling, smoothing the stone. It spoke to her heart, stirring emotions long buried. And memories.

"How did she…" Zack was curious but could not finish the question. Lenie responded quietly, woodenly.

"I got sick. She took care of me till I was better," Lenie paused as Zack waited for the rest of her story. "Then, she got the fever herself. I tried – I couldn't save her."

The lost, desperate little girl shone briefly through the grown young woman's diffidence. As usual she tried to cover her vulnerability by scolding Zack.

"Why are you so skittish? It's not like you've never seen a dead body before." She grabbed handfuls of the earth with the plants still rooted in it, sniffing deeply. Zack was appalled.

"Lenie, that was your mother –"

"Everything that dies returns in another way. That's what she said." She offered the stalks to Zack. "Rosemary. It means remembrance."

Reluctantly, he gave the green stalks a tiny sniff.

"Breathe in the earth. This is what Texas smells like. Strong. Wild. And a little sweet." Zack inhaled more deeply. He looked into her face, now inches from his. Their eyes met.

"Like you," he murmured. He held Lenie's hand, with its cup of black earth, to his face, and breathed deeply. Their faces were so close he could see the tiny pores in the ivory skin, now glistening with a fine dew of perspiration that made her whole face glow.

Lenie's blue eyes darkened with a sudden rush of feelings she had never experienced before. Suddenly embarrassed, she pulled her hand away, crushing the tiny green shoots in her fingers.

"We have enough. Let's wash up and go back."

Silently, Zack watched as Lenie stuffed her leather saddlebags with the fresh herbs, wanting to speak but finding himself completely tongue-tied. With uncharacteristic docility, he followed her to the creek bank where they both washed the dirt from their hands. The icy cold water seemed to break her frozen thoughts into words.

"I still love this place. In spite of what happened here." She shook her head, as if to clear the bad memories.

Her face was pensive. Zack studied her profile. His heart rose to his throat. Still, he managed to croak out a sentence.

"Maybe you could settle out here, after you get married," he suggested, watching her response.

"That'll happen about as soon as you join the Army of the Occupation," she retorted. "Besides, who would I treat out here? All that medical education would be wasted. All those people shocked by a woman doctor, for no reason."

She sat down on the prickly ground, stretched out her legs,

unlaced her dusty boots and pulled them off to reveal white, soft-looking feet. To Zack, the sight of a woman's naked flesh – even a foot – was more shocking than full nudity is to us jaded folks, today.

"Wh – what are you doing?" squeaked Zack in alarm. Lenie hiked her skirts to her knees, revealing seldom-seen calves above her bare feet. Zack stared at them, hypnotized and horrified.

"Out here I can do anything I want and no one will know. Come on." Lenie waded into the cold creek. Overcoming his initial shock, Zack pulled off his own boots and followed her.

"It's cold!" He winced.

Lenie splashed him and he splashed back. Off balance, she slipped on the mossy stones, landing seated in the icy water.

"Still can't keep your balance?" teased Zack. She pulled herself upright, her drenched skirt and shirtwaist clinging to her slender form. Mesmerized by the sight, Zack was caught off guard. Lenie pushed him hard, and he also lost his balance, toppling into the rushing stream.

Surprised, they both burst into laughter, their cares and differences forgotten for the moment.

Zack thought to himself, "It's now or never." Pulling himself upright, he reflexively shook himself like a dog, as if preparing for a test of strength.

"Lenie – there's something – that's hard for me to say–" he began, his voice suddenly hoarse with nervousness.

Lenie's carefree attitude evaporated as quickly as a desert puddle. Her face snapped closed.

"Don't bother. I know what you're going to say." Zack's expression was surprised and hopeful. Maybe she knows and he would be spared the agony of voicing his feelings. But Lenie had something else on her mind.

"Every time you see Charles looking at me, you look daggers at him. It doesn't matter what you think, I'll be friends with whomever I please." Her tone would brook no argument. From anyone but Zack.

"But why him? He destroyed our house! He –" Zack couldn't

bring himself to mention Helen. He went on, "Besides being a damn Yankee, he's rich and disreputable and doesn't care about anything but himself."

"Oh really? Isn't he the one helping build a hospital for this town?" countered Lenie, shaking her skirt vehemently to emphasize her irritation. Turning away from Zack, she began wading to shore.

"His money is. He's trying to buy his way back into people's hearts. Is that what he's doing with you?"

Zack didn't really mean to say that Lenie was mercenary – he knew the opposite was true – but it was too late to take his words back.

Furious, Lenie stopped beside the bank, and began to scoop up water and splash it on her sweat-stained face, then – to Zack's horror – pour handfuls inside the neck of her blouse. Decades of good breeding won out over more sensual curiosity and he averted his eyes from this shocking spectacle. Lenie's words reached his ears anyway.

"What I like about Charles is that he's so different from you! He doesn't tell me what to do. He accepts me just the way I am," she retorted.

"I like you the way you are!" exclaimed Zack, risking a glance her way.

"Hah! You've been criticizing me since the day we met. Just leave me alone."

Despite her words, her expression was indecisive. But Zack – stung by her rejection as if by a slap – didn't see this as he stormed away, for once complying with her demands.

He got as far as the tree where his horse was tethered when Lenie's scream shattered the air.

Zack whirled around. His worst fears were realized. While the two cousins had argued, two renegade Indians had crept from their hiding place behind the house. Yes, I know today we say "Native Americans," but back then they were Indians so that's what I call them.

And that's the dreaded word that popped into both Lenie and Zack's minds as these two warriors charged toward Lenie, who was

121

trying to run through the creek waters in her sodden clothes, heading for the bank. These Indians didn't look like Zack had imagined – they had no war paint, no feathers, and no warning war cry. If he had looked closely, he would have noticed they were more thin than muscular, their bare chests showing each rib. However, he saw none of this as he realized their danger. As their tawny bodies streaked towards Lenie, Zack reached for his gun – and realized he had no weapons but his hunting knife.

Within seconds he had raced to the creek and made a flying leap onto the back of one of the Indians. They fell to the ground in a writhing heap.

Startled, his companion turned his attention from Lenie for a few moments, giving her time to clamber onto dry land and grasp the spade that minutes ago had harvested her life-saving medicines. Now it was a weapon. With a piercing war whoop, she leaped onto the second Indian, one hand covering his eyes and the other raised to attack with the sharp spade.

Twisting like a bobcat, he unseated her and she fell to the ground. Then he was on her, holding her arms back, squeezing her wrist to force her to drop the iron spade. Held seemingly helpless, she nevertheless managed to sink her teeth into his forearm and hung on like a wolf to its prey.

Rolling to their feet, Zack and his opponent charged each other. The Indian tripped over the tombstone and was off balance just long enough for Zack to topple him. On the ground again, the two wrestled for advantage.

Meanwhile, Lenie's teeth in her opponent's arm succeeded in loosening her assailant's grip on her wrist. She fought like a desperate animal, using her feet, fingernails and teeth, and in spite of his size and strength, he could not pin her again. Lenie's nails raked the side of his face, opening a long scar on his cheek from an old battle. Infuriated, he gave up his efforts to subdue her and reached for his tomahawk, raising it overhead. Lenie used both hands to hold his upraised arm away from her. For a second their eyes met – startlingly deep blue with impenetrable dark brown. Something passed between them in that gaze.

An explosion of sound erupted, echoing across the empty countryside. As Lenie glared defiantly at her attacker, the light in the Indian's eyes died away. He loosened his grip on her slender arms, sagged and collapsed on top of her.

Zack's opponent wrested away from Zack's hold and raced back to the little house, leaped upon his horse hidden behind it, and galloped off, his companion's mount galloping riderless behind him.

Zack ran to Lenie, rolling the dead Indian's body off her. She continued to stare at the scarred, now bloody face, shock finally overtaking her.

Standing alone at the crest of the hill, Charles lowered his rifle. As Zack pulled Lenie to her feet, she spied Charles' slender figure silhouetted against the sun, motionless for a moment before he broke into a run to reach her.

"He's – he's dead," Lenie gasped. To Zack's amazement and chagrin, she turned to Charles and collapsed into his arms. She and Charles both stared at the Indian's body, an undefined emotion in their faces that Zack could not understand. He only knew that it was Charles's arm, not his, that encircled Lenie's slender shoulders protectively. Why was this cursed man so lucky?

It was midnight when the somber picnickers returned to the Lewis house, tired and bedraggled. Lucy and Caroline waited in the wagon as Charles escorted the Lewis party to the front porch. Dr. John met them at the door, puzzled and suspicious at their serious expressions, and then downright alarmed when he saw Lenie's drawn, pale face and disheveled clothes.

"What happened?" he queried.

"Nothing, Father. Only some renegades," replied Lenie, woodenly.

"Indians?" Dr. John clutched Lenie to him in a fierce hug, glaring at the men he had trusted with his most precious possession for an explanation of this shocking news.

"John, it was my fault. You were right. I should not have allowed the ladies to make this trip. I believed the reports…" Charles tried to apologize to his old friend, but his guilt lent the tone of an errant schoolboy caught in an embarrassing prank.

"I never should have left her at the creek. She just made me mad –" explained Zack.

"You were supposed to be watching out for her!" sputtered Dr. John. "You said it was safe! After what she went through – How could I have let you talk me into this!"

"Zack fought them off, Uncle John." Nan tried to explain and give credit to her crestfallen brother at the same time.

"Charles shot them," Lenie responded tersely, yet touched by her father's anger on her behalf. "It's all right, Father. Truly it is."

Dr. John's furious expression said he didn't think it was all right at all. Pulling Lenie and Nan into the house, he slammed the door, leaving Charles, Zack and Alden standing on the porch steps. Zack glared at Charles, who shrugged, turned, and left, returning to the wagon and his weary nieces, now longing to spend the night in the safety of their own beds. Zack and Alden pondered their options.

"Ah – guess we can sleep out back in the barn," suggested Alden. "We'll be camping after all."

However, Cook took pity on the two young men and let them in through the kitchen door, from where they slunk up to Zack's room.

But the events of the day were too much for Zack and although Alden snored away, he lay sleepless, tossing and turning as if he reclined upon a bed of cactus instead of his customary well-worn pallet.

Finally, he conceived of a solution – a glass of port to quell his racing mind and strangely excitable heart. He stole downstairs in the dark, unerringly directed himself toward his uncle's side table where the coveted beverage resided in a glass bottle from New Orleans.

But he was not the only one who could not sleep. Lenie sat so quietly in the shadows before the lifeless fire, sipping a dark beverage and wrapped in a blanket, that at first he did not see her. Making out her silent form, he took it as a sign. It was time. He took a deep breath to steel his courage and walked to the mantle, where he stood with his back to her.

"I'll try to say this without making you angry." He stopped, groping for his words, and once again not finding them. "Charles will not make you happy. He's – he's not a gentleman."

This was not what he had meant to say, but it was too late. "Maybe what you consider to be a gentleman doesn't matter to me," retorted Lenie. "Maybe a kind heart is more important to me."

Zack turned around to face her, desperate and for the first time in his life, vulnerable. "I can be kind."

Lenie lifted her dark brows in a quizzical look.

"The way you believe what you believe – you need a man of honor for a husband," stammered Zack.

"Didn't they all die during the War?" asked Lenie sarcastically. Again the ghost of Samuel stepped between them. Dismissively, she rose, her blanket wrapped around her, and headed for the stairs. Desperately, Zack watched her retreating form.

"I didn't die," he protested.

"What are you going on about?" Lenie questioned, not turning around.

She was getting away. Suddenly Zack's courage surged, drowning his fears. He quickly crossed the room, followed her to the stairs, and took her arm, turning her to face him. But his tongue lay in his mouth like a stone, rendering him speechless. So instead – shocking them both – he kissed her.

Despite their mutual inexperience in such matters, his rough lips locked with her smooth ones in a perfect match.

Lenie's insides turned to a liquid rush that shot through her body from head to toe. Too shocked even to try to label this bizarre reaction in medical terms, she pulled away with a sharp intake of breath as soon as her mouth was free. The back of her hand flew to her lips as if to protect them from further assault.

Oblivious to her reaction, Zack blurted out, "We love the same things. We understand each other. I would never betray you. On my word."

"Did that Indian hit you in the head? You and I – we'd kill each other," said Lenie, trying to make a joke of this strange encounter. She turned away, for once in retreat from danger.

"I'm sorry for all that's past. I know now – I do love you. Please, think about it," begged Zack. He touched her arm; she studied him for a long moment, before pulling away and running up the stairs into her room.

Inside, she quietly closed the door, touching her lips which still throbbed pleasantly from Zack's touch, and futilely trying to quell the strange vibration that still quivered within her. Never in her life had she felt so confused – that type of affection that is both painful and glorious. She fought the urge to awaken her sleeping cousin Nan to tell her of this tumultuous experience. Instead, she opened her dresser drawer – there was Zack's old uniform, cleaned and folded. She held the worn fabric against her cheek, savoring its familiar texture.

Lenie's movement woke Nan.

"What is it?" she inquired sleepily. "Can I get you something?"

At Nan's words Lenie started guiltily, quickly replacing the worn uniform in the drawer. "Nothing. I'm sorry I woke you."

Abandoned on the staircase, Zack studied the closed door for a long few minutes, hearing the light sounds of Lenie's furtive movement and Nan's whispers, although he could not make out the words. Finally, all was silent. There was nothing more he could do. Willing his tired legs forward, he retreated back to his own room and Alden's snores.

But he had surrendered his position too quickly. A few moments later, Lenie's door opened quietly. Maybe the tingling on her lips would not let her rest. Lenie stole back to the staircase, her eyes searching for a familiar form with a new meaning, unsure of what she sought but compelled to look for that unnamed disturbance.

But Zack was not there.

Chapter 22
The Language of Flowers

After that unsettling skirmish, Lenie and Zack established an emotional no man's land between them, never gazing directly at each other but stealing furtive glances when they thought others were not looking. Everyone but Nan assumed another of their frequent arguments had ensued and the prickly feelings were the result of that altercation, soon to blow over like the many disagreements in the past.

Lenie confided to no one that her emotional defenses had been breached. Not even her cousin Nan, whose sympathetic ear was more than attuned to any clues on the sentimental landscape.

Zack, on the other hand, had an almost physical reaction to this tsunami of feelings, reminding him sometimes of his first stomach-churning voyage across the choppy waters of the bay, now some years in the past.

In deference to Dr. John's anger with him and mayhaps out of his guilt concerning that narrow escape on the ranch – and perhaps also due to Zack's ever-present antipathy – Charles made himself scarce around the Lewis home. No doubt to Zack's great relief, and Nan's disappointment.

Meanwhile, the players in this romantic drama danced through the quicksand of their conflicting infatuations as they carried on with what is known as real life. I hear these feelings are pretty darned confusing – painful and glorious at the same time. Must have been a hellish time for both of these blunt and honest souls to lead a secret life.

Despite the hidden emotional drama, real life did continue. Like all her endeavors, Lenie's campaign for a new hospital had been crowned with success, aided by Charles' behind-the-scenes influence and funds. Construction of this red-bricked shrine to healing finally reached completion.

On the opening day of the new edifice, the honor of cutting the ceremonial ribbon fell to Dr. John. The entire town, it seemed like, attended the ceremony, pleased and proud of this example of the city's renaissance and its hard-won position as the West's bastion of civilization, commerce and culture. They also came to honor their beloved physicians, especially Dr. John, whose cane tapped more slowly these days as he made his rounds.

As family members of the illustrious father-daughter physician team, Zack and Nan occupied places of honor on the hospital steps. Lenie and Charles were placed opposite them. The crowd completely failed to notice that none of these honorees seemed able to look the others in the eye.

Instead they gazed outward, standing frozen, Dr. John with scissors at the ready, while the photographer hid under a dark cloth and readied his camera. A blinding flash and accompanying explosion signaled their freedom from the tableau. Using both hands on the scissors and with Lenie's hand on his arm for balance, Dr. John snipped the massive ribbon cleanly. It fell to the ground as the onlookers burst into applause and cheers.

Incongruously, Zack remembered Lenie's remark from so long ago, about the surgeon's knife sliding through flesh as easily as butter. His own heart felt like that soft mound of yellow butter right now, with Lenie wielding the scalpel as she allowed Charles to escort her down the steps. No one – including Zack – perceived the longing in Nan's face when she studied Charles's tall figure beside her beautiful cousin.

"I have to go home soon. We haven't much time. I have an idea," Nan confided to Zack.

Entirely missing the double meaning in her words, he turned to her beseechingly, looking to her feminine insight for an answer to the romantic dilemma that confounded this once intrepid warrior. He had complete confidence in his younger sister, much as her students and friends relied on her intelligence and her character throughout her life. Facing stormy emotional seas in the voyage to true love, however, was as foreign to her as to Zack. She just hid her fears better.

Nan indeed had a plan whose ingenuity Zack found most impressive. The next morning found the two siblings inside the city's finest floral shop. Nan carefully consulted a list of available blooms, directing the florist in making her selections. The delivery boy waited impatiently while Zack penned a note under Nan's direction.

After much whispering, Zack's note was completed. Nan read it over his shoulder. "These flowers say what is in my heart – I pray that it mirrors what is in yours."

In the custom of the day, he addressed it to "L" and signed it "Z". As Zack sealed the fateful letter, both knew their futures rested on the message of these blossoms.

For that afternoon, as Nan well knew, the lady volunteer guild for the new hospital was to gather at the Delacourt family home, where Lenie would tutor Lucy, Caroline, Nan and a dozen other women in the fine art of tearing and folding bandages.

"Turn it like this, and pull them tight," instructed Lenie, "That way they won't come undone."

The ladies examined each other's techniques as they struggled to imitate Lenie's skill. Nan, knowing what was about to happen, hid the excitement and fear in her heart with studious attention to her task. Peter, Charles' elderly black servant, went from one to the other, offering sandwiches.

"Mizz Pauline, Mizz Lucy, Mizz Caroline, Mizz Nan," he pronounced formally, offering them the refreshments on a silver tray. Too nervous to eat, Nan declined.

As Peter left the room, the doorbell rang. Nan started, almost dropping her basket, and then quickly recovered her composure, attending to the white strip of cloth in her hands.

Puffing out his chest with importance, Peter opened the door to find the florist shop messenger boy. Puzzled, he accepted the delivery, examining the envelope with its flourished "L" with rheumy eyes.

With a crash, a gangly young boy holding a large tray tripped and fell in the hallway. Peter hastily set the flowers on the highly polished side table and turned his attention to this domestic disaster.

"Didn't I tell you to be careful? What a mess!" he scolded the clumsy youth.

Hearing the noise, Charles emerged from his study, eyebrows

raised in inquiry. Relieved that the mishap was minor, his eyes fell on the bouquet and its accompanying envelope. Suspicion was aroused. While Peter was preoccupied, he quickly opened and read the note, replacing it with his long slender and silent fingers in the envelope while he contemplated what it meant for his own future. As he studied the "L" on the envelope, the solution came to him.

"Flowers for Miss Lucy, I see. She'll be pleased," remarked Charles, innocently, his face a perfect masque for his deception. Peter straightened up, picked up the flowers and the letter and headed for the parlor.

"I reckon she will, Suh," he agreed. The die was cast, with Charles wagering more than he had ever dreamed of in any gambling table.

"Flowers for you, Mizz Lucy," Peter announced grandly. The ladies let out a collective gasp of pleasure and excitement. Lucy accepted the arrangement, pleased and tremulous with anticipation, as Nan watched, at first puzzled and then with growing alarm.

"Oh, look! Red roses for love, camellia – my destiny is in your hands – and ivy – a wedding! Oh, Lucy, a proposal!" cried Caroline. Lucy, her blush deepening, opened the envelope. A look of joy stole over her face.

"Well, who is it?" asked Caroline eagerly.

"Zack!" said Lucy. Nan and Lenie's faces registered their shock, albeit for very different reasons.

"Oh, Sister! It's what you've wanted!" cried Caroline. Nan struggled to repress the horror on her face as she looked at the envelope in Lucy's hand and realized the mistake.

Her face as flat as polished glass, Lenie rose stiffly and embraced Lucy in congratulations. Viewing the scene from the hallway, Charles's anxiety evaporated as he watched the success of his ruse. He entered the parlor to seal his victory. A royal flush, some would say.

"What's this? My niece has a suitor?" he asked brightly.

"Zack has proposed to Lucy!" exulted Caroline, perhaps seeing in her sister's romantic success with one Lewis brother, the hope for herself with the other.

130

"Ah! And – you will accept?" Charles inquired with bland solicitude.

"Yes – Yes, I do, I will," said Lucy shyly, struggling in vain to control her elation.

"I know your father would have been so pleased." Charles embraced her as Lenie quietly disappeared into the study. While the ladies congratulated Lucy, Charles also slipped out of the room. Nan watched him go, helplessly, seeing the loss of her hopes in their retreating figures.

In the study, Lenie glared out the window, her face a battleground between grief and anger, her shoulders set rigidly against the emotions that roiled her soul. How dared he touch that tender place in her heart, only to wound it yet again? She roundly berated herself for momentarily forgetting what Zack was really like – wrongheaded, arrogant, and unreliable.

As Charles walked in, one glance – and a lifetime of experience with women – told him her mood.

"Are you happy for Lucy?" asked Charles, carefully keeping his tone light. Lenie tried to swallow the prickly lump in her throat so that she might give a suitably polite response, but it stuck there, burning her with its cactus-like spines. So she was silent, furiously blinking back the hot tears that lurked behind her stony expression.

Charles stepped closer, seeing the opportunity in her vulnerability.

"I have not had the foresight to prepare an appropriate bouquet, but I can offer you my heart –" he began gallantly.

A rush of anger stifled her emotions where willpower had failed. Lenie whirled to face him.

"DON'T. Don't even say that if it isn't true."

"It is true." For once his expression was completely sincere.

Unconvinced and even more confused, Lenie dropped her eyes. She would have turned away but Charles caught her hand, forcing her to face him. Still, she could not meet his gaze.

"You would accept me – as I am?" she queried, despite herself opening her heart gate – just a smidgen.

He gently tilted her chin up so that she had to look at him – dark

131

blue eyes gazed into brown ones that were, for once, completely devoid of charm and that façade of Southern gallantry.

"Exactly as you are," he promised, his heart leaping to his throat in a way he thought he had long outgrown.

Lenie looked deeply into his eyes, his soul, for a long moment, and was surprisingly satisfied with what she saw. Despite her grief, a new and very foreign vision of her future began to take shape in her mind. Could it be –

Then, like quicksilver, the stubborn ghost of Brave Wolf slipped into her soul, rebelling against any confinement or loss of his ancient freedoms. The familiar defiance suddenly returned and her forehead creased into a determined scowl.

"I won't be a wife like other women. My work comes first," she replied stubbornly.

Charles smiled, grateful for even the moment of tenderness they had shared.

"I know. I know you. With those eyes like your mother's." Charles leaned toward her. She pulled back, cutting off his romantic overture.

"Well, you'd best understand that I'm not like my mother. She was – a lady. If you want someone like her, you should marry Nan," Lenie challenged him, testing.

But Charles was not dissuaded. He had thought about this liaison deeply and long, before committing to his course.

"You are like your mother. You have her soul. Her goodness. And I would be pleased to have you as my wife, on any terms you choose."

For once, the master dissembler spoke from his heart. But Lenie was still too recently crushed by another's betrayal to trust it.

"Don't do this because you feel obligated," she retorted. "Because you saved my life. Or because you helped me into medical school. Or – because you feel sorry for me." This last admission was wrung from her very soul.

Tempted to smile at her lack of logic, Charles knew better. He alone understood the full meaning behind her angry, defiant words.

"I promise I feel no sympathy for you whatsoever. Only

admiration," he assured her. "Perhaps I can share your dedication. Perhaps – we can be partners in your mission."

He could have thought of nothing better to win Lenie's allegiance – a business offer to further her dreams. Their discussion of his allegiance during the War, his long friendship with her father, his generous guardianship of Lucy and Caroline, all flashed through her mind in a second. Despite his past reputation, she decided that this was a man who acted according to his own code of honor – not the traditional kind according to society's rules, perhaps, but someone who could be trusted to follow his conscience, as he saw it. The kind of man who could be a worthy successor to Samuel. In their commitments to right as they saw it, they were kin. She took in a deep breath and made her decision.

"Well then, we have an understanding."

They gazed at each other for a moment. He took her hand, knowing he'd won – and that she didn't truly love him. Yet.

Chapter 23
Reversal of Fortune

That was the longest afternoon of Zack's life. And the most disastrous. At first, though, he was hopeful when Alden entered the Lewis home and offered him a bouquet of jasmine.

"I'm told they mean 'yes.' Congratulations, Brother. You're engaged," proclaimed Alden. Zack accepted the flowers as he sank into a chair.

"I can't believe it was that easy," he gasped. "I'd rather face a thousand Yankees single-handed than go through this again."

Alden poured two brandies, both to celebrate and to steady Zack's nerves. He offered one to Zack in a mock toast.

"I must compliment you on your ingenuity. No female could resist such a proposal. Especially Lucy."

"Lucy?" asked Zack, perplexed.

"If you'd seen the look on her face, you'd have known she's been waiting for you to declare yourself."

"Lucy got the flowers? And the note?" Horrified, Zack began to understand that all was not what he thought. Alden forced the glass into Zack's hand.

"She did. What's wrong with you?"

"Does Lenie know?" queried Zack.

"She and the whole city, by now, I'll reckon. About Lenie and Charles, too," added Alden. Zack downed the brandy in one gulp, stunned and speechless. Alden clapped him on the shoulder.

"It must be catching. Charles proposed to our hellcat cousin. She said yes."

Zack's response was to drop his glass on the worn rug, turn and race out the door. Alden stared after him in surprise. Yet unschooled in the ways of love, he shrugged, assuming that Zack could wait no longer to be with his beloved.

In record time Zack arrived, breathless, at the Delacourt home. No messenger from Sparta ever made better time. But instead of knocking to request entry, he found himself nervously pacing in a small circle, his hands crushing his hat beyond recognition in his agitation. His own heartbeat sounded in his ears like distant cannon fire. How could this have gone so wrong?

Finally, he rang the bell, backing off quickly as if it might explode in his face. Peter answered all too soon.

"Good evening, Suh. And congratulations," Peter greeted him with a conspiratorial grin, as if he had played a role in Zack's romantic imbroglio.

"Peter, could I see Miss Lenie, alone? Please?" croaked Zack.

"Miss Lenie?" queried Peter, confused.

"Please – tell her someone needs her. Don't tell anyone else I'm here."

However, there was no need to fetch Lenie as at that moment, she appeared in the hallway. Puzzled and sensing something was wrong, Peter withdrew.

As Lenie realized her caller was Zack, her face froze but her eyes blazed with a fury that would have quailed any man except her stubborn cousin. She turned to swiftly retreat up the stairs. Zack followed her, taking the steps two at a time, and grabbed her arm.

"Lenie, please listen…"

But Lenie snatched her hand away.

"How dare you tell me those things when it was Lucy all the time you loved!" she spat at him.

"That's not – I meant – but Lenie, you can't love that – that Yankee!" Zack protested.

"You killed the only man I could ever love! At least Charles is honest. And he wants me just as I am. Don't ever speak your lies to me again."

Hearing their raised voices, Charles stepped into the hallway, and realized instantly what was happening – and the danger of untimely revelations. He moved quickly to consolidate his victory by taking Lenie's hand.

"Lucy! Caroline! Come out here!" he called.

"You've heard Lenie has accepted my proposal? We are to be one family," Charles announced suavely, as if Zack were a well-beloved relative instead of his worst enemy.

Zack's face turned red – part with rage, part with frustration – as he realized how his rival had turned this case of mistaken identity to his own advantage.

Lucy appeared in the doorway, radiant and shy.

"I can't tell you how happy I am, Zack, that my niece will have an honorable Southern gentleman for her husband," said Charles, with that sardonic grin that always incited Zack to a murderous rage.

Delighted with this romantic event, the ladies in the volunteer group burst into genteel applause. Lucy walked slowly to Zack's side, her face glowing.

"I was so surprised – so happy. I'll be the best wife any man ever had," murmured Lucy, her voice low so that only Zack could hear. She stood so close that Zack couldn't help but put his arm around her. She rested her head on his shoulder. From the stairway, Lenie watched them – happy for her friend, furious with Zack.

"Are you sure? It really is me you want?" Lucy whispered, her liquid dark eyes both adoring and beseeching. Zack stared into her face, his own expression confused and desperate. Clearly Lenie was lost to him. And he couldn't bring himself to disappoint Lucy.

"Yes, of course. I'm sure," he replied with whatever false enthusiasm he could muster. Lenie looked away. Zack was trapped. His eyes met Nan's, who watched the scene, hiding her own private grief and despair as her future and her dreams also slipped away.

Chapter 24
A New Generation

And so it was that, tricked by fate and trapped by his own sense of honor, Zack found himself facing a very different future than he had imagined. Even worse, he was forced to watch the woman he had finally come to love and desire, become the wife of the man he hated. His duty demanded that he accept this latest blow of a cruel fate, like a lamb led to slaughter as the offering to an indifferent God.

Lenie and Charles wed in the stately old cathedral in the center of the city, a month before Zack and Lucy. Charles Delacourt, that debonair and sophisticated rake, looks positively gobsmacked in the old photos of this momentous occasion. Disbelieving of his good luck, no doubt, stunned at this change in his fortunes – even though he had engineered it – and perhaps a little uneasy about the divine retribution that may befall him for the deception that brought about this union. Lenie looks as farseeing and calm as the figurehead on the prow of a ship, sure of herself and her direction.

Dr. John, on Lenie's other side, her arm through his instead of linked to her husband, seems to be both proud and relieved. He has bequeathed his legacy, his heritage, his treasure, to his trusted best friend – the man who has never let him down.

Zack and Lucy are there too, Lucy as the maid of honor, as demurely excited as a shy little girl about to dig into an ice cream sundae. And Zack looks as close to numb as I've ever seen a human seem –his face a granite mask shielding his feelings from everyone, even himself.

 Knowing that the woman he viewed as his true love was forever taken by his nemesis removed whatever excuses Zack may have had in dragging his reluctant feet to the altar.

Although Lenie cared not a whit for the pomp and circumstance accompanying her nuptials, she acquiesced to this formal affair in deference to her father's wishes. Both being physicians, they knew the inevitable outcome of the illness that had overtaken him, sapping his strength and health. Dr. John had the comfort of seeing his beloved only daughter married to his best friend, in one last grand event with all their friends and family.

Within a year of that celebration, Dr. John passed away, leaving the small ranch, the little house and office, and his post as chief medical officer at the new hospital, to his capable and independent daughter. This young lady, now technically a Victorian matron, once again buried her grief in her work. Charles seemed content to be at her side whenever possible, languidly tending to his business affairs which removed any possibility of want from their lives and any obstacles from her path.

This was not the case with Zack and Lucy, who struggled to get by on her slim patrimony and Zack's law earnings, half of which he continued to send home to his family in Virginia, and a goodly portion of what was left found its way to the Confederate Widows and Orphans fund. If sometimes Lucy wondered whether Zack loved The Cause more than he loved her, she never voiced her fears.

It was some solace that in the years that followed, Lucy proved herself an admirable wife, and a devoted mother. Lucy regained her old home after the Yankees left, and she and Zack moved in to start their married life. To her delight, her sister Caroline captured the affections of Zack's brother Alden. They too married and pursued Alden's dream of raising cattle on the open Texas range, setting up house on lands left them by the sisters' father. Fortunately, they were not so far from town that frequent visits and reunions were a hardship.

In time, Zack accepted this new phase of his life as yet another debt to honor, another sacrifice at the altar of the chivalry of the southern gentleman. The serendipitous way in which he ended up with one woman, and not the one he wanted, he attributed to another betrayal of the God who had capriciously abandoned the righteous and favored the iniquitous. Inside, the resentment that he never voiced slowly eroded his soul and heart, like a drip of water making a stalactite.

On the bigger world stage, the occupying forces eventually left Galveston, and its citizens began to heal from the wounds of the War. After all, the fighting had ended twenty years ago. For most people, that is. For some, it was as if the War were yesterday.

By the time the revered British Queen Victoria entered the fifth decade of her long reign, Zack had matured into an officious-looking businessman, his solid frame leaning toward stockiness but still radiating a wiry energy and determination. I have often studied the photos of that time, till I can see how they captured Lucy's adoration of her husband, Zack's preoccupation and fidgety filial dedication, along with the (momentarily) serious expressions of their offspring, facing the photographer's flash for the first time.

On this hot July day, some twenty years after he had first limped into Galveston, Zack stood at attention on the porch of Lucy's old home, now shabby with neglect, examining his watch and frowning his familiar scowl. A Confederate flag hung limply from the flagpole in the humid air as children emerged from the house, each banging the door after them like staccato gunshots.

"Hurry up! Helen, Sarah, Ellie, Billy," he barked, like a drill sergeant. The eldest, Helen, a demure 12-year-old with her mother's air of sweet gravitas, came first, followed by her more rambunctious sister Sally, two years younger. Ellie, a shy seven-year-old, followed in Sally's wake. Lastly came Billy, at five Zack's pride and joy, hopping down the steps like a rabbit. A very pregnant Lucy walked out more slowly. Zack stiffly offered her his arm and escorted her to the waiting carriage. The driver, a grizzled veteran with an eye patch and a wooden peg leg, climbed into the driver's seat.

"We're all here, Corporal. Drive on," ordered Zack.

Zack settled back into the seat and surveyed his offspring. Sometimes he missed the quiet of his single days, before these dependent creatures has settled noisily into his life. But, being from a large family himself, he quickly got used to the constant activity. As his children's feet pattered up and down the stairs, and through the rooms of his marital abode, sometimes he fancied he heard yet another set of small feet – the light, mischievous tread and the Rebel yells of another little girl he knew many years ago. But he told himself it was just his imagination.

"Will Aunt Pauline have new dresses from Paris? I so long to see them," chattered Sally. Her blue eyes, dark hair, and most of all her independent spirit reminded Zack too much of Lenie for him to feel real affection for her. Somehow Sally sensed his disdain and delighted in provoking him just short of punishment for herself.

"I expect she will, Sally," replied Lucy. Zack examined Sally's excited face with disapproval.

"Aunt Nan will want to know how well you're doing in your lessons. She'll be proud of you all. Except Ellie," he pronounced grimly.

Ellie's pale little face crumpled as she burst into tears. If she had had any spirit, this child might have reminded Zack of his little sisters, Millie and Helen. But Ellie was a shy, fearful girl, lacking any sort of what Zack thought of as backbone. Zack imagined that she was a throwback to some forgotten ancestor of Lucy's. Certainly no one in his family.

"She tries, Zack. Truly she does," murmured Lucy.

"Not hard enough," Zack muttered.

"Mother, tell the story of how Ellie got her name," suggested Helen, always eager to keep the peace. Her soft manner mimicked the gentleness of her mother and her Aunt Nan. Zack unconsciously relied on her, as he did his wife, as an emotional center for the family while he was about his professional duties.

"I'll tell it, I'll tell it!" Billy grinned proudly. "Her real name is Lucy, like Mother's. But Father proposed to Mother with a bouquet addressed to 'L', so we call her Ellie."

Although he tried to hide it, Zack was inordinately proud of his bright, lively only son, seeing him as the heir of the family heritage. Careful not to spoil the boy – who in Zack's opinion had far too much female influence around him already – he went to the other extreme and was overly strict. At Billy's remark, Zack frowned.

"William, tell me about the battle of Antietam," Zack commanded.

Billy frowned in concentration. Sally rolled her eyes in irritation to show her ennui at this perpetually boring topic.

"Well, it was a hot July day," Billy began tentatively.

"Who was the Confederate Commander?" Zack interrupted.

Billy looked upward as if the answer was written in the carriage roof. He was saved from Zack's disappointment as the carriage arrived at the harbor. Another vehicle disgorged Alden, Caroline, and their three unruly sons.

"Now, we're in the city so try to act civilized. Johnny, Jimmy, Char – Lee," begged Caroline. It was hopeless; her boys were gone, screeching their welcome to their cousins with rebel yells.

With a long, nasal hoot, a gigantic ship glided into the harbor, well-dressed passengers waving and lining the railings. The crowd on the dock cheered its arrival. The waiting relatives recognized their kin, waving enthusiastically from the ship's deck – Lenie, Charles, Nan, and Lenie and Charles' twelve-year-old son, Sam. As the ship docked and the passengers descended, the intermingled Lewis and Delacourt families were reunited in an orgy of hugs and tears.

Lenie's hand rested lightly on Sam's shoulder, conveying her fondness for her only child but without the emotional clinging that another woman might have shown. Her fingers slipped off gently as, hands in his pockets, Sam sauntered over to Sally. His smile was an echo of his father's debonair grin.

"Hey, Sally," he said casually.

"Hey, Sam," she responded in kind, concealing her unseemly excitement at seeing her cousin with feigned nonchalance. "Did your mother get her dress in Paris?"

"Yes. And lots more. We have so many trunks we had to pay extra to store them. You'll see," promised Sam.

Sally clapped her hands in delight.

The two children watched Zack and Lenie greet each other with a cool kiss on the cheek.

"Guess they still don't like each other," observed Sam. Sally shrugged off the scene – she had no interest in her elders, only her charming and well-traveled cousin.

Truth was, Lenie had barely aged in the ensuing years. Nor had motherhood slowed her in her inexorable dedication to her patients or challenged her vitality. She claimed her work kept her young, and maybe she was right. Even after the long, exhausting days at the hospital, she always found time for her child every evening, even if it meant waking him up for late good night prayers or a story about the olden times, before his birth.

In these stories, if Zack appeared, he was one of many cousins and a comrade during the War. No one would have guessed their emotionally tumultuous past from her cool and correct behavior toward him. However, her restraint told another story to uninformed observers, who saw two adults and cousins who for reasons unknown, just didn't get on.

Meanwhile, Lucy and Caroline greeted Nan warmly.

"Was the trip everything you hoped for, Sister?" asked Lucy.

"Oh, yes. I can never thank Charles and Lenie enough for taking me," responded Nan. Her calm, good-humored expression and demure dress proclaimed her profession as beloved schoolmarm. No trace of her disappointment in love so many years ago showed in her face, only a placid acceptance of her lot in life and gratitude for her family and her students. "I have so many things to show my classes at home."

"Now, we're expecting all of you at the house," announced Charles. "Peter will have cake and lemonade for everyone.

Charles, like his wife, remained relatively unchanged by the years – a little more grey at the temples, but still graceful and vigorous. Zack had his own dark suspicions of Charles' source of vitality, which he was too polite to voice.

At Charles' announcement, the children cheered and ran to the waiting carriages. Zack escorted Lucy at a more sedate pace.

"Sam! I can't believe they named their son Sam. Sounds like something you'd call an old horse," muttered Zack.

"Samuel was Lenie's first beau. But you knew him, didn't you?" asked Lucy.

Zack remembered Samuel too well. "Does Charles know that?" asked Zack.

"I'm sure he does. Charles and Lenie tell each other everything," replied Lucy. Zack squinted suspiciously at Charles and Lenie, wondering just how much Lenie did tell her husband.

As the returning travelers arrived, the Delacourt home came to

142

life. Children hung like monkeys from the limbs of trees while the adults enjoyed refreshments on the terrace.

"Mother! Mother!" cried Sam. No one paid attention.

"Dr. Delacourt!" called Sam. Lenie immediately turned to him. The adults laughed.

"Mother, have our trunks arrived?" asked Sam.

"Yes, they're in our rooms," replied Lenie. Unnoticed by the adults, Sam and Sally slipped away. An aging Peter, hair grizzled grey and weakened eyes squinting, poured champagne for the guests as Charles rose to his feet in one graceful movement.

"A toast – to the reunion of our families." As he raised his glass, the tree branch Ellie straddled broke under her weight, falling to the ground. Ellie lay motionless on the hard dirt, her eyes wide open and frightened. The adults rushed to her. Lenie quickly examined the frail body with practiced hands. Even in this emergency, Zack's eyes fixated on Lenie's long, graceful fingers working their medical magic.

"It's all right, Ellie. Just lie still," Lenie commanded. Finally, Ellie gasped, drawing in a shuddering breath. The crowd relaxed.

"What were you doing up in a tree? That's no way for a girl to behave," scolded Zack.

"We were escaping from the old plantation. Before the Yankees burned it," explained Billy, as if this explained – and justified – everything.

"Come on the porch, Ellie, and have some lemonade," suggested Lenie, helping her sit up.

Amidst the excitement, Charles observed Lucy's tired expression. "Lucy, come inside and rest. It's too warm for you out here."

"I think I shall," Lucy agreed, her voice betraying her exhaustion.

Inside the quiet, cool home, Zack escorted Lucy up the winding staircase to the second floor. The view of the luxurious house stretched below them – all polished woods, deep carpets, and luxurious drapes and wall hangings. Lucy paused, taking a deep breath. Her hand rested on the gracefully carved railing.

"Caroline and I used to slide down this banister, when we were children. Uncle Charles would stand at the foot and catch us," she mused fondly. Zack surveyed the opulent surroundings.

"Do you miss all this?" he asked, as if this question had just occurred to him. Lucy smiled.

"No. We have our own house, our family. But I wonder about you."

"About me?" asked Zack, puzzled.

"Are you happy? You've never said... that you love me," she said softly, hopefully.

"I'm not good at that type of thing, Lucy. You know you're the best wife an old Confederate could have," replied Zack. So Lucy had to be content with his evasive response.

Childish voices drifted from one of the bedrooms, where the door was ajar. Suspicious, Zack pushed it open.

There stood Sally, dressed in one of Lenie's new gowns, simpering before a mirror while Sam tried to arrange the bustle. The dress hung on Sally's slender body, but it did not take much imagination to see the lovely woman she would become one day.

"It's supposed to stick out," said Sam, frowning in puzzlement and giving the mysterious lump of cloth a boost with his hands, as if this would restore it to its proper position on Sally's anatomy.

"It's so cunning! Don't you think?" asked Sally, twirling her slim figure back and forth.

"What are you doing?" shouted Zack. Both children started guiltily. Sam snatched his hands away and put them behind his back.

"Aunt Lenie brought this from Paris! Can I have one like it? Please?" begged Sally, going on the offensive to diffuse her father's wrath.

"Certainly not! You look ridiculous. Take that off immediately. You, young man, should be downstairs with the other boys," ordered Zack with an intimidating scowl. Sam slunk off obediently, the spots of color on his cheeks betraying his embarrassment for his unknown offense.

"That boy is too much like his father," Zack muttered, thinking that Lucy could not hear him. Lucy did, but as always, she let his judgment pass unchallenged.

The sky was lit by bright Texas stars by the time Lenie and Charles said good-night to their guests, leaving them alone in their parlor.

"Are you going to the hospital tonight?" Charles asked Lenie, nonchalance masking his secret hope that she would prefer his company over her work.

"Tomorrow will be soon enough. Aren't you going out?" inquired Lenie. It was the era of gentleman's clubs, and Lenie did not mind in the least Charles' frequent visits. It gave her more time and freed her of worrying about a husband missing her presence. If Charles would have preferred her to ask him to stay home, he never voiced this wish but accepted the terms of marriage to his brilliant, independent wife.

No. Here we are – at home, together. How unusual." Charles poured himself a glass of port, offering Lenie one.

"That is our arrangement," said Lenie offhandedly, sipping the rich bronze liquid.

"Is it still enough?" asked Charles. He watched her closely, as if waiting for something.

"It's what we have," replied Lenie, without a trace of the regret she might have felt in her younger years and seemingly unaware of the meaning behind Charles' questions. Her husband said no more. Lenie had kept her bargain made at the start of their marriage, and gave him no more than that duty. He too accepted what he had, enjoying this rare moment with his mercurial spouse.

If you could have transported yourself across the neighborhood to Zack and Lucy's home, the first thing you would have noticed was how different their décor was from the gracious Delacourt mansion – homey, lived-in, almost shabby – but comfortable. And of course, the most prominent decoration was their Confederate flag, draped over the mantle.

In the small parlor, a scene unfolded that would have shocked Zack's respectable Galveston clientele. Here was their staid lawyer,

145

on hands and knees, crawling between the legs of the dining room table, flanked by Ellie and Billy.

"Yankee campfires to the right. What'll we do?" barked Zack.

"Come 'round the other side, and then surprise them at dawn," suggested Billy.

"Good. What's our plan of attack?" Zack queried. Billy gave an excellent rendition of the Rebel yell. Ellie cowered fearfully under the table as Zack grinned his approval.

Seated in a circle around the unlit fireplace, Helen, Sally, Lucy, and Nan labored with nimble fingers, making wreathes for the revered Confederate cemetery. Helen attended dutifully to her task, but Sally's face wore a look of mutinous boredom.

Lucy, hiding her weariness behind her customary good nature, put down her work.

"Time for bed, soldiers," she announced. Ellie and Billy scampered over to the circle of women to say goodnight.

"Were you in the Wilderness, Aunt N-n-Nan?" asked Ellie fearfully, clinging to her aunt's skirts.

"Not in the battle, sweetheart. But we saw the fires and heard the cannons," responded Nan.

"And when they came to burn your house, you said to them 'Damn the Yankees!'" crowed Billy. Lucy threw a gently reproachful glance at Zack, who looked guilty.

"No, dear, that was my little sister. But your grandmother reprimanded her immediately for using such language," explained Nan patiently.

"And then she d-d-died. Oh, Billy, don't you talk like that," whined Ellie, burying her face in Nan's lap.

"And all that was left of your house was this!" crowed Billy, standing on tiptoe to reach the lopsided lump of molten metal that graced the mantle. He proudly held up the revered relic from the old family home.

"Ouch. Mother, I'm bleeding. I can't work anymore. Look." Dramatically Sally showed her mother her reddened finger.

"What – what are you doing?" asked Ellie.

"Making glorious wreathes for the glorious graves of our

glorious dead. Don't we have enough yet?" begged Sally.

"Show some respect, young lady," snapped Zack. Lucy winced and sharply drew in her breath; Nan noticed her sister-in-law's pained expression.

"Lucy, are you all right? Would you like to go upstairs?"

"Is the baby coming?" asked Helen eagerly.

"Maybe so," replied Lucy. The children exchanged excited looks as Zack helped Lucy out of her chair.

"All right, all right, it's just a baby. No need to break ranks," ordered Zack.

Zack' seeming indifference to the arrival of another child reflected his understanding of the demarcation between the world of men and women. Babies and sundry subjects clearly belonged in the women's sphere. Not so his children, who shared a common sense of excitement over the coming addition to the family.

And so it was that next morning, the four children waited expectantly at the breakfast table as Zack seated himself at its head and put his napkin in his lap. Even Corporal peered in curiously from the kitchen.

"Is my little brother here yet?" Billy asked the question on everyone's minds.

"No, not yet," snapped Zack, focused on his breakfast and his newspaper. "These things take time." He peered over the paper. "I have to go to Houston to a meeting of the Confederate Veterans Society. When I get home, it will all be over."

Looking at the four crestfallen faces, he added, "And you have your studies. Who were the commanders of the Battle of Fredericksburg?"

Chapter 25
A Light Goes Out

I wonder if all tragedies begin like this, with the human players oblivious to the coming blow? Or maybe at some level, we know, and simply pretend our ignorance. Surely there is no hint that anyone that morning knew that within a day, their lives would be ripped asunder like a sapling in a hurricane.

While Zack attended to business as usual, the drama unfolded on the domestic front. Late in the afternoon, a chestnut horse cantered quickly down the street where the Lewis's lived, the carriage it pulled bouncing dangerously as the wheels hit each pothole. Before the horse had completely stopped, Lenie leaped out of the vehicle, hauling her ubiquitous black bag with such force she almost fell. She caught her balance and ran up to the door, entering without knocking.

Inside, the frightened children and servants clustered at the foot of the stairs.

"Where is Nan?" asked Lenie abruptly.

"Upstairs. Is Mother going to be all right?" begged Helen fearfully.

"Yes, yes. I'm going to her now," replied Lenie as she darted up the stairs two at a time, her haste canceling the effect of her words of reassurance. The children clung together in mutual fear and dread of the unknown, watching her disappear into their parents' bedroom, slamming the door behind her.

It was long after sunset when Zack strode up to a strangely quiet house, weary and tired from his day's journey. Despite his exhaustion, he noticed that the house was eerily silent, absent its customary air of familial activity. He felt no sense of alarm. Yet. He entered and climbed the dark stairs. Everything was still quiet. Only when he arrived on the landing did he see another person, as Nan emerged from the bedroom he and Lucy shared.

"Well? Is it over? What's wrong?" asked Zack, as Nan stared at him, stricken. Lenie walked stiffly out of the bedroom, her black hair unruly with humidity and sweat, her face a frozen mask, her skin stretched so tightly over her bones that, suddenly, she looked old.

"Zack. I'm sorry. The baby died. Lucy lost a lot of blood. I couldn't stop it." Lenie's voice was flat, emotionless, as she struggled to control herself.

"But – you're a doctor! You're supposed to fix these things," protested Zack, stunned at this unexpected, tragic development.

"I couldn't. I can't save her," said Lenie, her voice breaking at last.

"It must be God's will, Zack," said Nan, tears spilling onto her cheeks as her arms encircled his neck. Instead of returning her embrace, Zack stood motionless, staring at Lenie in shock and disbelief, his briefcase still in his hand.

Nan released him, blinking back her tears so she could speak.

"Come in and speak to her. Quickly. You haven't much time." Nan took Zack's arm, leading him into the room. He dropped the briefcase to the floor, where it spilled its content of papers down the steps. No one noticed.

In the bedroom, Lucy seemed to be sleeping, her face white and almost waxy in the faint light cast by the lamp. As Nan guided Zack into the chair by the bed, she weakly turned her head toward them.

"I dreamed my brother William was here," Lucy murmured, trying to smile. "I'm sorry, Zack."

"You did well. You did your best," Zack replied woodenly. Lucy groped for his hand. She spoke softly; he leaned closer to hear her.

"Zack, the children –" Her voice faded. Zack replied, 'I know, I know." Lucy seemed to understand. With great effort she spoke again. "Please – be happy," she whispered. She looked from Zack to Lenie, her eyes eloquent with one last request.

Zack sat by her side for the remaining few hours of her life, along with Lenie, silent with grief and rage at her inability to alter Lucy's destiny – to give her the right to grow old with her family, cuddle her grandchildren, and savor the long golden days of old age. It was not to be. Lucy's life would be a story, always told with the preface, "I remember." And the stories would be fewer and fewer

149

over time, until all that remained of her precious life would be faded photographs and a cold stone marker next to the small granite angel labeled "Baby Zachary Lewis".

Nan withdrew to be with the children, and from time to time a faint cry or whimper could be heard from their rooms, or whispers that could have been prayers. Zack did not seem to notice. Just as night was slipping away, so did the spirit of Lucy Lewis.

Chapter 26
Revelation

As the sun considered its rise for another day, its weak rays found an aging, stocky man slumped in his worn armchair before the cold fireplace. The parlor no longer resonated with children's laughter. Its eerie silence punctuated the tragedy that had just occurred. He stared into the dead embers as if they held an answer for this earthquake that had rocked his life.

Upstairs a door clicked in closing. Lenie walked slowly down the stairs. Even as exhausted and defeated as she was, she was struck by the incongruous sight before her: her cousin Zack appearing utterly helpless to her, like a floppy stuffed animal that could not move on its own. He lifted his eyes, not to look at her but to gaze at a vase of fresh flowers on the mantle with dawning understanding.

"Nan is with the children. You should go to them. Tomorrow, there will be arrangements to make." Lenie announced, forming her words with an effort of will while at the same time, drawing from her many experiences of mobilizing the bereaved to return to the responsibilities that would keep them anchored to their earthly lives, despite their despair.

But Zack just stared at the flowers in wonderment.

"She knew. She knew it was all a mistake," murmured Zack, as if at a revelation. Lenie stared at him, puzzled.

"The flowers were meant for you – but Peter gave them to Lucy. I tried to tell you – but by then you were set on Charles. And I couldn't disappoint Lucy. It wasn't the honorable thing to do," Zack blurted out.

Slowly Lenie absorbed what he was saying, her face a battleground of emotions as she realized that Zack, maybe, had not betrayed her, and what they might have lost – a life of passion instead of a life of compromise, but for a trick of fate that altered their destiny. Like mercury, her quick intelligence registered a flight of emotions – shock, anger, sorrow, even bemusement at the irony of it all.

151

"So, so – you're saying – you mean –" Her voice slid from incredulity to anger. "Your damned honor made a mess of our lives once again."

He finally turned his graying, tousled head to face her. Incredibly, his face looked younger, his eyes sparked with the memory of happiness, the scowl lines smoothed.

"Lucy wants us to be together. She said so. The way things happened – it must be God's will," he pleaded.

"You don't know what you're saying. Drink some brandy," Lenie retorted. He stood up shakily.

"You can't love Charles. If you care for me…" He took a step toward her. Lenie took a step back, holding her hands up as if to stop his advance and speaking to him as if he were a slow-witted child.

"Zack – listen to me. I am married to Charles. Your wife has just died. Your children need you. You have to tell them…"

"No. No they don't need me. They're afraid of me. If I were gone, they wouldn't even miss me. I have no one," he confessed, baring the loneliness that for years he had camouflaged with irritability. He reached out for her as if for salvation. His warm, strong fingers wrapped themselves around her cool ones, shocking her with their powerful physicality. Suddenly she wanted to be embraced, to be held, to be smothered, to be safe within this frightening sensuality.

"You and me, Lenie. We still believe the same things. Our hearts know each other. We should have been together. Now, we can. Please -0" His pleading broke the spell that rendered Lenie silent. She drew a quiet steadying breath to bring her back to reality – her reality.

"Those flowers – that was a long time ago. Lucy – Charles –" Despite her resolve, a painful lump of grief stuck in her throat, prickly and indissolvable. Although she knew anatomically that this was impossible, its bulk forced tears into the corners of her eyes. Angrily she wiped them away with one long elegant finger as she pulled her hand away from Zack.

Zack stood still, expectant – his heart barely beating as he realized that she, too, shared at least some of his feelings. His voice went soft with pleading.

"Please, think on it."

Neither of them noticed the upstairs door closing as an eavesdropper silently withdrew.

Lenie's response was to grab her bag and quickly rush from the house, almost stumbling as new tears obscured her vision.

By the time she arrived home, the tears on her cheeks were dry but her heart still stirred with a riot of emotions. Oblivious to the feelings within his mistress, a sleepy Peter greeted her at the door, taking her bag. Behind them the sun was barely peaking above the horizon, sending pale yellow shoots into the dark sky.

"Should I send someone up to help you, Mizz Delacourt?" he asked, yawning.

"No, Peter. That won't be necessary."

Lenie slipped through the house and into the garden behind it. Here was her retreat from lost battles of her life. Exotic flowers with healing properties imported from all over the world were nurtured carefully along with shoots at the home-grown herbs from her parents' old farm. She stood amid the foliage, breathing the perfume of the blooms and the stronger scents of the green plants, seeking to make sense of this tragic day and the awakening of feelings she had long thought dead. Had these beautiful flowers betrayed her, on that fateful day? Gently she touched one long strip of rosemary – the same plants she and Zack had harvested in her mother's deserted garden, so long ago. Was this bizarre proposal from Zack meant to be her destiny?

Her reverie was interrupted when Sam appeared in the doorway, in his nightclothes, gangly arms and legs poking out of the sleeves and hems as testimony to his beginning transition from boy to man. Charles followed him, his hand proprietarily resting on his son's shoulder.

"He wouldn't go to sleep till you got back," explained Charles, wryly cheerful as always.

"Is the baby here?" asked Sam, his voice still that of the little boy Lenie had taught letters to and played with in the nursery. Lenie

153

reached for him and he went to her. She held him fiercely, her long fingers stroking his thick dark hair, so like her own.

"Sam, I am so sorry," she said brokenly, squeezing her eyes tightly shut for a moment – just a moment – to regain control. "I'm afraid – the baby died. Your Aunt Lucy – she – she wasn't able to – we lost her, Sam. She went to the Lord. Her last wish was for us all to be happy."

Over Sam's head, Lenie watched Charles' grin vanish and his tanned face turn pale as he sat down heavily in a garden chair. Sam took in this devastating news in his own way.

"Now Sally has no mother. Just like you," he noted, looking up into his mother's dark blue eyes with his own, wide with the recognition of another's grief.

"Yes. That's right. I was her age when my mother died. Your age," agreed Lenie, wondering at his concern for Sally.

"We must go to her tomorrow. She needs us. Mother, please don't ever leave me," Sam begged, clutching her tightly, his face buried in her skirt.   Lenie held him close, gazing over his shoulder, at the flowers, at Charles. Her arm around Sam's slender shoulders, she began to walk back into the house to lead him to bed.

"Lenie, wait," asked Charles, raising his hand as if beseeching her.

"Go on up, Sam. I'll be there in a minute," said Lenie. Sam released her, reluctantly. Charles, too, stared into the foliage, not meeting Lenie's eyes.

"Was it – did she suffer?" he asked huskily.

"No. Not at the end. Charles, I am so very sorry –" said Lenie, realizing belatedly the depth of his loss too. She reached out for him. But instead of responding to her, he rose abruptly and walked away from her.

"So, now Zack is free." His voice was harsh with unexpected bitterness.

"What?" asked Lenie, incredulously.

"If you had been the one he meant those flowers for, years ago, what would you have said?" he asked, almost angrily.

"What are you saying?" she asked, puzzled but with a growing

154

suspicion.

"They were meant for you. When I saw the note, addressed to 'L', I had Peter take them to Lucy," confessed Charles, still not looking at her. Lenie, stunned at his admission, covered her face with her hands, as if to stop this flood of new and shocking revelations.

"It was the only way I could have you. But – you deserved better. You deserved – an honorable man."

Finally, he turned to her. The sardonic mask was gone. His face was open, grief-stricken, and ready to face her rejection now that she knew the truth.

"Now you can. I'll give you a divorce, if you want, and half of everything."

"A divorce?" echoed Lenie, stunned. The word was harsh and heavy – a violation of the civility that ruled their world. And this man – this man she trusted, this man she admired – had betrayed her. The feeling slowly spread through her body, like a wave of winter's cold.

"It's not done in polite society, but then, what have you ever cared about that?" said Charles. He smiled a ghostly version of his old grin.

"You – you caused all this?" asked Lenie, still struggling to take it in. Now a thousand memories flooded her soul – from her lonely childhood, her odyssey to Virginia, her war years, her return to Texas as a broken soul, and the life she had lived with this man for years – what did it all really mean? Was he the loyal friend she had thought him to be, or a traitor?

I can almost imagine how she felt – though I am unlearned in the psychology of the female human. What a refuge he had always been to her. The stab of loss for her father – who else could she rely on? Who else really understood her? Or was it all a charade – a lie?

"Yes. Now you know, and you have a reason to hate me." Stoically, he steeled himself to receive her scorn.

Slowly, Lenie walked to him. Charles stood his ground as she stopped, looking deeply into his eyes.

"Is that what you want? A divorce?" she asked.

"I wanted you to love me. Now, at least – I want you to be happy." He gazed into her eyes, with love, longing, and grief at a future without her.

"All right. You have what you want." Her voice was firmer now, her decision made.

Charles smiled sadly, stroking her cheek.

"I'll always remember – how beautiful you are. In every way."

Lenie placed her hand over his, stopping the movement. The very earth seemed to still.

"You have your wish."

Charles stopped breathing as his world tilted. Then, her next words righted it again.

"I do love you. And I forgive you."

Astonished, Charles was truly speechless. This was not what he had expected. One tiny part of his heart began to sing with joy as he realized the meaning of her words. His face glowed like a man resurrected. Now it was Lenie who touched his cheek.

"Maybe you haven't always been an honorable man. But you are now."

That awful morning, Zack finally dropped into an exhausted sleep in his armchair, unwilling to accept what lay upstairs – the sleeping children who were now his sole responsibility, the loss of Lucy, and the terror at his own boldness in at last confessing his feelings to Lenie.

He woke with a start to a knock at the door, just as the city was beginning to awaken. Groggily he opened it. A messenger handed him a flower – a yellow tulip – and a note. His heart in his throat, he opened it. But his hopes curdled into bitterness as he read it.

"We each made a choice. It's too late for us now. L."

Behind him, the grief-stricken children and Nan appeared on the landing. Their sad and frightened eyes sought him out as if he held the answer to this storm that had destroyed the center of their world. Dazed, he gazed up at them helplessly. This was his future. And he faced it alone.

Chapter 27
The Finest School in the South

No one clearly remembered the awful day of Lucy's funeral, and the laying to rest also of the tiny baby – Zack's longed-for second son – whose blue eyes never opened. Zachary Lewis had been furtively baptized by Lenie, at Lucy's instructions, her memories of a long-ago Papist heritage stirring her to this desperate act. Now, if her beliefs had been correct, the lost child frolicked in heaven with his mother. Perhaps he was the lucky one, escaping the temptations and tribulations of the mortal family he never knew. And perhaps he was the happiest of the children – frolicking with a little girl with spunk and spirit who loved to play war games as much as any boy.

With Lucy gone, and Lenie's rejection sealing off his one route to happiness, Zack's emotional anchor reverted to what it had been since the War – his duty and honor as a Southern gentleman. He spoke of neither his grief nor his crushing disappointment delivered by Lenie's single bloom and its message. The flash of passion he transformed in his mind into a mere mirage, an aberration from the tragedy of that awful night.

Lenie was determined to likewise pretend as if this deathbed drama had never occurred. She treated Zack with the same dispassionate tolerance that had marked all the years of their married lives, if albeit a bit less prickly than before that momentous night.

Determined to bring his children up as proper Southerners, Zack sent them back to Aunt Nan's school in Virginia. This also served the purpose of removing them from under his roof and relieving him of the responsibility of day-to-day parenting.

Although his love for his childhood home never dimmed, he refused to return to Virginia himself. Perhaps he preferred his memories to the reality that he would see.   Perhaps it was too painful to give up his dreams of his sisters being married and mistresses of their own domains. Now they were confirmed spinsters and beloved teachers, destined to live out their days under their parents' aegis in the little house at River's Rest. From his distance and old-fashioned vantage, he failed to see the dignity and worth of the different type of family legacy they were creating.

When his children were at home in Galveston, Zack maintained a distant eye on his three daughters and a stricter one on his only son. Helen quickly grew into the role of surrogate mother, trying to provide the nurturing and understanding that Zack could not. Nevertheless, they sorely missed their mother's affection, but as children do, learned to carry on without it.

In the midst of her busy multiple lives and as best she knew how, Lenie did what she could to watch over them, with frequent invitations to visit at the Delacourt home. On those occasions when their father and their "aunt" were present together, the familiar stiffness between them drew no comment.

Samuel Delacourt joined his cousins at the little school at River's Rest, an experience that bound them almost as close as siblings. More than any of his cousins, Samuel grew to love the gentility of Virginia culture and manners, and responded to the sweet affection of his aunts and especially, the aging James and Sarah. When it was time for his higher education, he chose the venerable school founded by Thomas Jefferson – the University of Virginia – where he did credit to his childhood education by excelling in his studies, his sports, and his friendships.

But neither Samuel's achievements nor his affection for the state of Zack's birth and boyhood endeared him to his curmudgeonly uncle. Zack continued to view Samuel as the scion of his bitterest enemy and a constant reminder of his unrequited affections for the boy's mother. Consequently, in his eyes, Samuel was untrustworthy and bound to be a black sheep in the Lewis family tree.

As for his own offspring, Zack mentally noted – and sometimes lectured them about – the contrast between their comfortable lives and the privations of his own youth, the daily struggle for survival at home and on the battlefield, the sacrifices made without complaint for the greater Cause that – he felt – was almost forgotten now. But at least as long as Zack Lewis lived and breathed, that glorious Cause would remain the ideal for at least one Southern family.

As the so-called "Gay Nineties" celebrated the century's last decade, and with his children poised on the edge of adulthood, Zack welcomed an event that he believed would tie his family even closer to his Southern heritage. It began at the Galveston train station, as Zack, Alden, and Caroline – all now in late middle age – loaded Billy, Johnny, and Jimmy – now strapping teenagers – onto the train bound for the Old Dominion.

Amidst the bustle of departing passengers and shouted good-byes, vendors hawked fireworks for the upcoming Fourth of July celebrations. An American flag waved above the station's tile roof.

Watching the rowdy boys and their horseplay, Zack reflected briefly on his own youth, and how he and his brothers had faced death and captivity when they were even younger. Like so many other parents, he rued the easier options facing his own offspring.

"Remember, Son, you're going to the finest university in the world. Make me proud of you," Zack admonished his restless boy.

"I'll do my best," promised Billy as he patiently endured hugs from each of his sisters. Ellie clung to him the longest.

"I'll miss you, Billy."

Samuel, now a handsome young man with dark sideburns and a fashionable bowler hat, demonstrated that he had inherited the physical grace of his father by running up to the platform as the train whistle sounded. With a flourish he presented the departing scholars with a bottle, passing it through the narrow window.

"To toast your arrival. At the finest University in the world," he panted.

"Thank you, Cousin Samuel!" beamed Johnny. As the train pulled out, the boys waved enthusiastically from the windows, leaning out way too far for the comfort of their female relatives.

As the train receded into the hazy distance, Samuel turned to Sally, who eyed him admiringly in a most uncousinly way. She had grown into the promise of her early beauty, with striking dark hair, dancing blue eyes that easily flashed with anger or flirtatiousness, and a slender figure that tended to fidget with suppressed energy.

"Come down to the harbor with me tomorrow and watch the fireworks," Samuel invited her with a charming grin. Zack was the only one to see the shade of the lupine Delacourt smirk – a

159

perpetual reminder of treacherous intent.

"Absolutely not! We do not observe any Yankee holiday in our house!" pronounced Zack sternly.

"Well, the children have always enjoyed it," suggested Caroline. Zack silenced her with a glare.

"I'll see you this afternoon, Uncle Zack? For our interview?" asked Samuel, diplomatically changing the subject.

"Oh? Yes." murmured Zack, absentmindedly. Sally defiantly took Samuel's arm, whispering to him as they walked away.

"I will come with you tomorrow! I'll be hogtied if I'll wear black just because it's a damn Yankee holiday."

"I think it's rather quaint, the way he observes all the battles throughout the year," remarked Samuel, displaying a tolerance of his uncle that was never reciprocated.

"Well, you don't have to live in the past," complained Sally. "And if he'd have a proper law practice, instead of giving his services away to those old veterans – we could afford to go to Europe like you." Resentfully, she tugged at her bonnet laces, drawing them tighter under her determined chin.

"Someday, I'll take you abroad. You'd be the belle of Paris," Samuel promised gallantly.

Sally rewarded Samuel with a coquettish smile at this enticing prospect.

But before Samuel and Sally's secret evening rendezvous, there was work to be done.

Later that afternoon, Samuel dodged small boys waving miniature American flags and stealing fireworks from an irate street cart vendor. He stopped before the doorway to Zack's law office, easily identifiable as the only entry flying the Confederate rather than the American flag. Squaring his shoulders, he prepared to enter the lion's den.

A clerk ushered Samuel into Zack's office. Worn books lined every wall, emitting a comfortable aroma of old leather mixed with the mustiness of a humid climate. Zack sat imperiously, like an emperor behind an ancient wooden desk he had purchased early in his career from the estate of a deceased sea captain. He peered sternly over the set of small spectacles he was now forced to wear.

"Thanks for seeing me, Uncle Zack," said Samuel, suddenly nervous as he faced his uncle's habitual scowl.

"Just what am I seeing you about?" asked Zack grouchily. Samuel opened the valise, taking out pencil and paper.

"Well, I'm interviewing veterans of the Civil War," explained Samuel.

"The War Between the States," corrected Zack.

"Yes. About their experiences. On both sides. Why they fought. What happened to them during the War," Samuel went on.

"Your Father too?" asked Zack, raising his graying eyebrows.

"Yes. That's what makes it so poignant, doesn't it? How friends fought against each other, even brothers."

"Oh yes, it was very quaint."

Samuel completely missed Zack's sarcasm. "Shall we begin at the beginning?"

Chapter 28
Temptation

As the interview between Zack and Samuel began, Jimmy and Johnny thirstily guzzled Samuel's gift, a bottle of champagne, oblivious of its patrician origins.

"Cham-pag-ney. Pro-doo-it of France," pronounced Jimmy. "Hmm. A little sweet – but not bad."

"Hey, we're supposed to save that for when we arrive at the University," protested Billy.

"We're Texas boys. We're not meant for a Southern education," replied Jimmy.

"Sure you are. Our family –" Billy began the refrain and his cousins finished it.

"Has gone to the University of Virginia since Thomas Jefferson founded it."

"That was a long time ago," retorted Johnny.

"It's almost the 20th century. Times have changed," pronounced Jimmy. The Iron Horse screeched and slowed down for its first stop. Johnny and Jimmy grabbed their suitcases.

"Come on, Billy. We're going out to Aunt Lenie's spread. We can hunt wolves. Break in mustangs. Chase Indians." Jimmy gave an Indian war whoop that caused startled passengers to swivel their heads to see the cause of the commotion.

Billy couldn't believe what he was hearing. Fear of his father has always kept him on the straight and narrow, unlike his more adventurous cousins. As the train stopped, Jimmy and Johnny leaped nimbly down onto the platform.

"Come on, Billy," taunted Jimmy.

Billy hesitated. The choice was difficult: adventures with his cousins and facing the eventual wrath of his father, or leaving his home for the confines of a classical education in the old Dominion. The train began to roll again. At the last minute, he grabbed his valise and jumped off.

Meanwhile, back in his Galveston law office, Zack was oblivious to his only son's betrayal. Preoccupied with his own bitter thoughts, he stared out the window as Samuel wrote furiously. That young man's fashionable coat was off now, his hands splotched with ink as he ended his notes with a flourish.

"That's quite a story, Uncle Zack," he commented, the excitement of a young writer discovering his voice underlying his compliment.

"It's not a story. It's true," growled Zack. His own children would have recognized the danger in his ominous tone, but Samuel was not attuned to such clues.

"It was over 30 years ago. And you still remember like it was yesterday," marveled Samuel.

"Yes. I remember the death of everything good and beautiful. I remember the look in my little sister's eyes when she died. I remember how it feels to hate," mused Zack, his voice cold with bitterness.

Samuel, chilled by his words and the implacable emotion behind them, fell silent. Leaving Zack to his reverie, he quietly picked up his jacket, his ink-stained notes, and with a deferential nod of his head that went unseen and unacknowledged, left the office.

If Samuel was intimidated by Zack's temper, it did not dissuade him from keeping his surreptitious meeting with Sally that evening. The two young people had a rousing evening with fireworks, popcorn, and sundry other delights, spiced with the growing attraction between them. They stayed till the last celebratory spark had died out. The long leisurely stroll home finally brought them to Sally's somber home.

The door to the Lewis household slowly opened as Sally peeked in, shushing Samuel as he followed her inside. The two cousins tiptoed into the parlor, Sally giggling softly as Samuel put his arm around her. Suddenly, Zack's forbidding form appeared like a menacing apparition. Quickly Samuel and Sally pulled apart.

"We were having such a good time at Aunt Lenie's, Father, I didn't realize how late it was," explained Sally with false gaiety. Zack grabbed her arm and pulled her away from Samuel.

"It's my fault, Uncle Zack. I should have gotten her home earlier," apologized Samuel quickly.

"I know where you've been! You disobeyed me. Stay away from my daughter, do you hear me?" commanded Zack. Sally yanked her arm from Zack's grasp.

"I'll go where I please! Besides, Samuel is my cousin!" Sally retorted.

"He's just like his disreputable father, and I won't have you consorting with such a man," ordered Zack.

"Consorting? Just what does that mean?" asked Samuel, vaguely insulted.

"It means your father was a damn Yankee and he can never forget that," snapped Sally.

"Don't talk back to me! Sarah, go to your room. Now!"

Sally's bravado evaporated before her father's glare, and, with one quick look at Samuel, she darted upstairs. No match for Zack's wrath, Samuel replaced his bowler hat on his head and meekly departed.

Chapter 29
Perfidy

A more insightful man than Zack Lewis might have realized that this particular battle – instigated by what they called once the "generation gap" – was not over; it was merely beginning.

At first, life seemed to revert back to its customary routines. The next morning saw Zack, Helen, Ellie, and Sally partaking of another silent breakfast so typical in the Lewis family. Neither Sally nor Zack mentioned the altercation of the previous evening. Yet it hung in the air like an invisible cloak, weighing down their spirits and reminding everyone to tread lightly or risk another explosion.

However, after a night of serious contemplation, Sally had adjusted her tactics from confrontation to negotiation. Mid-way through their silent meal, she innocently gazed up at her father over her porridge to make a startling proposal.

"Father, I've been thinking."

Raising a quizzical eyebrow at this pronouncement, Zack peered over his paper into Sally's wide, guileless blue eyes. She continued, "My life is entirely too frivolous. I need to make a change."

Her family reacted to this news with surprise and, it must be said, a little suspicion.

"Well, if you'd applied yourself to your studies –" scolded Zack.

"Yes, you're right again, Father. I'd like to ask Aunt Nan if I can help her with the school."

Zack and Helen exchanged amazed looks. Then, the unthinkable happened. Zack put down his paper and actually paid attention to his offspring.

"Sally, I'm proud, and I must say surprised, that you are so concerned about your family. I guess breeding does tell," he commented cautiously.

"If she'll have me, Father, may I go?" asked Sally, beseechingly, her face aglow with sincerity.

"Yes, Daughter, of course," agreed Zack, caught completely off balance. Sally smiled demurely, dropping her eyes so only Helen saw the trace of slyness in her dutiful smile.

Zack had already picked up his omnipresent morning newspaper and addressed his comments to its crinkly pages. "And I'm sure your brother will appreciate having family a little closer."

Poor old Zack Lewis's parental intuition surely was as dormant as a hibernating bear. His direct and blunt honesty was no match for his daughter's schemes, or for the influence of his uncivilized nephews on his only son. Zack had no idea that Billy was getting a very different kind of education from what he had envisioned for his heir.

Later the same day that Zack saw Sally off at the train station, supposedly departing for her new career at a teacher in Virginia, Billy stood poised on a gigantic boulder, somewhere in the Texas hill country. Steeling his nerves, he leaped into space onto the back of a wild dirty white mustang, held captive with ropes by Johnny and Jimmy. They released the ropes. The angry horse reared, jumped, and kicked wildly as Billy hung on for dear life.

"Hang on, Cousin. He's gettin' tired," yelled Johnny. Sure enough, the horse paused, breathing hard. Scarcely believing his good luck, Billy loosened his hold on the saddle horn. This was a mistake. The wily mustang suddenly kicked and bucked again. Billy flew through the air, landing on his back in the dust. The horse trotted off, tossing its mane in defiance – not far, because he was trapped in a corral with a dozen other rebellious beasts. Johnny and Jimmy ran to Billy, picking him up from the dusty ground. Billy shook out his limbs to be sure there were still attached and functional.

"Almost, Billy. You almost had him," congratulated Jimmy. Billy nodded ruefully, peering off in the distance where a speck appeared on the horizon, moving toward them over the scrubby terrain. He pointed to it, fearfully.

"What's that? It's not my father, is it?"

The three boys looked closely, their alarm apparent as they faced the possibility of discovery and, undoubtedly, punishment.

"No, it's just Samuel's rig," said Johnny with relief. The carriage reached the makeshift corral. Samuel, still wearing his city bowler hat, alighted first, then turned to lift Sally down, her petticoats

166

swirling in the dry air.

"Hello, Cousins! Need some help with the round-up?" asked Samuel heartily.

"From you? I thought all you did was read books?" Jimmy was dubious.

"Actually, I was looking for a quiet place to write and I thought of Mother's spread," Samuel admitted.

"You're not going to make us go back, are you?" asked Billy, nervously.

"What? Oh, don't worry – your secret is safe with us," promised Samuel. At this assurance, the boys relaxed. Sally gazed at the barren landscape, her face as enraptured as if it were the Garden of Eden.

"Sally, you won't like it here – it's, uh, pretty primitive," cautioned Billy.

"Oh, that's all right. Actually, I thought I could do the cooking." Her airy tone belied her complete lack of knowledge of the culinary arts. She continued to take in the rugged landscape, romantic fantasies of cowboys, Indians and fair maidens dancing through her agile mind, completely missing the dismayed looks the boys exchanged at the prospect of her as their chef.

So far oblivious to his children's perfidy, Zack continued his routine in the city, with Helen and Ellie dutifully performing their household and community roles. On yet another quiet evening, he sipped port alone in the parlor, reading his beloved newspaper. Corporal entered with the day's mail on a tray and formally offered it to him.

"No letters yet from Master Billy or Miss Sally. But there is one from Miss Nan," he announced formally.

"Thank you. Have you read it yet?" asked Zack.

"No, Mr. Zack. That's your job," Corporal explained, ignoring his employer's sarcasm.

As Zack read the letter, his pleasure at hearing from Nan and anticipation of news of his offspring transformed into first surprise, then dismay, and finally, rage. He dropped the letter, leaped up as fast as a man of 50 plus years could who got little or no exercise,

167

and stormed up the stairs.

"Helen! Ellie!" he brayed like an angry longhorn. "Where are your brother and sister?"

Helen stepped out on the landing, her brown eyes wide with concern.

"Why, Father, they're in Virginia."

"No! They are not! Where is Ellie?" barked Zack.

"At the hospital. Helping Aunt Lenie," replied Helen, startled at this news of her siblings – and in the case of Sally, not completely surprised. Zack turned and charged from the house as Helen watched him fearfully, fingering the crucifix around her neck.

Chapter 30
Discovery

In the years since he had first met Lenie during the yellow fever epidemic, Phillip had indeed realized his dream to also become a physician. Due to the prejudices in the land of his birth, he traveled abroad for his studies, funded by Charles with Lenie's complete understanding and support.

Upon his return, Lenie would brook no opposition to his presence in "her" hospital. With his European manners and continental education, many locals assumed he was an immigrant from an exotic country somewhere in that mysterious place referred to as "abroad," never recognizing the handsome mulatto boy, his skin the color of cinnamon in warm milk, who had once roamed the city streets. And although Charles made no effort to hide his fondness for the hard-working young man, no one outside the immediate family seemed to suspect there was a relationship here other than as his wife's employee.

Except Zack. He knew – or surmised – the truth about Phillip's parentage when he had first met the boy. Not only the physical resemblance, but also Charles' proud gaze on the few occasions Zack saw them together, gave away that secret. Zack kept his own counsel and added this fact to his private arsenal of outrage about the demonic Charles Delacourt.

Telling of Philip's success, I still get a bit tingly with pride. Maybe it's because I too am an outsider, though without the kind of obstacles he overcame. Truly, I wish I had known him.

Anyway, on that warm October day Phillip labored inside one of the hospital's operating rooms, intent on closing a wound for an elderly white woman who – if he had known the history that she genteelly concealed – would have known that she had lost all three of her sons in the services of the Confederacy.

He was assisted by Zack's erstwhile shy daughter, Ellie. Her pale, delicate skin was even whiter than usual as she swallowed hard to quell her nausea. Yet she willed herself to remain upright by Phillip's side, not only from a sense of duty but an ever-growing desire to be this young doctor's right hand. This most dutiful of daughters, whose timidity lured Zack into a false sense of confidence in her decorum, was quietly demonstrating a strength of character to defy the norms of propriety in ways that her conservative father could not even imagine.

"You're a fine nurse, Ellie. You really should go to nursing school," Phillip reassured her as he cleaned his hands, a mandate from the hospital's head physician, who had early learned how to fight deadly germs with cleanliness. Ellie's compassion and her healing, gentle ways had not gone unnoticed by him, along with her shy smile and heart-shaped, vulnerable face.

"Oh, no. Father wouldn't allow it. He thinks it's not p – p – proper," Ellie stammered, desperately trying to control this childish frailty but finding that her nervousness only made it worse.

"Your father isn't always right," pronounced Phillip. Ellie started with surprise, shocked at this heretical thought. Indeed, more and more, Phillip opened new vistas of ideas and emotion to the sheltered young lady. Maybe it was the attraction of opposites, maybe the recognition in each other of misfits, but the two had become good friends, enjoying long talks during their quiet times at the hospital, talks that began with a common interest in healing and spread with vine-like tendrils to the finer realm of feelings, hopes and dreams.

Suddenly, the bubble of their private connection burst as Zack stormed into the room, trailed by an elderly spinster who served as the hospital receptionist. Her hopes of romance fell among the carnage of Chickamauga decades before

"You can't go in here!" cried the horrified woman, flapping her arms as if to frighten Zack away like a wayward chicken.

"Ellie, where are Billy and Sally? Answer me!" roared Zack, his voice as deep the bellow of an outraged bull.

Ellie froze, the expression on her face proclaiming her guilty knowledge. It was one thing to spread her wings under the encouraging eye of her trail-blazing aunt; quite another to be caught out by her terrifying father.

Zack suddenly took in Phillip's presence and the old woman,

with her flaccid ivory skin, sleeping on the table.

"What's going on here? How dare you touch a white woman!" he growled, outraged and exasperated at this violation of his code of behavior.

But while Ellie felt as if she might faint in the face of this parental rage, Phillip was unperturbed by Zack's eruption. "They don't seem to mind when they get well."

"You remember your place!" snapped Zack. A cold voice spoke up from behind him.

"Phillip is a doctor here and this is his place."

The speaker was Lenie, a little older, imperious, clearly in command, but still beautiful – handsome perhaps is a better word. The streaks of grey in her hair contrasted with eyes still the color of bluebonnets. As usual, strands of it framed her face like a windblown halo, as if she flew faster than the wind itself on her mission. Her upright carriage and air of authority briefly reminded Zack of his own beloved mother. But he was no boy to be intimidated by a strong female presence. Even the awkwardness he usually felt in her company vanished in the face of his rage.

"Don't you have any respect for propriety?" asked Zack, flinging his arm toward the offensive scene.

"Apparently not," retorted Lenie. Behind Zack's back, Phillip smiled quietly to himself. Suddenly remembering why he was here, Zack grabbed Ellie's arm.

"I know you're hiding something! Where are they?"

"Let her go, Zack. If you're looking for the children, they're at my ranch," responded Lenie calmly.

Zack's grip on Ellie's arm tightened as she winced in pain. "You knew this and you didn't tell me?"

Suddenly Zack had an even more disturbing thought, causing him to release his daughter just as Phillip moved forward to rescue her from his clutches. "Where's Samuel?"

"He's there too, working on his book," Lenie answered, still unperturbed by what, to Zack, amounted to moral outrage beyond description. What could he expect, he thought, married to that amoral cad for all this time – but the urgency of the crisis at hand

171

drew his attention back to the present.

"At your ranch! With my daughter! How could you allow this? It's scandalous!" Zack stormed out, knocking over a tray of instruments in his wake. Lenie followed him into the hall, calling after him.

"I'm going with you! If you don't calm down you may need a doctor."

Ellie watched them go, her demure mouth a perfect "O" of terror at the prospect of a confrontation more awful than she could imagine. Phillip, bemused, grinned to reassure her. When she didn't notice, he gently slipped his arm around her shoulder to return her attention to their patient and was rewarded by a swift, fleeting smile of gratitude.

"You know his bark is worse than his bite," murmured Phillip. "Besides, Lenie will protect them if he gets out of line."

So Ellie was comforted, if not convinced, and definitely distracted by the warmth of Phillip's touch.

Chapter 31
Accusations

Unconscious of the approaching danger to what she thought was her safe refuge, Sally wandered out into the afternoon heat at the old ranch house beside the stream where Lenie and Zack had waded many years ago. The humming of the cicadas, the cloying heat of an unexpectedly hot Indian summer, were almost hypnotic. And truth be told, she had treated herself to a long, dream-filled siesta as she stayed alone in the adobe-cooled ranch house, ostensibly tending to the housekeeping.

Barely awake, lazily and somewhat clumsily she lowered a bucket down the well, its underground coolness like a breeze on her glistening skin. Then, in the distance, she spied a movement, watching with growing alarm as it came closer. It was a carriage. Who in tarnation...

As she recognized the occupants, the rope slipped from her hands. Bereft of her guidance, the bucket discharged a series of echoing clangs as it hit the sides of the well on its downward descent. Oblivious to its loss, Sally raced back into the house to give the alarm. Startled lizards scampered aside at her frantic approach.

"It's Father! He's here," she yelled in warning, with all the terror of the Atlantans welcoming the arrival of the devil Sherman. She retreated into the house just as Zack and Lenie pulled to a stop in front of the old adobe. Zack leaped out of the carriage as fast as his advancing age would allow. Ignoring the sharp pains to his back and knees, he stomped to the door, with Lenie only a step behind.

The startled boys, who had been relaxing from a hard day of mustang wrangling with a friendly game of cards, only had time to leap to their feet, knocking over their card table, as the door was flung open by an enraged patriarch. Zack glared at each one, accusingly. No one met his eyes. The silence hung ominously in the suddenly airless room.

"Sarah, William, get your things and get in the carriage." Zack's voice was like a funeral bell to the crestfallen and terrified young people.

"Father, I'm sorry, but I don't want to go to Virginia. I want to stay here," confessed Billy, his voice squeaky with fear.

"You are going to the University of Virginia! You are my son, not some cowboy. And you" – he glared balefully at Sally – "After this scandal, I'll have to send you to New Orleans to find a husband!"

"I've already found a husband!" she announced, tossing her dark curls in that all too familiar gesture of defiance to parental authority. "Samuel and I are in love. We're going to get married."

Zack stared in horror from Sally to Samuel and back to Sally again, then whirled around to Lenie as if for an explanation. But she only watched him with wary eyes, as if he were an unpredictable mountain lion. Her silence, to Zack, confirmed her complicity in this outrage. Zack approached Samuel menacingly, his words like the angry growl of an enraged bear.

"If you have…" threatened Zack.

"Oh, no, Sir," stammered Samuel defensively at Zack's implication. "We were going to ask for your permission to marry as soon as – uh…"

Zack grabbed Sally's arm and pulled her across the room, snarling.

"You will never marry him! Never! I won't allow it!"

"Yes I will! I'm of age and you can't stop me! I won't be like you!" Sally retorted.

Maybe his authoritative touch enraged her, or perhaps her spell of freedom at the ranch had given her courage, as an animal let out of its cage can get downright uppity. She broke free and screamed at Zack.

"I heard you the night Mother died! You loved Aunt Lenie! You meant those flowers for her! You just married Mother because you were trapped! You don't want me to have Samuel because you couldn't have what you wanted!"

In the sudden, complete and horrified silence, her revelations seemed to echo off the old adobe walls in the small room like bullets. Within the minds of the each young person, clues from the past suddenly shifted into position like a kaleidoscope to explain this mysteriously prickly relationship and all its contradictions. In a twinkling, something died in that room – call it illusion, security, naiveté. Nothing would ever be the same.

Appalled at her accusations, Zack was for once absolutely speechless. Lenie, shocked and embarrassed by the brutal revelation of this ancient secret, was too honest to deny it.

"But – Mother loved my father. Didn't you?" queried Samuel, for the first time questioning a truth he had always taken for granted. Lenie only regarded him mutely, her eyes begging his understanding. She could not comfort him by uttering the lie she had thought was hidden in her heart. By her silence, Samuel understood what he did not want to know. I do believe, with the foundation of his world shattered, Samuel grew up at that moment.

"Sally, do as your father says. Get in the carriage," he said calmly. Sally, suddenly frightened by the potential consequences of her outburst, reluctantly acquiesced. Billy followed her obediently, giving his father a wide berth as if expecting a blow at any moment.

Nary a word was spoken on that long ride back into town. Each occupant of the carriage was silent with his own thoughts, and either too mortified, too horrified, or too frightened, to speak. Maybe all three.

Zack dared to believe that the entire event was an aberration in his carefully ordered existence, and if he ignored it, the whole sorry episode and its embarrassing implications would disappear. That was not to be.

Even in the midst of great turmoil, the daily life of humans has a way of going on. Dinners are eaten, newspapers are read, duties call and those calls are answered. No punishment had yet been meted out to the miscreants, as if the adults themselves did not want to acknowledge that painful confrontation. So, several evenings later found Zack back to his old routine, sipping port while his four children sat silently in the parlor. The emotions of the last few days had subsided somewhat, but they still feared arousing their father's anger again. Sally alone acted normal; in fact she wore an expectant look of suppressed excitement. Corporal stepped in the doorway, looking very important.

"Mr. and Mrs. Delacourt to see you," announced Corporal. The family seemed startled by this surprise visit. Except for Sally, who dropped her eyes to hide the sly and excited little smile she could not suppress.

However, it was not Lenie and Charles who appeared in the doorway, but Lenie and Samuel. Zack frowned at them over his glasses, then grudgingly nodded toward the worn sofa. Samuel and Lenie seated themselves, as civility demanded.

"I'd like to speak with you, Uncle Zack," said Samuel nervously. Beside him, his mother sat with rigid posture and an impassive expression.

Helen was the first to realize that something of import was about to happen, and quickly rose to herd her siblings from the room. Sally shot Samuel a meaningful look as she withdrew. The room hung pregnant with excitement and fear, as the ancient ritual of bartering for a daughter in the family was about to begin.

Samuel swallowed and somehow found the courage to look Zack in the eye. "I'm very sorry about what happened, Uncle Zack. I know it was wrong of us to deceive you."

"It certainly was," allowed Zack, guardedly, his brows reflexively drawn together in disapproval.

"I should have insisted that they be honest with you, from the beginning," admitted Lenie, in a carefully neutral tone. Everyone carefully avoided the specter of Sally's horrible accusation, yet it was on their minds.

Samuel took a breath, crushing his prize bowler hat in his nervous hands. "The fact is, I love Sally. I would like to ask for her hand in marriage."

Now it was out. Samuel froze as he waited for Zack's response. It was immediate.

"Samuel, with all due respect to your family, I'm afraid you do not have the background or the maturity to be a husband for my daughter," Zack pronounced definitively, setting down his glass of port as if that ended the matter.

Samuel of course protested vigorously. "But I do, Uncle Zack! My career is going well. Soon –"

"A career scribbling stories? This is no way to support a wife. The answer is no."

Lenie placed a cautionary hand on Samuel's arm. Shaking it off, he stood up.

"I'm going to change your mind, Uncle Zack. We won't give up."

Replacing the battered bowler on his head, Samuel turned on his heel and left.

If Zack had paid more attention, he might have noticed the same air of determination that had propelled Lenie into and through medical school in his retreating figure. But, now alone with Lenie, he was annoyed and discomfited to find himself distracted by the same old feelings her presence still engendered in his heart.

Zack braced himself for an argument. But Lenie surprised him by the softness of her speech, and her daring to speak of the old festering wound.

"Zack, please don't punish them for what you think you have lost. Don't dishonor what you love with hatred."

A rush of the old emotion rendered Zack momentarily speechless, despite his rancor. For a moment, Lenie dared hoped that she had reached his somnolent heart. Then, Sally peeped in the half-open door. Zack quickly set his features in their familiar stern expression. Sally interpreted this as bad news.

"You said no, didn't you? I told him you're too stubborn to ever change your mind!" she wailed in disappointment and frustration.

"He's not the man for you," said Zack with finality.

"Why? Because his father was a Yankee? Because the Lewis's never "consort" with the enemy from that damned war you can't forget?" Sally accused him, tossing her head for emphasis in the way that absolutely infuriated Zack.

"That's right. You are a Lewis and you will act like one," he commanded in that tone that brooked no argument.

"I'm going to marry Samuel no matter what you say," retorted Sally just as forcefully.

"Sally…" pleaded Lenie, half rising from her chair in a vain attempt at peace-making.

But Sally was beyond reasonableness. Bless her heart, she was young and selfish and full of the belief that happiness could only be found in the present moment, the impervious now. She flung her hateful words like rocks.

"Don't try to stop me! You both throw your lives away on the cripples of the world because you can't have each other! Well, I'm going to have the man I love!"

Lenie recoiled as if slapped by Sally's harsh words. But her unruly niece wasn't finished yet. In a frenzy of frustration, Sally ran to the mantle, pulled down the Confederate flag, and hurled it on the floor. Zack started for her menacingly as Lenie tried to stop his advance toward the hysterical girl. Drawn by the shouting, Helen, Billy and Ellie ran into the room with Corporal behind them. Helen quickly rescued the sacred flag from the floor.

"Sally…" begged Helen.

"He wants to marry us off to one of those old ugly veterans, like Corporal. He'll only be happy when we're all in caskets, like his glorious war, dead!" shrieked Sally.

"Sarah, I demand that you apologize this instant," roared Zack. Instead, she faced him, raging.

"I hate you! I hate your damn War! It's ruined all our lives!"

In her fury, she grabbed the revered melted doorknob off the mantle and hurled it at her father. It missed his gray head and sailed through a window, shattering the precious glass.

Sally raced for the front door to escape the home that had become her prison. But Zack, surprising everyone with his speed, sprinted after her, caught her around her slender waist, and slung her over his shoulder like a sack of grain. As he mounted the stairs, Sally kicked and screamed and beat her fists against his back, but to no avail.

Zack staggered into Sally's room and deposited her on the bed, her skirts and petticoats akimbo. While she struggled to right herself, he strode to the door.

"You will stay here until you are ready to apologize. And until I am assured that you will not dishonor this family," he stormed, slamming the door and quickly turning the key, firm in the belief

178

that his will would prevail. From inside the room, his enraged
daughter banged and kicked the unyielding door.

"You can't keep me here! I'll get out!" yelled Sally.

Dropping the key into his pocket, Zack faced the spectators;
slowly, they backed off before his implacable anger. Lenie,
realizing that there was nothing she could do in the face of Zack's
stubborn righteousness, wordlessly withdrew. The curse of those
fateful flowers visited itself more firmly on yet another generation.

Chapter 32
Billy's New Cause

Sally's career as a prisoner threatened to become permanent with each passing day that she remained incarcerated, her isolation only interrupted with the three times daily visitation of Corporal's tempting culinary morsels.

Tension hung in the air like an approaching thunderstorm. But the fickle weather, as usual, was a deception. For it was an earthquake that secretly quivered just below the surface, its danger undetected until it was upon them.

Life on the "outside" of Sally's prison continued. Having missed the start of the university year, Billy had no choice but to follow Zack's instructions to report to his office each day to help the law clerks. Unfortunately, Billy's taste of ranch living had shown him another way of life that he sorely missed, but he was too afraid to confide his feelings to his father. To Zack's chagrin but no one else's surprise, Billy was less than industrious in his legal duties.

On that one fateful morning, Billy lounged at his desk, avidly reading a newspaper whose glaring headline read, "Maine Sunk in Cuba". Zack lumbered out of his office, carrying a satchel and talking with an old veteran with one arm, a stubbled chin, and ropey neck. The veteran reached into his pocket, fumbling for money.

"Don't you worry about that, Captain. I'll take care of everything," Zack assured him gruffly.

"Bless you, Mr. Lewis," rasped the grizzled old man. Billy dropped the paper and tried to look busy, but Zack was not fooled.

"I need you to take this money for the Confederate Widows and Orphans Fund to Mr. Van Houten at the Mengers Hotel in San Antonio. Can you handle this without sneaking off the other side of the train?" asked Zack sarcastically.

"Yes, Father, of course," Billy took the satchel obediently, taking the first decisive step toward a fate neither father nor son could envision.

Despite Zack's concerns, Billy had no trouble finding the venerable Mengers Hotel after an uneventful train ride through the dusty Texas prairie. Thirsty from his long journey and with some time to spare before he had to make his delivery, he found himself in the hotel's luxurious bar, with gleaming wood fixtures so shiny you could almost see your own reflection. As Billy sipped his root beer, an energetic, rotund man with round glasses addressed the group of young men likewise refreshing themselves with various beverages.

"Here's rich, corrupt, mighty Spain, oppressing poor little Cuba! And they've blown up an American ship, killing innocent citizens!" the excited speaker exhorted the rapt crowd.

"What can we do, Colonel Roosevelt?" asked one young man seated next to Billy, clearly swept up by the passionate oratory of the enthusiastic speaker.

"Sign up for my Rough Riders! Let them know they can't push us around. America for Americans!" Roosevelt nodded so vehemently Billy thought the tips of his waxed handlebar moustache waved in acquiescence.

The orator then addressed Billy.

"Young man! Do you have a horse?"

"Uh, yes," replied Billy, startled.

"Do you believe in America?" asked the ebullient newly minted colonel.

"Yes sir. I do. My family –" spoke Billy, prepared to launch into the patrician legacy of his family, but Roosevelt gave him no chance.

"Have you got a hundred dollars?" queried Roosevelt. This gave Billy pause. He glanced at the satchel.

"Uh – Yes," he responded.

"Bully! Well, then. Join us!" declared the Colonel enthusiastically. Carried away by Roosevelt's passionate invitation, Billy took the pen offered him and added his name to the list of volunteers. Thus, the first Lewis since the Revolution enlisted in the American army. For Billy, it was an act of patriotism. For his father, it was a betrayal.

You might think that by now Zack has developed some kind of sixth sense, some emotional or psychic sensitivity to the perfidious activities of his errant offspring. Well, you would be wrong. Zack carried on with his duties in his state of chronic irritation, in complete ignorance of the treachery of his only son.

That night as the Lewis family dined and awaited Billy's return, Corporal approached Zack with a tray of food.

"This all right for Mizz Sara?" asked Corporal, critically eying his lovingly prepared creation.

"Yes, yes," murmured Zack, betraying no concern for his imprisoned offspring, still confined to her room.

"Made a special strawberry tart for her. She doesn't eat much these days," bemoaned Corporal. His sympathy went unrequited by his stern employer.

Finally, from the hallway came the sound of the front door opening. Corporal withdrew into the entry way to welcome the new arrival, then re-appeared in the dining room, an uncertain look on his face.

"Master Billy's back, Mr. Zack."

"Well, it's about time," muttered Zack. Now Billy stepped into the doorway, wearing the olive-green uniform of a Rough Rider, the pants flaring at the thigh and the Canadian Mountie-like hat dwarfing his young head.

The effect was as if a lightning bolt had struck the dining room table. Zack, Helen and Ellie froze in mid-bite, shocked and stunned at this invasion of the hated government of the North into the sanctity of their home. Zack rose like an avenging menace, his napkin dropping to the floor.

"Is this some kind of joke?" he thundered.

"No, Father. I've enlisted," quavered Billy. "We're going to free little Cuba from the oppression of Spain. Fighting for our rights, just like you did."

"Take that thing off! How dare you wear a Yankee uniform in this house!" stormed Zack. Billy's face set stubbornly. Ellie ran to her brother, as if to protect him, but stopped short of embracing him. Instead she clutched her hands helplessly, her mouth an "O" of silent terror.

"No. I've given my word, and I'm going to Cuba with Colonel

Roosevelt. It's a matter of honor!" declared Billy, to everyone's amazement standing up to his father for the first time in his young life.

"Then you are not welcome in this house! Get out!" roared Zack, his face a deep vermilion with outrage.

Billy hesitated only a moment, then mustering his newfound adult dignity, he turned and left. Ellie looked after him, distressed and terrified. The door had barely clicked shut with ominous finality when Corporal stumbled down the stairs and into the dining room.

"She's gone, Master Zack!" he croaked. Zack's already overburdened heart gave another lurch as he realized what Corporal was saying. He raced up the stairs, followed by Helen and Ellie.

But Sally's room was empty. The bedroom curtains swayed desultorily in a cold breeze. Zack ran to the window and leaned out. A ladder led down to the ground. Helen picked up a note on the dresser and read it aloud, questions in every word.

"Tell Aunt Lenie and Corporal that I am very sorry for what I said."

Her eyes met her father's, beseeching him to make it right. Brows drawn into a ferocious scowl, Zack was untouched by her silent plea.

"Should I call the police?" asked Corporal deferentially. Zack's face set in stubborn anger.

"No. Let them go. Just let them go."

Chapter 33
Loss

Colonel Roosevelt and the charge of his Rough Riders are history now. No more than a footnote, really. But, for the Lewis family, this little skirmish accomplished what four years of the War Between the States could not.

Only a few months after this disastrous evening of Billy's betrayal and Sallie's escape, Zack, Helen, and Ellie silently observed a train pulling into the Galveston station. Watching them, no one could have imagined their state of mind. There were no smiles of greeting, no excitement about a pending arrival, no eyes watching the windows searching for a familiar face. No expressions at all on their pale faces. Oddly for those times, the two girls silently held hands. An astute observer might have noticed how tightly they gripped each other's hands, as if by that contact they each held the other upright.

As passengers debarked, blue-garbed soldiers unloaded a long box draped with an American flag. Zack watched their movements, his face a blank mask and his eyes dulled with a deep wound. When he spoke, his voice had the finality of hard metal.

"Take that thing off my son."

The soldiers exchanged puzzled glances. Zack grabbed the flag, pulled it off with a violent quickness that made the air whistle, and threw it on the ground as if it were infected with a deadly disease.

"What should we do with –" asked a soldier.

"Put it on the train to Virginia. My son will be buried there," ordered Zack in a fierce, gruff voice. Another soldier offered Zack an envelope and a small box.

"The Government of the United States has awarded your son this medal for bravery. He died serving his country." Smartly he saluted.

Zack merely stared at him, at the box in his hand, then turned and walked away, his walking stick tapping in heavy, rhythmic intervals on the brick pavement, like a slow grandfather clock. Helen stepped forward and accepted the item from the confused soldier. The other soldiers lifted the casket and headed for the northbound train.

"Father, can we go with Billy? Please?" begged Ellie, running after her father.

"No. No. We cannot go back." Zack's tone was as final as death.

Ellie paused for one last look at the casket, then – helpless to disobey – followed her father.

But Helen quietly lingered, making the sign of the cross as she watched the men loading the coffin. As the box slid into the railcar and the doors clanged shut, she spied Lenie approaching the platform, rushing as usual, darting through slower passengers with a small valise in hand. Her fine-boned face bore the ravages of the grief Zack refused to acknowledge. As her aunt reached her, Helen offered not a greeting but only the box and the envelope.

"Please keep these – safe for us," she asked quietly. Lenie accepted them wordlessly as Helen pulled her black shawl closer and followed what was left of her family.

The engine whistle blew, and the metal cars shifted on the tracks. Lenie boarded the train just as the cars began to pick up speed. She staggered down the aisle, lugging her valise and clutching the precious box and envelope, until the conductor came to help her.

"Where are you bound, Ma'am?" he asked.

"Virginia," said Lenie woodenly. He helped her into a seat across from two elderly women, who eyed her with sympathy, both of them old enough to recall the many losses women had suffered in the long-ago War Between the States. One reached out and gently touched Lenie's black-garbed knee.

"Pardon me, Ma'am, but is that your boy you're taking back to be buried?" she asked in a high, quavering voice.

The well-meant question embedded itself into her heart, like a poisonous arrow. Although she had not fought for Billy's life at a sickbed, nevertheless Lenie still felt the familiar sharp pain of defeat, just as when she had failed to save his mother. The gods of healing truly mocked her.

"No. No. But he might have been," she responded enigmatically. Ignoring the women's puzzled looks, she stared out the window at the blurry scenes rushing past, silently praying that Billy had found his mother at last. I know she believed in her heart that the two were reunited, yet still she ached for them both. Once again all the victories in her life paled before this searing failure.

Chapter 34
Hurricane of Hearts

They say Zack never spoke of Billy or Sally, as if by silence he could blot out the memory of their loss. He knew Sally was with Samuel, but never inquired of Lenie, and certainly not of Charles, of their whereabouts.

However, feelings – like a flood – cannot be contained forever. And a storm was brewing in the new century that would be his last and worst battle.

It was Saturday, September 8, 1900. Grey clouds scudded across the sky, blown by high winds. In the yard at the quiet Lewis home, water covered half the lawn. A dog loped up to drink, tasted brackish liquid, and backed away at its salty flavor. Afterwards people would remember that the air was heavy and ominous, foretelling a disaster to follow. But truth be told, they really only thought another late summer storm might be blowing in.

The new century had not changed life at the Lewis household. It had only grown smaller and quieter, as if the very air had been sucked out of the unhappy home by all the sorrows it had seen.

That morning Zack and Ellie ate breakfast, in their customary silence. Or rather, Zack read the newspaper while Ellie stirred her cereal, seemingly unable to eat it. As Zack turned the page of the newspaper, the crackling sound made Ellie jump. Zack did not even notice. She had become as nondescript to him as a piece of furniture. He did not even seem to note the many hours she spent volunteering at her Aunt's hospital, even late into the night.

The faithful, grizzled figure of Corporal appeared in the doorway.

"The wagon's all ready, Miss Ellie," he announced officiously, his voice cracking with age.

"You're going out? A storm is coming," groused Zack.

"I promised H – H – Helen we'd bring food to the orphanage," she explained, timidly.

"Well, be quick about it and get home right away," Zack ordered, not looking up.

"I'm to help at the h – h hospital this afternoon," Ellie responded furtively.

"I hope you're not in the way over there," warned Zack, now glaring at her over the top of the page. "Just get home at a decent hour," he added with a belated deference to propriety. Ellie was spared the agony of a response when Corporal interrupted.

"Mr. Lewis, there's rising water in the yard."

"Humph! If the damn Yankees had left us any money we could have built a proper sea wall to keep that water out," He folded his paper with decisive disgust.

Ellie quickly darted outside to escape his scrutiny, leaving her breakfast untouched. As Zack left the house a few moments later, he skirted the standing water in the yard, but did not pause on his way to work and his duty.

Ellie was strangely silent during the entire ride across town, past the Gothic buildings that symbolized Galveston's prosperity, the sedate brick mansions that mimicked the opulence from before the War, the children chasing their hoops in the street, the other carriages pulled by the fine horses that clopped in unison through the broad boulevard. Corporal regularly tipped his ragged Confederate hat to the passersby, making up for Ellie's disinterest with exaggerated courtesy.

At the orphanage, the nuns and children alike ran excitedly to greet Ellie and Corporal and their wagonload of provisions. Ellie alighted and embraced one of the nuns. It was her sister Helen, her serene face framed by the black habit of her order. She alone of the little family had found peace, radiating the quiet calm that was also her Aunt Nan's special gift. Not even Zack's raving about the invasion of Papist influence from New Orleans (born like a disease, he implied, from that shameful Delacourt connection) into his family had stayed her quiet resolve to follow her vocation.

"Boys, take the goods into the storeroom," directed Helen.

Outside the orphanage grounds, neighborhood children laughed gaily as they sailed makeshift boats in the rising water at street level. Noting the envious looks from her little charges, she admonished, "And stay out of the water."

"Yes, Sister," chorused the small boys, disappointed but obedient. A few fat raindrops fell on their tousled heads; they paid no attention. It was Ellie who erupted, suddenly bursting into tears like the proverbial geyser and falling into Helen's arms.

"Ellie, what's wrong?" asked Helen, both startled and alarmed at this uncharacteristic outburst from her quiet little sister.

"I – I – let me stay here with you!" sobbed Ellie.

"Why, Ellie, your place is with Father. He needs you," comforted Helen. "You must have a calling to enter the religious life."

But Ellie only cried harder. "Let me stay! Or help me run away!"

"What troubles you?" asked Helen, deeply distressed by the violence of her shy sister's emotions. Enfolded in Helen's arms hidden somewhere in those long flowing black sleeves, Ellie slowly stopped sobbing.

"Helen, you're s-s-so good. Just like Mother. I w-w-wish I was like you."

"You are good, Ellie. You are so helpful to everyone. And you take care of Father," soothed Helen. Ellie pulled away from Helen's embrace, not meeting her eyes.

"Father doesn't need me. I bother him."

"Of course he needs you. We all do. Ellie, please tell me what's troubling you."

Heedless of this emotional interchange, the children ran up to Helen, demanding her attention.

"Sister! Can we have lunch now? We're hungry."

"I'll be right there."

Ellie dried her eyes, dabbing them with the handkerchief Helen offered. "I'm s-sorry. I'm just so – frightened."

Helen glanced up at the darkening sky. Perhaps her worry over a coming tropical storm blinded her to the possible reasons for her sister's deep distress.

"It's this weather. You should be getting home. Ellie, bring your troubles to God. He can help you." Despite her sister's advice, Ellie looked doubtful that her solace would be found in the Divine.

By early afternoon, the storm was raging in full force. Or so they thought. The rain fell in long, smooth gray sheets. On the streets, pedestrians' umbrellas were collapsing like children's toys. The water ran knee-high in rivers between houses and shops. The small children were now inside, called to safety by their mothers. Some of the bigger boys and girls still saw the rapidly rising waters as their playground, swimming and sailing down the rushing waterways, enjoying this respite from the summer heat.

For hours, even the people living in those houses on stilts, near the water, continued to feel safe. But with the rising tide that crept inexorably up those pillars, and the powerful, shrieking winds pounded the doors and shutters, the homes began to creak and groan in alarming ways. Some retreated to the upper floors for safety, while others overcame their fear to brave the elements in a flight for safety with friends and family further into the city.

But inside Zack's office, it was business as usual as far as he was concerned. To his chagrin, the clerks wasted precious time peering out the window with apprehension. He expected considerably more diligence from young men he had handpicked from the graduating class of the University of Virginia. Of course, their tiny moustaches and straw hats bespoke – to him – a lack of gravitas. But shouldn't breeding and education win out over frivolity?

"Haven't you ever seen rain before?" asked Zack scornfully.

"It's very bad, Mr. Lewis. All the other businesses have closed," replied Clarence, in a timid voice that may have reflected either his fear of the storm, or of his employer's wrath, or maybe both. Abruptly the telephone rang; Isaac responded to its tinny summons. He called out to Zack.

"Sir, it's Dr. Delacourt. At the hospital. She says it's urgent." Zack crossed to the phone and picked it up.

"Lenie? Lenie? Hello?" He shook the phone, then hung up in disgust. "Useless contraption."

"The hospital could be flooded," observed Clarence, a worried frown rising above his round glasses.

"Well, I guess we should go," agreed Zack grumpily. With relief the two young men tidied their desks and prepared to leave.

Outside, the winds were now so strong that it took the combined strength of all three men to close and lock the office door. Their journey quickly became a battle not only against the wind and rain, but the waist-high water than ran swiftly with a mind and strength of its own. The only other humans they encountered were a family that was, inexplicably, floating a bathtub filled with children to an unknown destination. The wind had not yet reached the force that could tear off a person's clothes in a second, but clearly this was no ordinary storm. A walk that usually took ten minutes lasted almost an hour, before they finally reached their destination and dragged their tired legs and sodden clothing up the steps of the hospital.

Their relief at reaching their destination quickly evaporated at the scene inside that venerated institution. The chaos of the staff running to and fro, the roar of the wind, and the screaming patients all created a scene like those of bedlam, or one of those scary movies they show at Halloween. In the darkness, Lenie's familiar slender figure appears. Her relief at their arrival was palpable; even her usual calm shattered by the emerging catastrophe. Strands of black hair, streaked with grey, escaped her bun and stood out from her head like a halo in the humid air. After all this time, Zack still felt his frozen heart thaw – just a little – at the site of her graceful figure darting between the beds of the frightened patients. He did not even notice Ellie's wraithlike figure behind her.

Seeing the fear in Lenie's eyes, Zack finally realized that this was a real emergency.

"Thank goodness you've come. The old hospital across the yard is flooding. We've got to move the County patients in here," she shouted above the melee.

She rapidly led them to the back door. Across the quadrangle through the sheets of rain they could see the old infirmary. The tall, spare figures of Charles and Phillip protruded from the raging lake that separated the two buildings. Each carried an elderly woman on their backs. The two rescuers waded in chest-high water to the door of the newer edifice and staggered up the steps. Zack and the clerks helped pull them inside while Lenie and Ellie took charge of two terrified patients.

191

Charles' birthdays now passed the 70 mark. His once sleek dark hair was now completely grey and his skin stretched like fine dried leather over the bones of his face. His slender frame now gave him an aura of fragility rather than feral strength. Relieved of his burden, he leaned against the wall to catch his breath. Despite the heat of the late summer afternoon, he shivered. Zack, from his 15 years younger vantage point, allowed himself a moment of superiority.

"Well, old timer, wind got the best of you?" He razzed Charles. "You stay here. We'll handle this."

Calling on the courage and bravado that had taken him through countless cavalry charges against impossible odds, Zack motioned to his troops – er, clerks – to follow. Phillip offered his arm to Charles, but Charles shook it off. Grimly he turned to the raging winds, unwilling to concede the field to his old rival.

Still, no one could imagine how bad the storm was going to be. Despite the darkness and dense rain that made it impossible to see more than a few feet ahead, many still fought their way through the flooded streets, trying to complete their daily errands. Then word began to spread through the city of early disasters. The roof of a favorite restaurant collapsed, killing the city's elite businessmen there enjoying lunch. The sea ravaged the venerable old bathhouses at the beach. Along the coast, the waters flooded the ground floors of even the raised houses on their stilts, prompting their inhabitants to seek shelter with relatives and friends who lived further into the city. Fear spread like fog from house to house, street to street, feeding the terrors inspired by the relentless winds and rain.

Even the orphanage, under the direct patronage of the Divine, was under siege. Belatedly Helen and the other nuns led the terrified children up the narrow circular stairs to higher ground, away from the relentless tide that had engulfed the ground floor. The smaller children sobbed in fear; some of the older ones may have still thought this was all a great adventure, but not many.

"All right, children. Hold hands. Let's sing. This is a song my father taught me," announced Helen with false brightness. Slowly, she began singing the only tune she could think of, the one she and her siblings had sung daily in childhood:

"Oh I wish I were in the land of cotton
Old times there are not forgotten
Look away, look away, look away, Dixieland."

With quavering voices, the children joined her in the Southern anthem.

Outside, the relentless storm systematically continued its destruction of the city of Galveston. Homes toppled under the relentless pressure of swirling water. The people who had taken refuge there were disgorged into the sea; they swept by in the rushing current, screaming for help until their voices were silenced. Uprooted giant trees were added to the swirling debris. People, animals, and homes spun by in the angry waves that showed no mercy to any living thing.

The ancient lighthouse crumbled under a gigantic wave, its light permanently extinguished. Ships in the harbor collided against each other, disintegrating with the force of the impact.

Starting at the beach, a wall of debris, like a giant dam, began to swell. Propelled by the hurricane gale, it slowly inched its way toward the city – first a few feet high, then high enough to reach the floors of the raised homes, then another story, then above the roofs. Like an implacable bulldozer, it crept forward, collapsing everything in its path.

Outside the hospital, the rain slammed into the water, now shoulder-deep, with the force of bullets. Hurricane winds blew so hard, no waves could form. The flat surface of the floodwaters disguised the churning maelstrom underneath, hiding the remnants of fallen buildings, uprooted trees, and fences, all spinning with deadly force.

Inside the hospital quadrangle, somewhat protected from the gale, Charles, Zack, Phillip and the clerks crossed the courtyard again, hands clasped as they struggled on in single file, each with a petrified elderly person clinging to his back. Suddenly, despite their efforts, Phillip was torn free and went under the water.

Watching from the doorway, Ellie screamed in terror and would have jumped from her perch of safety to rescue him had Lenie not stayed her with an iron-like grip. But God smiled as Philip and his patient were caught in the gnarled branches of a dislodged tree. Ellie still could not breathe, even as Zack and Charles reached out and pulled them both to safety.

But when they broke the chain of hands, they gave Fate the chance to strike again, as Clarence and his charge, an old man whose mouth formed a soundless scream, were caught up and swept away outside the quadrangle and into the tempest.

As Lenie and Ellie pulled the men and their frail charges inside the hospital, Ellie threw herself into Phillip's arms, heedless of any Victorian proprieties. He did not push her away, only looked back into the storm as the doomed pair disappeared into the wailing darkness, shaken by his narrow escape and the randomness of their loss.

"God help them," he murmured.

Water now covered the first floor of the hospital. Orderlies, civilians taking refuge from the storm, and patients moved in a steady, if disorganized, stream upstairs to what they imagined was a safe refuge. Once on the second floor, some used bedding to tie themselves to furniture so that they would have something to cling to should the floodwaters breach the walls of the building once thought to be invulnerable.

Every few moments – with the force of a hybrid thunderclap and earthquake – the hospital's thick stone walls shuddered as pieces of buildings and masonry assaulted them. Amidst the screaming winds, a groaning – like a thousand mourning souls – added to the surreal scene.

On the second floor of the orphanage, the terrified children were all crying now. One nun tried futilely to lead them in the rosary, but only her quavering voice was heard amidst the din, "Deliver us from evil, as we forgive those who trespass against us."

The more practical nuns, including Helen, used the rope belts around their waists to tie the smaller children to them as the winds raged outside, and the old walls moaned before their power. Each time a piece of debris hit the sides of the building and blocked the windows, the dying daylight was shut out and blackness fell over the frightened souls inside. Shadows obscured the smiles of the beloved faces in the orphanage's prize possession: a stained glass window of the Holy Family, with the long, narrow faces of Jesus, Mary and Joseph staring impassively out over the children's damp heads.

"Holy Mary, Mother of God, pray for us sinners now and at the hour of our death–" With a crash, the roots of a gigantic magnolia tree shattered the sacred glass window. The children screamed as the shards of glass flew into their midst. But only for a moment. With a malevolent roar, an avalanche of water burst through the now open window.

Outside, the building swayed like a shimmying dancer, listed, and the walls slowly collapsed leeward. The shrieks of those inside were swallowed up by the crash of wood and stone disintegrating as the edifice dissolved into the flood.

Unaware of this latest catastrophe, Lenie comforted the patients as best she could in the dark hospital wards, using reassuring pats and touches when her words could not be heard.

"Doctor, are we all going to die?" gasped one old woman.

"Hush. This is the strongest building in the city. We're safest here." Lenie squeezed the trembling hand in reassurance, but could not meet her terrified eyes.

Amidst the din and the shadows, no one noticed as Phillip drew Ellie aside, near a window where the shutters rattled ominously against the gale outside. Protectively he took her hand, squeezing it tightly, commanding her to meet his eyes and lean closely to hear his words.

"If the building falls – hold on to me. We'll jump out the window together." She nodded her understanding, her light eyes huge pools in the darkness, clinging to his hand as if for her life.

Their rescue mission complete, Zack and Charles now sagged against the groaning wall, both thoroughly exhausted. From outside, cries for help wafted over the roar of the wind. Like that day in the fiery inferno of the Wilderness so long ago, Zack's need to rescue these lost souls once again overcame his instinct for self-preservation. He pushed himself upright and opened the shutter to the raging storm.

The force of the wind caught Charles full on like a blow, pinning him to the opposite wall like an insect displayed in a box. Zack crawled across the floor to him and slowly, limb by limb, pealed him away from the wall.

Using reserves of strength released by their survival instincts, the two old veterans forced the shutter out the window into the hurricane, hoping to catch the victims being swept by in the flood. But again the all-powerful wind felled Charles, and he collapsed on the wet floor. Zack, oblivious to Charles' plight, concentrated on his futile rescue attempts.

Charles struggled to stand, but after a lifetime of daredevil adventures, his strength finally failed him. The malevolent tempest had accomplished what no battle or conflict had ever done: made him afraid.

"Zack! Zack!" cried Charles. The howling winds obliterated his words. Charles grabbed Zack's arm to get his attention and when Zack finally turned his head, Charles half-gasped, half-yelled into his face.

"I'm not going to make it. Please look after Lenie."

His gray wavy hair blown back from his face like wings, Zack was in no mood for anyone's last wishes.

"Stop it, you Yankee reprobate. Old buzzards like you never die," he barked.

Charles didn't believe his assurances for a moment. Guilt weighed on his soul. He used the last of his strength to be heard above the screaming storm.

"I have to tell you! I – I told Peter to give the flowers to Lucy."

Zack stared at Charles, trying to take this in above the noise of the tempest, the tragedies of that day and of a lifetime. Finally, Charles' confession registered in his brain. Zack understood that it had not been an accident, all those years ago, that had deprived him of his happiness, but another betrayal by this deceitful nemesis. His piercing glare at Charles was murderous. Releasing the shutter into the maelstrom outside, he curled his hands into fists.

"You lying – I'll kill you myself!" he yelled.

Charles may not have heard his words but the intent was

196

unmistakable. However, screams from the patients distracted Zack from his vengeful intent. In the dusk, a huge shadow loomed over the hospital.

It was a section of railway track, a block long, sweeping toward the doomed building. Zack and Charles stared at this deadly apparition in helpless horror. At the same time, both men reached for Lenie, standing behind them, and grasped her arms just as the iron track crashed into the hospital. The thick walls snapped like dry sticks and the tsunami poured in.

In that split second, Phillip pulled Ellie toward an open window; they jumped into the wave as the entire structure collapsed upon the hundreds of souls trapped within it.

The underwater vortex hungrily sucked the intertwined couple downward into the depths, as their arms clenched around each other, kept them together. Ellie's long skirt snagged on a tree branch, holding them down despite Phillip's frantic kicking toward what he thought was the air. Feeling his way along the length of her body, Phillip ripped the cloth, freeing them both. Together they fought their way to the surface, gasping for air.

The relentless sea twirled them again, like a malevolent spinning top, round and round, up and down, not satisfied until the desperate couple was finally wrenched apart.

"Phillip! Phillip!" screamed Ellie, before she went under again. And then her screams were swallowed up in the everlasting night.

"HELP ME! FOR THE LOVE OF GOD!" shrieked one lost soul.

"Mama! Mama!" cried a terrified child piteously.

"I'm John Bullock, please tell my wife I love her!" said yet another desperate voice, over and over again, before the wind and water silenced the piteous last wish.

Heaven was busy welcoming too many souls that day to show mercy for those still trapped on earth.

But Fortune smiled at last upon Zack and Lenie, who found themselves clinging to a piece of masonry, riding the waves like a miniature raft. Zack grasped Lenie's hand, pulling her closer.

"Hold on to me!" he panted.

"Lenie! Lenie!" Faintly, they heard Charles' voice through the whining storm.

"Charles! Charles! Over here!" yelled Lenie with all the force she could muster. But her shout came out as a puny whimper, lost in the shrieking tempest.

She spied Charles floating by, clinging to one of the shutters, his hair plastered to his skull and his skin waxen with strain. He struggled to swim to them, was almost there when a piece of driftwood caught him in the head. He lost his grip on his makeshift life raft and slipped out of sight below the surface of the hungry waters.

Zack watched his disappearing form, thinking dimly that justice was finally done. His grip on Lenie tightened as she struggled to break free and go after her husband.

"Zack! Let me go for him!" cried Lenie.

Her frantic writhing convinced Zack that she would lose her own life in this fruitless struggle unless he intervened. Once again, the urge to protect his own overcame fear, and even his desire for revenge.

"NO! You hold on! I'll go!" ordered Zack.

He hesitated just a moment, then propelled himself out into the water toward Charles. Disoriented, buffeted by the winds and the pellets of sharp rain, Zack, too, went under. Lost and confused, he could only kick his exhausted legs and reach upward toward his old adversary with arms that felt like dead weights. Unable to hold his breath, his willful lungs sucked in the salty water.

"I'm drowning," thought Zack, his mind completely clear. In a second, his life appeared before him; he watched the scenes whiz by as he pondered the irony of dying in an attempt to save his worst enemy, especially after all the near escapes Fortune had bestowed upon him in the War.

On her violently heaving raft, Lenie swiveled her head looking in vain for either of the two men. The most fervent prayers of her life caught in her throat, unspoken but beating like drums in her desperate heart.

A few endless moments later, miraculously Zack emerged from

198

the sea, his arm gripping Charles' neck. Lenie silently gasped her thanks to the Almighty as she watched Zack struggle back to the raft, which was now twirling and bucking like a horse with an unwelcome rider. Unable to loosen her hold on the spiraling boards, Lenie stretched out her foot for him to grasp. Zack reached, missed, reached again, missed. Finally he grasped it, only to have the water-logged shoe slip off her foot into his hand.

Again Zack was adrift in the riotous sea. Charles' bony form pulled him downward like an iron statue. His head bobbed lower and lower below the water's surface. Lenie, in desperation, released one hand from her precarious hold on the slippery wood and offered it to Zack. He tried but could not reach it.

As his head sank again, she grasped a handful of thick grey hair. As she pulled it toward her, Zack's head came with it. Finally he was close enough to grab the edge of the raft and pull himself, and Charles, toward it. Together, he and Lenie managed to haul Charles' inert form up into the center of their fragile lifeboat. The threesome continued to swirl through the hurricane into the darkness.

They say it was sometime after midnight when the winds finally began to blow not quite so fiercely, the rains slacked off, and people still alive began to think that maybe, after all, this was not the day they would meet their Maker.

A thousand prayers later, dawn broke over a sky that was, unbelievably, clear and pinkish blue. At last the sea was quiet. Where the city of Galveston once stood proud and prosperous, only two and three story piles of broken lumber and steel rose above the water. In the far distance, the spire of a church reached upward with one bare wall, a symbol of God's abandonment.

On the raft, Charles lay unconscious as Lenie and Zack still hugged the precious wood, weakly surveying the horizon and the rising sun. Its rays revealed the body of a drowned woman in a gingham dress floating beside them. The blue water, as far as they could see, was a liquid graveyard, strewn with the carcasses of dead animals, corpses of all ages, sizes and hues, broken furniture, pieces of buildings, and the remnants of ruined lives.

Charles groaned, opening his eyes.

"Are they gone?" he murmured groggily.

Her arm still wrapped around him, Lenie responded soothingly, as if she knew exactly what he meant, "Yes, they're gone. You chased them away."

Zack had no energy to inquire about this cryptic remark. He snagged a floating stick and pushed it down in the bay. It hit bottom. Cautiously, he slid off the raft to stand in calm water up to his thighs.

"It's over," he said, in wonder at their survival. Lenie had no strength to respond or even smile, but her lips moved in a silent prayer as her exhausted body collapsed onto the flimsy wood, only her arm tight around Charles' spent frame. Dully Zack observed their cryptic, powerful bond, stronger than the elements themselves.

Chapter 35
After the Deluge

In the midst of death, life must be served. Anyone who has ever lived through a tragedy will remember the astonishing resilience of the survivors. So it was after the Great Flood. By evening, a ragged tent city had been erected on the beach. Here, volunteers and conscripts brought bodies to be buried and the wounded to be cared for. Flames from a gigantic bonfire reached to the blue-black sky, providing heat and light for people wandering through the refugee community, seeking friends and relatives. Police and soldiers forced men to work at gunpoint, searching the wreckage for more bodies, their mouths and noses covered with kerchiefs as protection against the smell of already decaying flesh.

Focused on the one constant in her life – her work – Lenie seemed almost normal as she walked among the prone bodies of the injured, asking questions and feeling for broken bones and hot foreheads. Zack followed her, dumbly, like a faithful animal, as she let him pretend that he was helping her.

Zack's attention drifted to a familiar blanket-clad figure lying on the sand, wondering for a moment who it was. The lanky old man opened his eyes.

"Lenie!" called Zack, trying to get her attention.

"Shhh!" whispered Charles weakly, "Don't bother her when she's working." He grinned slightly at Zack at this private joke, then closed his eyes again. Belatedly, Zack remembered Charles' confession from last night.

"Damn lying Yankee traitor," he muttered in weary disgust. "And I saved you."

"Volunteers" pulled up in wagons heaped with more casualties, unceremoniously dumping new victims in a pile beside a one–story high mound of unidentified bodies. The corpse of a nun rolled out across the sand, the lifeless bodies of four little orphans still tied to the rope around her waist. The nun's sodden habit slowed her progress and she rolled to a stop.

It was Helen, her face as serene in death as it had been in life, her eyes open as if seeking the Almighty.

Through the bonfire's flickering light, Zack slowly recognized his oldest daughter. His emotions frozen by the immensity of yet another tragedy, he could only stare in mute recognition of the loss of his firstborn. The repository of his sacred memory of his baby sister and his time of Camelot, was lost.

Now Lenie turned and saw the tragic tableau, as Zack slowly stepped forward and reached out to Helen, as if to touch her to be sure she was really, truly gone. Her hand went to her heart in wordless grief at the loss of this kind, gentle soul, the lost heiress to her mother's gentle patience.

Then behind Zack, an image flickered in and out of view through the dancing firelight. Slowly, an apparition appeared – a bedraggled, dazed, half-naked young woman, long light hair braided with seaweed, staggering toward Zack. As the flames illuminated the bodies littering the sand, the girl stopped. Her face crumpled, and a wail of pure, hopeless grief erupted from her soul.

"Ellie!" cried Lenie. Zack turned and caught his surviving daughter in his arms as she lurched toward the pile of corpses, as if intent on adding her own frail body as a further sacrifice. Despite Zack's restraint, she still fought wildly to reach the flames. Lenie helped Zack hold her back. An unearthly shriek of despair emerged from her fragile, half-clad frame, giving voice to an entire city's devastation.

"Nooooooo!"

In the struggle to restrain the hysterical girl, no one noticed that it was not Helen's body she recognized, but Phillip's, his chiseled features and olive skin now pale enough in death to finally pass drawing room inspection. Only Charles' tired eyes focused on Phillip's lifeless face in the fire's light. His lined face crumpled in a quiet, despairing grief as he closed his eyes to the sight and to the loss of the son he had loved, but never acknowledged. Meanwhile the despairing young girl shrieked on and on in the surreal light, until she could no longer make even a whimper. Finally silent, she lay like a corpse herself, staring into the eyes of the only person who truly loved her.

Chapter 36
Aftershocks

When they started the accounting, after that Great Flood, there was not a house without a loss to mourn, and many entire families were lost forever. It was, and remains, the greatest loss of life in a natural disaster than America has ever endured.

In its aftermath, the survivors somehow walked and talked and went through the actions they had to undertake to keep on going, with bewilderment just beneath the surface like actors trying to remember their lines.

Zack's home, like the life he had once had, was swept away in the storm. Pawing through the wreckage, only one item was recovered – the treasured melted doorknob from his family's old mansion, following him like a ghost of lives past.

The Delacourt house was much damaged, but still stood. The surviving family members made it their residence, offering shelter to friends who needed it. With Ellie prostrate from her trauma, and having no home himself, Zack had no choice but to lodge there as well.

Though Helen's body was destroyed in the fires that raged to protect the survivors from contagion, Zack sent money to have a handsome stone erected in the family graveyard in Virginia, that little patch of ground that held a bereaved family's heart. What Charles and Lenie may have done for Phillip, Zack neither knew nor cared.

As a city elder, Zack was quickly pressed into service to help with the re-building and planning of a Great Sea Wall to keep the sea away forever. I imagine keeping busy helped him numb his personal grief and the sense he must have had of the loss of yet another way of life.

As soon as Charles was able to travel, Lenie surprised everyone by deserting the ruin of her beloved hospital for the sanatorium near San Antonio, where she took Charles to continue his recovery. Ellie, who had not uttered a word since that dreadful night, accompanied them, a silent wraith who moved among them like a ghost of the life that was past. Although grateful that she had survived, Zack had no idea how to help her with her convalescence and no words of hope to share with her. He was probably secretly relieved to have her sad presence removed from own his life while he himself tried to rebuild it.

As the months passed, Zack began to wonder about his stricken daughter. But she wrote no letters. Only Lenie sent vague and guarded communications that left much unsaid. Finally Zack received a letter that prompted him to action.

By then it was early spring. Life was returning to the hill country surrounding the sanitarium, although the air retained some of winter's chill. Lenie deemed it warm enough for Charles to take some air. And so, snuggly wrapped in a blanket, he dozed on the veranda overlooking those reawakening hills.

But it was Zack's sister Nan, not Lenie, who sat beside him, studying his lined but still patrician face, her book lying unread in her lap. Putting it aside, she gently tucked the blanket tighter around his slender, now fragile frame.

Unnoticed by Nan, Lenie watched the scene from the doorway, surprise and understanding dawning on her face. Suddenly she realized what she had been blind to all her life, even back in their days together before the War.

With a start Nan caught Lenie's gaze and sat back, embarrassed.

"It's all right. I just never knew," Lenie spoke wonderingly, realizing what Nan had lost all those years ago. "If it wasn't for me – you could have had a husband. Your own family."

"He loved you," Nan replied, her embarrassment evaporating in the face of Lenie's compassion. "You made him happy."

Charles stirred, awakened, and noticed the two women, who grew silent under his gaze.

"Am I interrupting something?" he queried sleepily, smiling the ghost of his wolfish grin.

"No. We were just talking about how happy we've been," said Nan. A look of deep understanding passed between the two women, bonded for a lifetime. Anyone viewing the tableau of the three old friends would have seen a trio of elderly people, hair grayed, faces lined, and bodies becoming brittle with fragility. But to the three comrades themselves, they had not changed from the days of their youth. The decades had passed in a few seconds, leaving their emotions young and fresh as their bodies aged. I understand the feeling well, myself. The soul never grows old.

Lenie returned to their ongoing debate.

"I was just going to say – what are we going to do about Ellie? We have to tell Zack. Eventually."

"I know. But how?" sighed Nan.

Abruptly, like an apparition conjured up by their words, Zack rounded the corner of the veranda in time to hear her question. His stocky frame and rolling walk reminded Nan, unbidden, of the approach of one of the black bears still seen in the Virginia woods. The three looked at him in consternation and guilt.

"Nan! Why didn't you tell me you were here?" Zack demanded gruffly, his tone and presence increasing his ursine resemblance.

"We didn't want to worry you," parried Lenie.

"Got a letter from Jim. At least some people in this family communicate," grumped Zack. Lenie stepped forward to wheel Charles inside.

"Well, we'll let you two talk," she offered, giving Nan a meaningful look. "I'm sure you have a lot to catch up on."

Zack sat down heavily in the chair beside Nan, looking closely at her tired face, her once plump apple cheeks now drooping beside her thin lips.

"Jim said you had surgery." His tone was demanding but the underlying worry was clear.

Nan smoothed her skirt over her lap, not meeting his eyes.

"I've had the X-ray treatment that they do now, and Lenie says it's just a matter of getting my strength back and seeing what happens," she responded, her deliberate vagueness fooling no one, including her suspicious brother.

"You've got to get well, Nan. If anything were to happen to you, I don't think I could stand it," begged Zack, his voice gruff with emotion. He bowed his head and blinked quickly to hide the tears welling in his eyes that he had thought would be dry forever.

Nan stroked the gray head with affection, thinking again that it was so like that of an old bear.

"Yes, yes, you could, Zack. We bear what we must." She paused, then said what she must say.

"I'm so sorry about Helen. At least we know she is in God's hands. As are we all."

Zack wiped his eyes quickly with the back of his hand, ashamed of his momentary weakness. "Humph. Yes, I guess so. Suppose I should go see Ellie."

"Yes. You must see Ellie," said Nan decisively. She tried to rise but stalled halfway out of her chair. Zack helped her up and to get her balance, her frailty another stab to his heart.

Once steady on her feet, Nan took his arm and led him inside and down the antiseptic-smelling hall. Lenie emerged from the room they were approaching.

"Zack is ready to see Ellie," Nan announced with quiet firmness.

"She's resting." Lenie stood implacably in the doorway.

"He must see her, Lenie. It's time."

"What's wrong?" asked Zack, suddenly suspicious.

"She's had a rough time, Zack. If you upset her – I'll make you leave." Lenie's strong words did not hide her underlying anxiety. Now thoroughly alarmed, Zack pushed through the door.

Ellie lay in the spare iron bed, her hair spread out around her pale face like the petals of a wilting flower. At the sight of her father, her eyes grew wide with fear. Instinctively, she huddled under the covers for protection, pulling them up to her chin.

"How are you, daughter?" Zack asked, struggling to put some semblance of joviality and concern into his habitual grumpy tone.

But Ellie only stared at him with growing terror. From the corner came a small, mewling cry. Now Zack noticed the small bassinette tucked almost out of site. His first thought was that this hospital must be really crowded, to have to house babies with adult patients. As the crying continued, the realization of what this really meant dawned as the pieces of the puzzle fell into place. Ellie's illness, her late nights at the hospital, the silence since she left Galveston. His face, too, turned pale with shock at the realization of this unspeakable breach of morality, then just as quickly his expression darkened in anger.

"A child! You have a – How could you –" he thundered. He whirled to Lenie and Nan.

"So that's why you didn't want me here. You've been hiding her." Lenie quickly positioned herself between Ellie and Zack.

"I warned you, Zack. Don't be angry. It's done. Just accept it."

"I will do no such thing!" Zack roared. "It's a disgrace to the entire family! Who is the father? I'll make him pay!"

At the sound of his angry voice, the baby wailed harder. Nan gently picked up the small bundle, making shushing coos as if she had mothered dozens of infants. Now Zack saw its face. He stepped closer and stared, unable to believe his own eyes. This could not be happening.

Round dark eyes with long lashes opened to stare back at him, as the crying abruptly ceased. But it was the baby's skin that caused Zack's world to tilt. This infant was not rosy pink like the other four infants of Zack's acquaintance. This one was beige – the color of New Orleans coffee with two servings of cream. The meaning of this observation sent shock waves through Zack's very soul. Horrified, he turned back to Ellie, who added her wracking sobs to the baby's renewed wailing.

"How in God's name – How could you –" His power of speech failed before this unspeakable outrage. He had to flee. Abruptly he stomped out of the room, storming down the hall, almost staggering with the shock.

The others in the room exchanged questioning glances. None were surprised by Zack's reaction. But none knew what to do. Then, Lenie turned and ran after him.

Once outside, he leaned on the porch railing, gulping air. Before his vision, the trees and hills swam as if he viewed them from a pitching ship. He closed his eyes to quell the rising nausea, still sucking in huge gasps of air.

Behind him, Lenie listened to his ragged breathing. Her hand reached out – but she was afraid to touch him. Her mind searched for the words to try to comfort him, to make him understand, and could only find them by going back a lifetime – to her own betrayal. Finally she spoke softly.

"Zack – when Samuel died – for a long time, I remembered the pain. Now I know he wanted me to remember the love."

She paused. It seemed to her that Zack's breathing was quieter. Encouraged that he was hearing her heartfelt words, she continued, her hands fluttering in the air as if she wanted to touch him, but was afraid.

"Zack, you have to look at this – with forgiveness, you can heal each other."

She finally placed her hand, timidly, on his shoulder. Zack stiffened as if he had been shocked, shaking her off like an angry, mortally wounded beast. He whirled to face her.

"Forgiveness? This is – is – a crime against nature. It's a sacrilege!" he cried, his voice high with outrage.

"That's not true. Anything can be forgiven –" argued Lenie, her voice still gentle in deference to his pain.

Even in his torment, Zack recognized this as a moment he had been waiting for. Finally, it was time to show Lenie what betrayal was all about.

"Anything? It was your scheming husband who kept us apart with a lie! He made sure those flowers went to Lucy instead of you! Can you forgive that?" he spat at her.

To his surprise, she didn't flinch. There was no expression of shock, no anger, no pain. She looked deeply into Zack's eyes.

"Yes. I did. A long time ago," she said quietly. Zack's face crumpled as he realized she knew – had known for a long time – what Charles had done. And it didn't matter.

All these years, and it still hurt. Unable to face her or the horrible truths of this grim day, he ran down the steps and into the velvet anonymous twilight.

Chapter 37
Crisis

That night, black clouds scudded across the sky. Thunder rumbled, the noise punctuated by the plopping of fat raindrops on the hard ground. The ominous weather forecast a hurricane of the heart that would finally reach its climax.

As Ellie slept fitfully in her narrow bed, the door to her room opened. Silently as a stalking Indian, a figure crept toward her, then tiptoed over to the baby's crib. The intruder quietly picked up the tiny bundle, with its skin like a dusting of nutmeg, and stealthily carried it away.

Outside, a fork of lightning illuminated the ghostly figure. Zack clutched the bundle of blankets and its contents close to his chest as he stole through the dark streets to the river bank. Swelling waters fed by spring rains flowed swiftly beneath the overhanging trees. Here, Zack stopped, his soul alight with white anger so deep it was icy cold. He watched himself as if from a distance, understanding dimly that he had crossed the line from sanity – and the constraints of civilized life – into madness. There were no more laws, no more justice, and no honor. He was free to do what he needed to do to erase the stain of this final betrayal. Curiously he felt totally free, almost weightless in the still, humid air, pregnant with the storm that mirrored his inner anguish.

At that moment, the heavens opened and the rain poured down as if God had dumped a heavenly bucket upon His earth. The force of the water proved to be the flood that finally broke Zack's poor tormented soul. He glared up into the angry sky.

"Why? Why did you take everything from me? Why do you destroy everything I believe in? I won't stand it!" he shouted angrily, his voice hoarse with rage.

There was no answer to his heartfelt plea, nor to his threat. Infuriated by the silence of an indifferent deity, he lifted the baby up to the sky as if in offering, and then held the little body out toward the rushing waters.

Who knew what might have happened if that baby hadn't

opened his dark eyes and looked directly at Zack. Those eyes were wise, yet beseeching – a gaze exactly like Zack's little sister Helen, so many years ago, as her spirit left this world. For the second time in Zack's life, Spirit spoke to him. Helen was there, passing through his being just as she had the day she died.

All nature grew silent. Even the storm and its fury seemed to disappear as Zack was captured by another pair of childish eyes. In them Zack saw reflected that lost child, Nan's tearful face as he and his siblings made their vows to their home and family, Lucy's gentle loyalty, and even Juno's devoted watchfulness. A lifetime of anger was caught and diffused by the power of that infant's loving expression as the ghost of his lost baby sister reminded Zack of what he really loved. At long last, his broken heart surrendered to the grace offered him.

Pulling the child back from the precipice, he clutched the baby to his chest as he fell to his knees, sobbing with a force that threatened to break his aged, ursine body apart at the seams. Old and wise, the baby watched him with knowing eyes as Zack's tears mingled with the rainwater and dripped onto the infant's round, mocha cheeks.

Near dawn, the rain had almost stopped when a Mexican porter knocked on the door of the priest's room at the old Alamo chapel.

"Padre, padre! Come quick!"

The friar rose from his prayers in answer to the urgency in his servant's voice. In the portico, he found a stockily built man, dripping rivulets of water onto the rough stone floor of the revered old mission. Soggy blankets hung from his arms, touching his soaked boots.

Fearful at what he might find, the priest pulled the blanket away to see a tiny form, unbelievably sleeping peacefully through the storm. As the wet cloth brushed his face, the baby opened his eyes and studied the friar's face with wonder.

"I baptized him in the river. But you could do it, officially. Please." Zack's voice rasped with emotion.

"Whose baby is this?" asked the priest, looking from the child to the man and back again.

"He is my grandson," replied Zack, as if amazed at this revelation. The priest withheld his questions and, perhaps fearing for the survival of a young baby who had endured such exposure to the elements, nodded assent.

"Juan, get some dry blankets."

At the ancient (even then) stone baptismal font, the priest placed the stole over his neck, preparing for the timeless ritual of taking a new soul into the family of God. He dipped the chipped glass vial into the font of holy water.

"What name do you give the child?" he asked.

Zack paused. He had not thought this far ahead. "William. To remember."

"Then, I baptize thee, William, in the name of the Father, the Son and the Holy Ghost." As the priest poured water over the baby's head, William blinked in surprise, but did not cry. From years ago, the words to the old psalm came to Zack's mind. He murmured the prayer in a hoarse whisper, his voice gaining strength with each word as if the old psalm poured the life-giving water into his parched soul:

"Behold my servant whom I uphold.
My chosen one in whom my soul delights.
I have put my spirit upon him;
He will bring forth justice to the nations."

The voices faded into faint echoes in the empty adobe church. Little William's sable brown eyes met Zack's watery blue ones, as if recognizing him across heaven and earth.

Chapter 38
Understanding

By this time, back at the sanitarium, Zack's long absence and the baby's disappearance had long since been discovered; fear of the worst was in everyone's hearts. Lenie, Charles, and Nan were frantic, but Ellie was downright hysterical, pulling her hair and beating her fists in frustration on the covers of the bed. Two nurses in white uniforms tried in vain to calm her. One attempted to force a draught into her mouth as Ellie squirmed in protest.

"Hush now! It's all for the best if you ask me," said one.

"We didn't ask you, and we don't need you here," snapped Lenie. Startled, the two nurses withdrew. Lenie barked into the telephone, her voice laced with exasperation.

"What do you mean, describe the baby? He's small. The man? About 60 years old —"

She broke off as she spied Zack in the doorway, holding an oblong bundle of dry blankets. All eyes turned to him. All breathing ceased. He walked heavily and slowly to Ellie and awkwardly handed her the infant.

"I had him baptized. William. I hope that's all right."

Back in his mother's arms, William began to whimper. No one spoke until Zack added, superfluously,

"I think he's hungry."

Ellie clutched the baby tearfully, covering his round face with kisses, baptizing him anew with tears of relief.

Lenie and Charles exchanged wary glances, not sure what to make of this new development — and a new Zack who was quiet, almost meek. Nan alone understood the essence of what had transpired; she watched the scene, eyes shining, tears sliding silently down her now withered cheeks.

Zack awkwardly patted Ellie's arm. She turned her gaze to him, and for the first time in her life there was no fear in her eyes — only love. And gratitude.

For Lenie, the center of her world shifted in a profound, quiet earthquake. Something that had always been off kilter, was now righted. As Zack slowly left the room, shoulders drooping with exhaustion, she followed him, unsure of what to say but knowing the time had come to open her heart to him at last.

Zack settled heavily into a chair on the veranda. The early morning landscape, the fresh crisp air, the chirping of awakening birds – it all seemed clean and fresh to him. He absorbed the scene as if seeing it for the first time, like a baby bird newly escaped from its shell. Lenie quietly sat beside him, intently studying her entwined hands in her lap. Her patrician face softened and looked strangely vulnerable; her piercing eyes relaxed into a wondering stare at the universe before her.

Zack glanced at her, then gazed silently back out over the spring landscape. Lenie took a deep breath, clasping her hands together so tightly her wedding ring dug deeply into her skin.

"I never told you why I married Charles." Her words echoed in his brain, but the usual emotional reaction was not there. Zack listened, rocking gently in his chair, as if to a bedtime story. If he was surprised that she chose this moment to reveal the reasons for this long ago decision, he said nothing.

"Before we went to Virginia – there was an epidemic, and Father – he thought Mother and I would be safest at the ranch. But the fever was already there. In the Indian villages. Mother tried to help them, but – they blamed us for bringing the plague to them."

She sat perfectly still but for her hands that worried themselves together, over and over. If Zack questioned the reason for this retelling of a story from her childhood, he gave no sign.

"I got sick. Mother nursed me through it. But, when she got ill, I – I could not save her."

Zack's newly sensitive ears now tuned in to the echoes of grief from a young girl, helpless, motherless, and broken by her failure to defeat death. Lenie stared out at the landscape as if looking for the small ranch house on that long-ago night. Zack also imagined that he could see it.

"We were alone. At night, the wolves came. I could see their eyes in the darkness. They wanted her. And me."

Zack's rocking stopped. He felt her fear, creeping up the back of his neck, as if he too saw those hungry, glowing orbs with a growing sense of horror.

"I shot some of them, and when the ammunition ran out, I tried to scare them off with the fire. But there was no more wood."

In his imagination, Zack pictured the tragic scene all too vividly – the young girl, the dying woman, the desperate fight to save a life and the courage he knew so well. Gently he placed his hand over hers. And listened. Truly listened.

"I knew they would come for us. But instead they ran away. When the Indians came."

Now Zack's stomach turned to water. He knew what the Indians had done to the settlers. His hand on Lenie's tightened. Finally, he looked into her soul and saw the effort it cost her to share these unspeakable secrets. He did not want to hear any more, longing to cling to his ignorance and his judgment. But instead, he waited.

"When one attacked me, I slashed his face. After that – whatever he had planned to do to me – now there would be no mercy."

Lenie swallowed. Into Zack's mind flitted the memory of the angry, defiant child he had known – refusing to conform, lashing out at restraint, and determined to go her own way no matter what. At last he understood the passion, the rage, behind that drive.

"But then, he came."

"Charles?" Zack rasped, understanding at last.

Now the face of the scarred, old Indian Charles had shot at Lenie's old homestead during their ill-fated picnic appeared as if a vision, before Zack.

Lenie swallowed, steadied her voice, and went on.

"He killed two, and the one I wounded escaped. Together we buried Mother. I wished I had died too. Somehow – it was my fault."

She stopped, bright tears in her eyes. "Charles never told anyone. He – forgave me, when I could not forgive myself. He accepted me. As I am."

Zack's newly vulnerable soul ached for her. He was deeply ashamed of his own criticism and his anger, for so many years.

Lenie placed her slender, pale hand over Zack's rough one.

"Forgiveness heals, Zack. Like you healed Ellie."

The two old adversaries – and perhaps if different paths had been chosen, would-be lovers – stared deeply into each others' eyes, for the first time seeing past the rough-edge, prickly personality to the kindred spirit within. I can feel it, in my soul, even though I wasn't there to see it.

Chapter 39
Rapprochement

Somehow Charles sensed that a meeting of hearts had occurred between his wife and his old rival. But rather than being angry or jealous, he found himself deeply pleased. His own heart beat in contentment with the summer cicadas as he rested on the veranda, smoking – despite Lenie's orders – one of his fine cigars.

Zack joined him, looking slightly frazzled I reckon, sinking down into the neighboring chair, wiping his perspiring forehead with a well-used handkerchief.

"Well, he's finally asleep. Never knew babies were so complicated," he sighed.

Charles grinned in commiseration. The two men silently surveyed the peaceful countryside.

"Want to go for a walk, old timer?" Zack offered. Surprised, Charles nodded.

With some difficulty Zack maneuvered the wheelchair down the steps. Charles accepted his bumpy descent with gentlemanly good grace. As the ride smoothed out on the path leading to the woods beyond, Charles savored the closeness to nature and the wilderness, breathing in the scents that Lenie called "Texas." The smell of the past, yet with the sense of a new beginning. He had one more thing to say to Zack. And it was easier for him to voice that thought over his shoulder, rather than face to face, as Zack pushed him in his chair.

"You know, I haven't said 'thank you,' for rescuing me. Especially after I told you I was the one who ruined your life." Underneath the familiar sardonic tone, Zack heard a strange note in Charles' voice. It was sincerity.

"Hummph," grunted Zack. "Well, I guess you did a good enough job, taking care of her, after all."

Charles' eyebrows shot up in surprise at Zack's grudging acceptance. He ventured another admission.

"You know, I didn't understand what you went through, losing a son. Till now."

It took Zack a moment to realize what Charles meant. "You mean – Phillip? You loved him like you love Samuel?"

"Yes. I did. I do. And I'm grateful that at least he left us William."

The two men were silent for a moment, each realizing the irony that they shared the loss of a son, and now shared a grandson. Perhaps they ruminated in their minds about the extraordinary circumstances that brought this new soul into their lives. Then Charles spoke again.

"I always envied you, Zack. So sure of what you believed. You and Lenie both, never doubting. You know how I decided which side to fight for in the War? I flipped a coin."

"Who won?" asked Zack, with a flicker of his old sarcasm.

Charles chuckled. And for once, Charles' response did not rankle as Zack confessed his own uncertainty.

"I'm not sure of anything anymore," Zack admitted, with a new openness. "Except that maybe with William, it might be different."

"You might be different," Charles pointed out.

As the chair bumped along the garden path, Charles took an envelope from his lap and offered it over his shoulder to Zack, his pale, veined hand trembling slightly.

"Here."

They paused under a gnarled oak tree as Zack inspected the letter and its unfamiliar stamp.

"From Paris?" he asked, quizzically.

"Samuel is there, finishing his book. Go ahead, read it."

Zack sat down heavily on the ground beneath the stubby oak and retrieved his reading glasses from his vest pocket. Charles watched him as he read, enjoying the warming sun, the path of a large industrious ant climbing the tree bark, and the low hum of a fat yellow jacket seeking nectar from the opening wildflowers. Slowly his eyelids drooped closed.

In a few minutes Zack finished the letter – read it several times, actually, so it all had time to sink into his brain. He removed his glasses to wipe his eyes, damp with emotion and relief. Awkwardly he replaced the letter into the envelope and offered it back to

Charles. But Charles did not move to accept it. Zack shoved the envelope back into his companion's palm, but the long slender fingers did not grasp it, and it drifted to the ground, like a wilted petal. Zack peered into the gaunt face and saw that life had quietly slipped away from his old adversary. A powerful emotion caught him by surprise.

"Damn Yankee," he murmured, overtaken by his deep surge of loss.

Chapter 40
The Return

All of Galveston – that is, all of the survivors of the Great Flood – turned out for Charles' funeral. Whether they came in support of Lenie or because they had actually forgiven the deceased for his long-ago perfidy during the War, it didn't matter now.

The physician in Lenie had known his demise was near, even as she fought for his recovery. Yet for once, Lenie did not rail at death as her eternal enemy but peacefully accepted the loss of her husband of more than 30 years. She had no regrets about their life. The coming together of hearts and the healing of old wounds gave her strength to see Charles' passing as not defeat, but the natural progression of life.

Those who watched her at the funeral marveled at her calm, yet it was what they would have expected from this larger-than-life woman who, more and more, was viewed as both a heroine for her bravery in the Flood and a legend for her accomplishments.

Peter's successor – the little boy who so many years ago had dropped the tray in the doorway as the fateful flowers were delivered – respectfully showed the mourners out the door as the crowded wake dispersed. Their whispered comments drifted back to the family members still inside.

"Did you see that baby?" hissed one wizened old woman in a shiny satin black dress and old-fashioned bonnet. "What are they thinking?"

Zack pointedly ignored their disapproval, focusing instead on Alden, Caroline and their sons bidding good-bye to Lenie. More and more, his once volatile emotions felt finally, tamed by time, leaving a smooth, placid calm that was unruffled by the vicissitudes of social interactions.

"Lenie, please think about coming to the ranch and staying with us," urged Caroline. "I hate for you to be all alone in this big house."

"I will. Think about it," responded Lenie, in a politely appreciative tone that left no doubt that she would do no such thing.

Zack and Lenie rejoined Nan, Ellie and William in the parlor. At last Lenie allowed herself to collapse into a chair, surprised at the weakness that suddenly swept through her.

"I wish Sam were here. Samuel," Zack corrected himself, "I don't like the idea of you being here by yourself either."

Lenie shrugged away her momentary frailty. "It's all right. I'm leaving to take Nan back to the sanatorium tomorrow."

But Nan shook her head. "No. I want to go home. I'm ready."

There was a painful pause; they all knew what she meant. Nan turned to her brother with that sweet smile that always moved his heart.

"Zack, please come home. It's time."

"Please, Father?" asked Ellie beseechingly. The others stared in amazement at the first words she had spoken since the Great Flood. I can still imagine that sweet voice I knew so well. No wonder his stubbornness dissolved before his sister's quiet insistence. Zack laid his hand across Nan's and nodded assent. It was, indeed, time to go home.

And so the survivors boarded the train that had taken so many of their family back and forth over the years. This time, Zack was with them. Life had sued for peace and won.

That journey home was nothing like Zack's heartbreaking trek to Texas, almost forty years before. Where he had seen only devastation and misery, now prosperous towns and cultivated fields sped by as he gazed out the train windows. During all the years Zack had been the last holdout for the Confederacy, the rest of the country had healed. Surprisingly, instead of resentment, he found the sight brought gladness and relief to his heart.

Virginia had changed too. There was even a railroad station close enough to his old home where Jim could meet the prodigal son. Over a gap of four decades, Zack and Jim eyed one another, each silently amazed at how the other had grown old. Jim's hand, spotted with age, shoved his thick grey thatch up his forehead in that old familiar gesture. The two brothers approached each other tentatively, awkwardly shaking hands. The air quivered with emotion but there were no hugs. It was not a time when grown men embraced each other.

As their fingers gripped each other's palms, Zack had a flash as if a psychic revelation. He saw and even felt, the decades of dedication his older brother had given to his family and his parents. Never feeling good enough with the loss of that keen mind that impressed his professors at University before the war. Wondering if it had been better if he had indeed lost his life in that long-ago battle. Slowly regaining his sense of self through year after year of hard, manual labor and dedication to two old people and two spinster sisters. At last finding joy in the eager young spirits who came to River's Rest for their education in body, mind and spirit, who universally called him "Uncle Jim."

Zack's hand closed even more intensely over the gnarled paw with the big knuckles, surprising Jim with its strength.

The rutted lane to their old home, where the Delacourt carriage had nearly run over Lenie so many years ago, had been widened into a real road. The distance home, which to the young Zack had seemed so long, was now but a short drive.

I can't say Jim leaped out of the old wagon, but he clambered down with considerable agility for his age to help Lenie, Ellie, William, and lastly, his frail sister Nan to the ground as Zack stood in the hazy Virginia sunlight, taking it all in. The smell of roses wafted on the warm air from his mother's garden where loudly buzzing bees feasted on a thousand blooms. Here he had ridden away to War as a young boy and returned a man. At the edge of these woods, he had run as Brave Wolf chased him and, a few years later, escaped the inferno that was the Battle of the Wilderness. On the wide lawn, now given over to fields of alfalfa, he had sipped tea with Helen and Mildred, and watched his baby sister die.

And there, before him, was River's Rest – smaller and shabbier, but still standing. And with some new inhabitants.

"My wife, Mary. Our children. Landis and Anne." Jim announced. A red-headed young woman – young enough to be Jim's daughter, was Zack's first thought – nodded shyly as she balanced a two-year-old boy on her hip. A little girl – also red-headed – peered out from behind her mother's skirt, at the strange man she was told was her uncle.

For it was in his sixtieth decade that Jim Lewis had finally taken a wife. One of the young students who came under the tutelage of Nan, Mildred and Sarah, Mary was a younger daughter of an impecunious veteran whose family went back almost as far back as the Lewis' did. That clan had not amassed the wealth as Zack's patrician ancestors had in the 200 years before the War Between the States, but it was just as well for they felt the loss of their patrimony less keenly. Nan and Millie, ever generous, took on the family's children in return for bartered produce and livestock. They delighted in Mary's keen mind and she grew up to become a skilled and beloved teacher. With this Celtic loveliness in his life every day, it's no wonder a heart even as numb to the finer feelings as Jim, was aroused to ardor. And miraculously, she returned his affections.

After a moment of surprise at his sister-in-law's youth, Zack's recent experience with small children prompted him to bend over to pat the heads of the two tykes. They suffered his touch with stoicism and refrained from bursting into tears at the site of this burly stranger.

Zack slowly straightened up to see a vision he had dreamt about for more than a generation. An old woman walked carefully down the porch steps, a very elderly person clinging to each arm. Zack's mind registered with a shock that this was Millie, escorting his parents, two slender wraiths with skin several sizes too large, yet held upright by indomitable will and grace.

"Mother. Father," Zack's voice cracked. A joy that he had not felt since his youth burst forth from his aged heart.   James placed his shaking hand on Zack's head in a blessing as Zack fell to his creaking knees on the ground.

"We thank thee, Lord, for the safe return of our son," rasped James, his voice hoarse with both age and emotion.

Sarah smiled through her tears, as with trembling hands she offered her prodigal son a lily.

"Our happiness is complete." Her voice was still low and clear as the syllables flowed gracefully in her Southern tones.

Unable to speak, Zack took the flower, and fiercely clasped her withered hand to his cheek. He was home.

His first few weeks at River's Rest were strange, almost painful. At times the rickety homestead seemed old and ramshackle, a relic from a bygone era, displaced into his present life. The hazy humid air, so different from the relentless, brilliant Texas sun, induced an almost dreamlike state. At other times, a glimpse of a copse of trees, a meadow of flowers, or the sound of woodland birds would stun him with a memory of childhood, sharp as a thistle. His old heart continued to break apart gradually, like a glacier falling into the sea. If he had put his feelings into words, he might have said he felt as much like a baby as William was, but with memories of a former life to which he had returned.

By silent agreement, neither he nor Lenie referred to or ventured into the still mysterious depths of the Wilderness. Maybe someday other children would play there, but for now, it was another world – a Valhalla inaccessible to ordinary mortals.

By appearances, he quickly fell into the daily routine of caring for the old home and helping Jim eke out a meager living from the land. Returning to the unfamiliar work of farming after his long years at his law desk was not an easy transition for his aging body.

While the two brothers labored together to repair a fence in the heavy Virginia heat, Zack straightened up too suddenly, groaning and bracing his back.

Jim pushed his hair back from his forehead and wiped the sweat off just before it dripped into his eyes. "Is it much changed from what you remember?" he asked Zack.

"It looks good, Jim. Very good," Zack lied. "But I didn't expect that Mother and Father would look so old."

Jim laughed, clapping Zack on the back. Zack winced.

"Why, Zack, they're not old – they're ancient. WE are old."

The two brothers gathered their tools and headed home, past the little graveyard with the now well-tended rosebushes. Zack peered at it, fixating on the small headstone he knew was Helen's. And the larger ones, not yet overgrown with grass, that housed his only son and the memory of his oldest daughter. As he always did when he passed, he tipped his hat in memory of the lost children and thought again of the irony that they were gone, while the relics of the family still lived.

"Sometimes I think about you and Alden and me, all we went through, and we're still here. And my son – killed in some pantywaist little skirmish fighting under a man who gives his name to a child's toy. Was it worth it?" he speculated, daring to ask the long-festering question.

"It was our Cause, Zack. What we believed," Jim assured him. "As long as you and I are alive, it is alive."

In the face of Jim's belief, Zack looked dubious, for the first time in his life.

His aged eyes spied two elderly women sitting in rockers on the porch. Two old neighbor women must be visiting, was Zack's first thought. Then, with a start, he realized the two women were Lenie and Millie. The shreds of a package lay at their feet.

As the two brothers reached the sagging porch, Lenie proudly held up a book for their inspection. The cover read, "Loyalties," by Samuel Lewis Delacourt, handsomely stamped into the leather in deep gold. Zack accepted the tome, and examined it with disbelieving eyes.

"It's our story. He's written it all down," announced Lenie, as if she couldn't believe it.

Jim studied the volume over Zack's shoulder, squinting as he struggled with his failing eyesight. "You and me in a book. Makes me feel kind of…" he mused.

"Old. The War is history. And so are we. Well, we know what to do with this." Zack's tone carried the finality of a lifetime of stubborn idealism. He strode into the house purposefully, carrying the book in front of him as if it were contaminated. Lenie recovered from her surprise, leaped up and ran after him.

"Wait! Don't you – my son wrote that!"

Ignoring her, Zack strode up to the old fireplace, where the family's treasured sword from George Washington gleamed, enshrined above the mantle. But instead of throwing Samuel's book in the fire, Zack carefully set it on the mantle beside the regimental flag, the sacred melted doorknob (imported from Texas), and the case displaying Billy's medal.

Lenie's emotion caught in her throat when she saw his intention.

"There's something else." She ducked into a bedroom, returning with a bundle of torn cloth which she offered to Zack. He recognized it at once.

"My uniform! You didn't burn it!" He fondled the ragged cloth, reliving in a flash the prickly emotions and unspoken longings that surrounded the circumstances of its disappearance.

"No, I couldn't – it belongs to the last Confederate soldier," said Lenie, almost gently. Reverently, Zack placed the bundle atop the mantle, another treasure of his family's heritage.

Chapter 41
A Truce at Last

That night, the family savored one of what they knew would be their few remaining evenings with their dear Nan. With his siblings and parents crowded into the small parlor, Zack read aloud from Samuel's new book.

"As my Uncle Zack and Uncle Jim ran from the cottage and the fastest Christmas dinner they'd ever eaten, my father let them go – after all, it was Christmas."

He looked up over the rims of his glasses, studying each of the beloved faces in the small circle, appreciating the story and each other's company. Nan's pale, thin face tugged at Zack's heart. Every day she grew weaker, despite a storm of prayers that besieged heaven on her behalf.

"Nan, it's time for you to rest," said Lenie softly. Millie helped her parents onto their feet and toward the stairs. Zack picked up Nan and carried her to her room like a child. Together Lenie and Zack settled her frail body into the bed.

"It's a wonderful book, Lenie. Please tell Samuel for me," murmured Nan. Zack took Nan's hand and sat beside her while Lenie perched on the opposite side of the bed Nan still shared with Mildred.

"You can tell him yourself. Soon as you are well, I'm taking you to Europe again."

But Lenie's false heartiness didn't fool Nan, who smiled her understanding and disbelief. Everyone knew Nan had no expectation of leaving the family homestead again. Zack sighed.

"Doesn't seem right, Nan. Alden and I left, and you never had a chance to have your own life."

"I've had everything, Zack. A wonderful family. Friends. Love," Nan reassured him.

"But you deserved to have this," said Lenie fiercely, pulling off her wedding ring and placing it on Nan's finger. Nan smiled weakly.

"Everything in its own time." With effort she joined Zack and Lenie's hands with hers. Their fingers – his rough and stiff, hers slender and veined – intertwined atop the old coverlet, as Nan's loving heart again brought peace.

Chapter 42
Peace at Last

The last day of the War Between the States began with a sunny morning. Too bright for the grief that the dozens of mourners gathered outside River's Rest held in their hearts.

Dressed in his Sunday clothes, which had become strangely baggy as his stocky frame had shrunk during the stress of the last year and unaccustomed exercise, Zack stood before the parlor mantle holding little William, explaining the family heirlooms. William's solemn face studied each one carefully. No longer a baby, he struggled to understand this world of giants that surrounded him and sometimes behaved so strangely. A light dusting of freckles now adorned the tiny beige nose, testimony to the strange genetic make-up that had gone into the makings of this little boy.

"This is the sword your great-uncle carried in the Mexican war and your great-great-grandfather used when he fought with George Washington. And the flag of our regiment in the War Between the States."

Zack picked up the uneven ball of metal and let little William hold it in his chubby hands. It felt strange – bumpy, hard, and warm.

"This is from our old house, lost in the War. Your Aunt Nan thought it was a doorknob."

William's tiny beige fingers plucked at the folded materials, the insignia on a ribbon, the gold embossed book.

"My uniform. Your Uncle Billy's medal. You were named for him, you know. And the book that tells all about our family. Your family," explained Zack, also reverently touching each sacred relic. A new thought struck him. "This is your inheritance."

Behind him, Nan's body lay in view in a wooden casket, her face eternally calm and beautiful. William laid his dark, curly head on Zack's shoulder, staring at her still body as if suddenly fearful.

"Grampa, when will Aunt Nan wake up?"

Zack drew in a deep breath and bravely turned to face his sister for the last time.

"Well, William, she will sleep for a very long time. Then she will wake up, and live forever," he explained, his voice soft with deep emotion that was part grief, and strangely, part joy.

Behind them, Lenie watched this scene from the doorway of her room. Jim, Alden, family and friends appeared at the front door as Millie and Ellie, leading James and Sarah, descended the stairs.

"Are you ready, Brother?" asked Jim. Zack nodded, handing William off to Ellie. Together the three brothers placed the lid on Nan's coffin and lifted it onto their shoulders. James, too frail to lend his weight to their endeavors, nevertheless joined his shoulder with theirs as the fourth pallbearer.

Outside, the mourners silently parted to make way for the procession. Slowly the Lewis men carried their beloved burden through the crowd – black and white, young and old, neighbors, former students, and friends who had come from far and near. Zack recognized Jeremiah, now white-haired and grizzled, and Juno, still statuesque even in her old age.

The garden at River's Rest was filled with more people who stood, silent and hatless, as the procession passed them in the unusually bright November sunlight. Thankfully, it was one of those warm days that sometimes happen at the end of the so-called Indian summer. Red and yellow leaves still clung to the trees in abundance, while the ever-present pines retained their deep green. Yet despite the unseasonably fine weather, a pall of grief hung in the air like a gray shade.

Beyond the crowd, a smart carriage pulled by four matching chestnut horses halted. A tall man and a slender woman, with two small children, alighted; dressed in the latest fashions, the new arrivals stood out among the simply clothed Southern folk. But despite their finery, the young family looked ill at ease, as if unsure of their welcome.

The mourners watched circumspectly as the family approached, but – being Virginians – they were too polite to whisper the unasked question about the strangers' identity. The foursome made their way to the gravesite where Nan's casket was now laid beside her open grave, standing a man's length behind Zack and the rest of Nan's

229

surviving family.

Although there was something familiar about the couple's posture and their thick dark hair, it took a moment for Zack to recognize Samuel and Sally, now that they were adults instead of rebellious teenagers. The shock of this recognition was a needle inserted into the deepest section of Zack's heart and then twisted like a fishhook. He almost gasped with the pain of it. Sally's flight, her betrayal of him, her absence at the deepest tragedy of his life – the death of his only living son – and her silence these long years as the Great Flood washed away what was left of his life – the grief of her abandonment hit him harder than the tsunami of Galveston Bay.

He turned away, setting his face to stone while he tried to will his heart to do likewise.

Behind Zack's implacable back, Lenie raced swiftly to embrace the young couple, to ooh and ahh over the children – who were after all her grandchildren too. Samuel and Sally, pretending to ignore Zack's rejection, embraced the aging figures of Sarah and James, and their beloved Aunt Millie and Uncle Jim, their affection from years of boarding at River's Rest still undimmed by a move across the Atlantic.

Behind his back Zack heard the discreet murmurs of greeting, the exclamations of delight. He feigned deafness to it all, willing his heart as well as his ears not to hear.

But not so little William. Drawn by the fascination of one child to another, his round sable eyes peered over Zack's shoulders at the strange newcomers, especially the ones as small as he was. Kicking his legs and climbing with small chubby hands, he propelled himself upward across Zack's stolid chest until he was leaning over Zack's shoulder, in peril of falling over and landing on his curly head.

Zack grabbed for him, but William was already beyond the tipping point where he could be returned to safety. So Zack whirled around, slipping the toddler off his shoulder and regaining his grip on the wiggling youngster.

So his eyes met Sally's. She held his gaze. In her soul, Zack finally saw not a defiant, angry girl but a poised young woman, who

230

had finally learned compassion through her own emotional journey.

She walked forward slowly, and greeted him in a low, firm voice as the others watched quietly.

"Hello, Father. You are looking well."

Behind her, the two children peered at this other stranger and the odd-looking dark-visaged boy he clutched. Sally gestured to them.

"These are my children. Zachary and Pauline."

Zack couldn't help but inspect the two children, who looked to be a little older than William. But he did not say a word. Sally swallowed and drew herself up a little straighter, as if for courage.

"Father, I'm sorry for the things I said. I was wrong."

Despite her elegant dress and her fine hat and gloves, part of her looked like she would like to run and bolt, fleeing this difficult scene with long legs flying. Nevertheless, she stood her ground, bravely looking her father in the eye.

Zack's eyes remained on the children, who clung to their mother's skirts as the stocky, scowling man examined them. Two pairs of deep blue eyes gazed up at him. Like their mother, they did not turn away. Images of Zack's own family, his brothers and sisters, and their games and exploits and love for each other popped unbidden into his stubborn brain. Especially, Helen's mischievous face seemed to stare back up at him, direct, questioning, curious. Across the decades, she reached out to him.

Zack settled William in his arms. That young man was now content to sit still also and study these strange new arrivals, one finger in his mouth. Zack finally spoke.

"Zachary and Pauline. This is your cousin, William."

Holding William in one arm, he embraced Sally wordlessly with the other. Sally clung to her father, a loving daughter at last, the old injuries forgiven. Slowly Zack released her and offered his hand to Samuel; with relief Samuel shook it heartily

Lenie watched the scene with thankfulness overflowing in her soul, marveling that Nan's gift for peacemaking reached beyond the grave. Little did she know that this rapprochement was engineered by the baby sister so long gone.

Now, finally, the family all faced the gravesite. The sunlight was still bright but soft now, caressing the blooms in Sarah's garden, the tombstones, and the bouquets of flowers that adorned Nan's casket. The very air stood still.

Millie stepped forward and offered Zack the worn family Bible. Zack opened it, then paused to retrieve and put on the narrow glasses he now needed, and finally, began to read in a slow, firm, voice.

"God is our refuge and strength,

A very present help in trouble.

Therefore will not we fear, though the earth be removed, and though the mountains be carried into the midst of the sea.

Though the waters thereof roar and be troubled,

Though the mountains shake with the swelling thereof.

There is a river, the streams whereof shall make glad the city of God, the holy place of the tabernacles of the most High.

God is in the midst of her, she shall not be moved,

God shall help her and that right early.

Finally, Zack's voice broke. His face turned red with emotion and his mouth twisted with repressed sobs. He looked up helplessly, his weakened eyes blinking rapidly and his throat constricting with grief.

In a brief second, Lenie stepped forward and stood beside him. She did not need the Bible to remember the words. Her voice was strong and proud, in tribute to her good friend.

Come, behold the works of the Lord, what desolations he hath made in the earth.

He maketh wars to cease unto the end of the earth,

He breaketh the bow, and cutteth the spear in sunder,

He burneth the chariot in the fire.

Her voice dropped, softened.

Be still, and know that I am God.

I will be exalted among the heathen,

I will be exalted in the earth.

The Lord of hosts is with us,

The God of Jacob is our refuge.

The crowd stayed quiet as her words faded. Zack swallowed,

gaining strength from her strong presence beside him. He closed the Bible and held it in his two hands, as if it were a delicate living thing. Strangely, his spirit soared with a gladness that he could not explain, as he began to speak.

"Well, if my sister were here today, she would explain to you the meaning of these flowers. Marigolds, for joy and remembrance; violets, for modesty; yellow roses, for friendship. This was her life. A life that could have been blighted in bitterness at what was lost, but which was instead enriched by what remained."

His gaze stopped on Lenie's face. Many listening to his words would assume that he referred to the economic hardships that Nan lived with all her adult life. But Lenie understood exactly what he meant.

"Once, we fought for the Cause we believed to be honor itself."

"We lost the War." Here Zack paused, almost in disbelief at the admission he had just made after his denial to admit this defeat for almost forty years. But there, he'd said it.

"But we never compromised our honor. It flourished in people like my sister, Nan. She never forgot what the true Cause was. No matter what happened, she never surrendered – her dedication to her duty, her commitment to her family, nor her loving heart. May we be brave enough to do the same. We will always remember and cherish her."

Millie stepped forward again. Gently she took the Bible from Zack, and offered him a perfect, velvet red rose. He accepted it and placed it atop the wooden casket. Brokenly he whispered, "We love you, little sister."

Sarah smiled through her tears – tears not of sorrow, but of happiness at her son's long-awaited redemption. James squeezed her hand in silent understanding.

Zack and Lenie were the last to leave the site of Nan's final resting place. Together they walked slowly back to the house as the carriages, the wagons, the horses, and the pedestrians left to go back to their homes, carrying with them only the memory of this exceptional soul who had touched so many lives. Even Samuel and Sally and their children went on ahead, understanding that this odd couple would be joining them soon.

Little William ran before Zack and Lenie, playing in the grass and chasing butterflies. Lenie looked at him, then off into the distant, mysterious woods.

"You know pretty soon, the children will be old enough to play Indian in those woods. Like we did."

Zack also gazed toward the playground of his youth. "If they do, they'd best be careful. I hear there are still Indians in those parts."

They fell silent again, enjoying the colors and scents of the wildflowers that had once populated Sarah's carefully tended garden. Finally Zack spoke.

"If you had gotten those flowers all those years ago, would you have said 'Yes'?"

"If I had, would we have been happy?" Lenie parried.

Zack chuckled. "I don't know."

And, just like that, in an instant, they laid to rest the wondering and the mourning for what might have been.

Lenie's foot sank into the wet ground and she stumbled. Zack caught her, but her foot remained mired in the greedy mud, her shoe held captive. Slowly bending over, with Lenie balanced precariously against him, Zack freed it and straightened up to a chorus of creaking bones rivaling the evening serenade of a hundred bullfrogs. Lenie very politely did not comment.

Instead she said, "I remember this place. It's where I fell in the pond, when we were playing scout, and you saved me." Lenie held Zack's gaze. "You know, I never said 'thank you'."

"Well – I never admitted you were the best scout in the family," acknowledged Zack. He did an imaginary tip of his non-existent hat to the skill of the legendary Brave Wolf.

"I declared war on you that day, remember?" murmured Lenie, as each reflected on the long decades of their conflict.

Zack paused before a rosebush, now wild and bushy. Pulling out his penknife, and avoiding the thorns, he carefully cut off a bloom – a yellow rose – and offered it to Lenie.

"Nan always said these mean… friendship."

Lenie accepted his offering, profoundly moved. It was as if she, too, was freed of a lifetime of griefs. And the old warrior spirit of Brave Wolf, finally at peace, slowly drifted away toward his final resting place with the Great Spirit.

The soft wings of butterflies swirled around me as my grandparents' conflict was laid to rest, transformed into the companionship and comradeship that it was always meant to be. So that's how I came to be present that day when the longest battle of the War ended in a truce. And peace finally came to River's Rest as Lenie and Zack, arm in arm, walked slowly back to the old homestead. And a little boy who had the honor of bringing forgiveness to the hearts of his Granny and Grandpa and who would one day tell their story, went back to chasing butterflies all the way home.

Book Club Guide

1. This novel spans more than 40 years. How have the three main characters changed and grown in that time? Who has grown the most?

2. What are the forces or events that precipitated the changes in the three main characters – Zack, Lenie, and Charles?

3. If Lenie had married Samuel, would she have been happy? What would her life have been like?

4. Do you think it is a tragedy that Zack and Lenie did not marry, or were they better off with the partners they had?

5. Which character did you like the most, and why?

6. Discuss the roles of women in this novel – Sarah, Lenie, Nan, Lucy, Sally, Helen, and Ellie. Did they make their own choices, or were they victims of society's expectations?

7. Discuss how "family" is defined by the actions and beliefs of the characters. Who was most devoted to their family, and how did they show it?

8. What does "home" represent to the characters in this novel? How are their views of home different? The same?

9. Today, symbols of the South are used to represent a white supremacist, racist point of view. Do you think the Southerners in this book fit that description? What were they like and what did they believe?

10. Discuss the life of Nan. Is her story tragic, or heroic?

11. Charles sees something in Lenie that no one else does. How does he see her? Is his view accurate, or is it his imagination?

12. What are the reasons for Lenie's pridefulness – in her youth and as an adult?

13. Are Sally's accusations of Lenie and Zack, and their motivations, accurate?

14. Is Charles Delacourt an honorable person, as Lenie says? Why or why not?

15. What do you think happened to dissuade Zack from drowning little William?

16. What characters grew the most in this story? Why and how?

To find more inspiration, visit **www.go-deeper-now.com**.

Made in the USA
San Bernardino, CA
15 June 2020

73093521R00135